MGK

D1029352

COMANCHE SUNRISE

COMANCHE SUNRISE

ETHAN J. WOLFE

FIVE STAR
A part of Gale, a Cengage Company

GALE
A Cengage Company

Farmington Hills, Mich • San Francisco • New York • Waterville, Maine
Meriden, Conn • Mason, Ohio • Chicago

LIBRARY OF CONGRESS CATALOGING-IN-PUBLICATION DATA

Names: Wolfe, Ethan J., author.
Title: Comanche sunrise / by Ethan J. Wolfe.
Description: First edition. | Waterville, Maine : Five Star, a part of Gale, Cengage Learning, [2018] | Series: A Youngblood brothers western | Identifiers: LCCN 2018014451 (print) | LCCN 2018015495 (ebook) | ISBN 9781432847197 (ebook) | ISBN 9781432847180 (ebook) | ISBN 9781432847173 (hardcover)
Subjects: | GSAFD: Western stories.
Classification: LCC PS3612.A5433 (ebook) | LCC PS3612.A5433 C66 2018 (print) | DDC 813/.6—dc23
LC record available at https://lccn.loc.gov/2018014451

First Edition. First Printing: December 2018
Find us on Facebook—https://www.facebook.com/FiveStarCengage
Visit our website—http://www.gale.cengage.com/fivestar/
Contact Five Star Publishing at FiveStar@cengage.com

Printed in Mexico
1 2 3 4 5 6 7 22 21 20 19 18

For Alice and Tiff, two great gals dear to my heart.

PROLOGUE

Two Hawks sat in his rocking chair and waited for the reservation doctor to tell him that his wife had died. Several years ago he purchased the chair for his wife at the reservation general store, but she never liked the feeling of the hard wood against her back so he made the chair his own.

He smoked his pipe and rocked while he waited for the black doctor to appear from the bedroom and tell him his wife drew her final breath. Two Hawks thought of many things while he waited.

As a young boy, he sat beside his father at the council fires and listened to Ten Bears tell the story of the Comanche's great victory over the whites in the town of Austin and along the Red River. Ten Bears was an old man by then, but still a proud and commanding presence to behold. He stood while others sat and told of the great raids. The war brewed for many years and had started with the false words of Sam Houston and his treaty at Fort Bird. While great chiefs like Buffalo Hump trusted and made peace with Houston, many whites living in the area still did not like Indians.

Raids on the reservation by whites were common, and many Comanche were murdered and butchered, their women raped and noses disfigured to show their disgrace. The Comanche, Kiowa, and Apache joined forces to take on John Ford and his Texas Rangers. The result was a bitter defeat for the Comanche and resulted in the Treaty of Medicine Lodge, whereby sixty thousand square miles were set aside by the government for the Comanche to live on. The government made no effort to stop buffalo hunting, and even encouraged the practice by offering rewards for buffalo hides. The Comanche, as most other native tribes, were a buffalo culture and needed the great animal for its very existence. To destroy the buffalo was to destroy the Comanche, and the American government was well aware of that fact.

The Comanche responded by launching the attack on Adobe Walls, only to suffer another bitter defeat at the hands of the whites. Two Hawks's father took part in that battle and was wounded, although he survived.

In the year of 1873, the last free Comanche, led by Quanah Parker, surrendered and were moved to the reservation at Fort Smith in Arkansas. Miserable with reservation life, two hundred Comanche led by Black Horse left the reservation two years later. Two Hawks and his father were among the two hundred.

It was Two Hawks's first real taste of freedom, having been born to reservation life eighteen years earlier. Black Horse led the two hundred to the Llano Estacado where they began to raid buffalo hunters' camps in the panhandle and along the Red River. It was even told in stories that horses were stolen from the famous lawman Pat Garrett. In the fight that followed, known as the Buffalo Hunters' War, Two Hawks killed his first man.

To kill a white man in battle was an experience Two Hawks described later as exhilarating, but was short-lived. A quarter of Black Horse's men were killed and the rest rounded up and returned to the reservation in Oklahoma.

Without buffalo hides to build their tipis with, cabins were built using government lumber and tools, and the Comanche lived as whites on their government reservation land. Two

Hawks's cabin had a porch that faced the sun. Every morning Two Hawks would drink his coffee, smoke his pipe, and watch the sunrise. The new sun brought the promise of a new day and hope. The setting sun brought with it the crushed expectations of the hopeless.

Two Hawks had two hundred acres of land to farm and six good horses that provided many colts. He often sold the colts to the army in Fort Smith. The white women in the streets would run and hide or cover their eyes at the sight of such a savage. He wore white man's pants and shirt and used a white man's saddle and yet was still mocked as a savage.

His pipe was empty and Two Hawks went to the table to stuff it with fresh tobacco from the pouch. There was a bottle of rye whiskey and a glass on the table, and he filled the glass and took it to the rocking chair.

He smoked and sipped the rye and listened to the black doctor moving about in the bedroom.

When he turned fourteen years, his father took him on his first buffalo hunt. There still were buffalo on the reservation land then. Only after he killed his first buffalo was a Comanche allowed to go to war. It was a pointless act, to be sure, as there were no wars left to fight, but still an important part of becoming a man nonetheless. One year later he was allowed to undertake his vision quest, the passage to manhood. He spent four days and nights alone in the mountains of the reservation where he prayed to the great spirits for strength and guidance. When he returned to the tribe, his visions were interpreted by Quanah Parker at the council fires. He had seen two hawks battling a great eagle in the sky and Parker gave him the warrior name Two Hawks to honor the vision.

The following year, Two Hawks met his future wife, Yellow Sky. She was fourteen and a member of the Kiowa people living on the Fort Smith reservation. She was beautiful, and Two

Hawks knew that when she came of age he would marry her and she would bear him many sons.

Only she never did. Three times she lost the baby she carried. The reservation doctor called it a miscarriage. After the third miscarriage, Yellow Sky began to cough. The cough worsened and she went to see the reservation doctor, the very doctor with her now. He told them she had what the whites called consumption, the tuberculosis of her lungs. It was a white man's illness that only whites should die of, like the famous Doc Holliday.

Two Hawks finished the glass of rye whiskey and went for another. The sun was low now, and he took the drink and pipe outside to the porch.

A few years back, Buffalo Bill Cody visited the reservation seeking fierce warriors for his show, The Wild West. Cody promised twenty-five dollars a week and the chance to tour the country and the world with his show. All you had to do was act like a screaming, ignorant savage. Two Hawks turned Cody down, but many did not and joined his show. Two Hawks considered those who joined Cody to be lowly dogs unworthy of the name Comanche.

As the sun touched the mountains in the background, the black doctor opened the door and came out to the porch.

"She will go any time now, if you want to spend the last few moments with her," the doctor said.

Two Hawks went inside to the bedroom and sat in the chair beside the bed. Yellow Sky had wasted away to practically nothing. Even close to death, he could still see the beauty she once possessed. Around her neck she wore a simple chain with the Christian crucifix attached to it. He removed the chain and placed it around his neck. He took her hand and watched as she drew a final breath and then went still.

Two Hawks returned to the porch where the black doctor waited.

"She is free of her pain now," the black doctor said.

"Free?" Two Hawks said. "What do you know of free? Your Ab-Ra-Ham Lincoln may have freed you of the white man's slavery, but you are not free. You are a doctor, but the white man won't allow you to treat them. Is that not why you work on the reservation?"

"If a man is free in his heart, he is free in his mind," the doctor said.

"Goodbye, doctor," Two Hawks said.

After the doctor got into his buggy and rode away, Two Hawks spent the night on the porch drinking coffee and rye whiskey and smoking his pipe. At sunrise, he picked his best horse, saddled him, and loaded as many supplies as possible into the saddlebags. He owned an excellent Winchester rifle and packed it and boxes of ammunition along with the supplies.

"Goodbye, my wife," Two Hawks said to Yellow Sky and then burned the cabin to the ground and simply rode away.

CHAPTER ONE

William Jefferson had been the reservation doctor almost since he first graduated medical school at the Negro College in Boston in 1867. Two Hawks spoke the truth when he said the white man would never allow a black doctor to treat them. After several failed attempts to establish a practice in Boston, New York, and Chicago, he took the position on the reservation.

What Two Hawks failed to understand was how young the country was and how far it had come in such a short time. You don't eradicate four hundred years of hatred and bigotry in two decades, white, black, or red.

Jefferson had never been a slave. He was born a free man in Boston some fifty years ago to parents who had escaped from Georgia on the Underground Railroad. Many slaves didn't make it to freedom; his parents did. They lived in the slums, but always saw to it that there was food on the table and clothes on his back. He went to the Negro school, and it was quickly established that he was an excellent student. When the War Between the States erupted, Jefferson was in his second year of medical school. He stayed in school until late sixty-three, when Lincoln opened up the army to black soldiers. He was one of the first to join the 54th Regiment out of Massachusetts.

At first they were assigned supply or burial details, but their commander, Colonel Robert Shaw, convinced the generals to allow them to fight. Jefferson was one of six hundred men who saw action at Fort Wagner in Charleston in South Carolina.

Colonel Shaw was killed in that battle along with one hundred and twenty others. Jefferson served mostly as a medic, but oftentimes had to use his rifle to defend his unit and once was slightly wounded in the right leg. After the war, he returned to Boston to continue his studies and graduated in sixty-seven.

As he traveled the well-worn road back to the settlement center of town where his office and cabin were located, Jefferson paused to light the two mounted lanterns on his buggy. The moon was full and the road well illuminated, so the lanterns weren't necessary to see, but they made the wagon visible from a distance.

It bothered him, losing Yellow Sky, but a doctor can only do so much. Her tuberculosis had troubled her for a decade, and in the end took her life. The look on Two Hawks's face when he rode away also bothered him. Two Hawks was a proud man and believed in the customs of his people, but Jefferson had never believed Two Hawks was a mean man.

At a fork in the road, Jefferson took a sudden left turn and traveled about a mile until he reached the home of the reservation police chief, Emmet Youngblood. His cabin was larger than most, as it had to accommodate his mother and two daughters. There was a corral out front with several horses in it, a toolshed on the side of the cabin, and a bar out back.

Jefferson parked the buggy in front of the cabin. Two lanterns mounted on the wall of the porch were lit, and he could see Youngblood open the front door and step out holding a Winchester rifle.

"Emmet, it's Doctor Jefferson," Jefferson called out.

"Doc, what are you doing out after dark?" Emmet said. "Is somebody sick?"

"Emmet, come here a minute," Jefferson said.

Emmet set the Winchester aside and stepped down off the porch and walked to the buggy.

14

"Yellow Sky passed tonight, Emmet," Jefferson said.

"I'm sorry to hear that, Doc," Emmet said.

"Two Hawks didn't take it well," Jefferson said.

"I expect not," Emmet said.

"I saw something in his eyes I didn't like," Jefferson said.

Emmet sighed. "I'll ride over and see him at first light," he said.

"I think that's a good idea," Jefferson said.

"Come in for a while?"

"Have to get home, but I'll stop by Two Hawks's cabin in the morning," Jefferson said.

"Good night, Doc," Emmet said.

"Was that Doctor Jefferson?" Amy Youngblood asked when her son Emmet returned to the cabin.

"Yellow Sky passed away tonight," Emmet said.

Amy sighed heavily. "I'm sorry to hear that," she said.

"I'll take a ride over and see Two Hawks in the morning," Emmet said.

"I will go with you," Amy said.

"That's not necessary, Mother," Emmet said.

"I will go with you," Amy said.

Emmet nodded. There was no use arguing with his mother; he'd never won an argument yet. "Okay, Mother," he said.

"There's coffee left in the pot," Amy said.

Emmet filled a cup and took it and his pipe out to the porch.

Amy went to the sink and cranked the pump to fill the basin with water to soak the dinner dishes.

She was close to sixty years old now, but still maintained the beauty of her youth, the beauty that attracted her husband to her so many years ago, even if her dark hair was sprinkled with gray. Her mother was a mixture of Irish and Sioux; her father was Mexican Apache and French. The combination bloodlines produced a woman of exquisite beauty.

Her childhood was turmoil. Her father was killed in the Comanche Wars in 1836 when she was still a child. Her mother, as a mixed breed, was an outcast in most Texas towns and was forced to take in laundry to put food on the table. Her mother also insisted that Amy receive a proper education. By the time she was eighteen, Amy spoke English, French, Spanish, Sioux, and Apache. In her eighteenth year, Amy also met a handsome, young United States marshal named John Youngblood.

They courted for two years before marrying because he was away from Austin so much, but finally they married and settled down. Their first son was named John after his father. The second was named Emmet. When John was just five and Emmet all of two, her husband took an appointment of marshal in Fort Smith in Arkansas. Her husband was killed just before the war started by outlaws he was tracking in the Ozark Mountains.

Left with two small sons to rear, Amy applied for a position of schoolteacher and was granted a license. The war years were hard, difficult times, but the family survived, and her sons grew to men.

John was appointed a deputy US marshal by Judge Isaac Parker when John was just twenty-five years old. Emmet was appointed a deputy on the reservation by Judge Parker a few years later because of his Native American blood and law degree.

Her sons, once as close as brothers could be, now hardly spoke at all. Amy took some blame for that, having seen the feud brewing long before it came to a head, and she kept silent about it, figuring incorrectly that brotherly love for each other would prevail. She didn't count on the love for a woman breaking such a bond.

A year after his appointment as a deputy marshal, Jack, as he was called then, met a young woman whose family recently settled in Fort Smith. Her name was Sarah, and she was a fine doll of a woman, with black hair and chiseled features. Jack immediately was smitten with her and asked her to marry him.

Emmet was away at school in Boston at the time. He returned home while Jack was away on assignment and upon Sarah and Emmet meeting, the two fell deeply in love at first sight. When Jack returned, he didn't take kindly to the news that the woman he wanted to marry had fallen in love with his kid brother.

Jack was a giant of a man, standing six-foot-three in his stocking feet, and came close to beating Emmet to death, and would have, had not Amy clubbed him on the back of his head with a bottle. The wound required seven stitches to close. When it healed, the hair never grew back, and the injury left a small, crescent-moon scar.

After Emmet and Sarah married, Jack avoided seeing his brother for years and would only see Amy if she came to town. Amy, a devote Christian, prayed every Sunday in church that her sons would one day reunite and be brothers again.

Emmet was no stranger to heartache. He knew exactly how Two Hawks must feel, having lost his own wife some five years ago when she hemorrhaged during childbirth and died giving birth to their second child.

The baby wasn't due for at least a month. She and Emmet's mother went to town to buy a rocking crib for the newborn. Their first child, a girl, accompanied them. As they shopped in the large mercantile store, Sarah felt a sudden, sharp pain in her lower abdomen. She started to bleed and collapsed. By the time Emmet was summoned to the town doctor's office, Sarah was unconscious and bleeding to death. The doctor had no choice but to take the baby, another girl, to save its life. Sarah died soon afterward from complications.

Jack came to the church service and the cemetery out of respect for their mother but stayed in the back and spoke to no one, not even his mother. Emmet believed that Jack secretly blamed him for Sarah's early death.

His older daughter was named Mary Louise, in honor of Amy's mother. The younger was named Sarah, in honor of his wife. Both of his daughters were hardly aware they had an uncle.

It was a hard task bringing up two daughters without a wife and mother but it was made easier when Amy quit teaching in town and came to live with him and the girls. She taught at the reservation school and was able to bring the girls with her every day and that helped Mary Louise recover better from losing her mother at so young an age.

Both his girls were his bond to Sarah, a bond that could never be broken. So he understood the loss Two Hawks must be feeling this very moment.

Amy came out to the porch with a fresh pot of coffee and a cup for herself. She filled Emmet's cup and took the chair beside his.

"I know what you are thinking," Amy said.

"Do you now?" Emmet said with a slight grin.

"You feel Two Hawks's loss as your own," Amy said.

"If you mean I know how he feels, I believe I do," Emmet said.

"The girls need a mother, Emmet," Amy said.

"The girls have you, Mother," Emmet said.

"I am almost sixty," Amy said. "How long do you think I will last?"

"Long enough to see both of them marry," Emmet said.

"And you? Do you plan to spend the rest of your life alone?" Amy asked.

"My plate is full right now, Mother," Emmet said.

"Not so full you couldn't court a young lady," Amy said.

Emmet sipped his coffee and looked at the moon. "It's a beautiful night," he said.

"Don't wind up like me, Emmet," Amy said. "I had three or four chances to remarry and didn't. A person can get used to being lonely to the point they know no other path in life."

"I'm not lonely, Mother," Emmet said. "I have the girls and you and a job that keeps my hands full sunup to sundown."

"Being lonely and being busy are two separate things, but as I have dishes to wash I will drop the subject for now," Amy said.

Amy went inside, and Emmet sat for a while longer with his coffee and pipe. It was always amazing to him how his mother could see clear through him and know exactly how he felt and thought at any given moment. It wasn't just a mother knowing her son, it was more than that. She knew his heart because she had lived half her life with the identical heartache and loss.

Tomorrow morning he would ride to see Two Hawks, as many others on the reservation would, and he hoped that so proud a man would allow others to share in his sorrow.

"Why do we have to wear our Sunday dresses, Grandma?" Mary Louise asked. "Today is Saturday."

"We are going to pay our respects to Two Hawks for the loss of his wife," Amy said. "After that we will go to church to light a candle for her soul."

"I don't like my Sunday dress," Sarah said. "It's hot and itchy."

"Never mind it's hot. Your father is waiting for us," Amy said.

Amy took the girls outside where the buggy was hitched and waiting. Emmet sat atop his pinto next to the buggy. He wore his sidearm and carried his Winchester rifle in the saddle sleeve, because he would ride to the office afterward to check in with his men.

"Let's go, girls," Emmet told his daughters.

Amy helped the girls into the buggy, and then she got in and took the reins.

"All settled?" Emmet asked.

"Yes, Pa," Mary Louise said.

"Let's go then," Emmet said.

He led on the pinto, and Amy followed in the buggy. The ride to Two Hawks's cabin took about an hour. Several hundred yards from the turnoff to the cabin, Emmet held up the pinto when he caught the faint smell of smoke.

"What is it?" Amy asked.

"Stay here, Mother," Emmet said.

Emmet yanked the reins and rode full out to the turnoff and along the road to Two Hawks's cabin. As he neared the cabin, the acrid smell of smoke filled his lungs. He pulled up the pinto near the corral and dismounted.

Two Hawks had burned his cabin to the ground. The charred remains of the wood smoldered and, as he got closer, the harshness of the smoke made him cough.

Emmet turned when he heard a buggy approach. It was Doctor Jefferson. Jefferson parked beside the pinto and jumped down quickly.

"Dear God, what did he do?" Jefferson said. "Is he . . . ?"

"No, Doc, he isn't," Emmet said. "I count five horses in the corral, and he owned six. Looks like he took the big stallion he always rides."

Jefferson shook his head. "I knew he was feeling pain, but not like this," he said.

"Two Hawks wouldn't speak what's in his heart, Doc," Emmet said. "It isn't his way."

"I saw your mother and girls on the road," Jefferson said.

"I best return to them and go to the settlement and see if anybody saw Two Hawks this morning," Emmet said.

Jefferson looked at the smoldering remains of the cabin. "My God," he said.

Emmet mounted his pinto and road back to the buggy.

20

"Go home, Mother," Emmet said. "There is nothing we can do now."

Amy nodded. "Come on, girls, we can go to church tomorrow."

The settlement was the hub of the reservation. It was actually a town with a large general store, a blacksmith, a saloon, a school and church, a livery stable, dozens of cabins, the reservation police office and jail, and Doc Jefferson's office.

Emmet rode into the settlement, dismounted at the jail, and tied the pinto at the hitching post. The streets were crowded, as they were most Saturdays. While the majority of its citizens wore white man's clothing, most of them also wore something of their heritage that said they were not white but Comanche, Kiowa, or Sioux.

Emmet entered the office and found two of his deputies on duty. Charlie Blackbear, Emmet's senior deputy, sat at the desk. He was writing in the logbook and drinking coffee. Sonny Davies, a Comanche with Irish blood, sat on the edge of the desk cleaning his pistol.

"Morning, Emmet," Charlie Blackbear said. "Didn't expect to see you in town today."

"Yellow Sky passed away last night," Emmet said.

"Sorry to hear that," Blackbear said. "She was a good woman."

"How is Two Hawks taking it?" Davies asked.

"He burned his cabin down around her and left on that tall horse of his," Emmet said.

"Left?" Blackbear said. "Left for where?"

"I don't know," Emmet said. "Into the mountains maybe, to mourn."

Blackbear and Davies exchanged glances.

"Want us to look for him?" Davies asked.

"He's better mounted that any of us and probably left last night," Emmet said. "You'd never catch him, and even if you could, it's only because he wanted you to. Better if you round up the rest of the deputies and tell them to take over for you. We'll ride to his cabin and see if we can bury what remains there are."

Emmet, Blackbear, Davies, and Jefferson found the remains of Yellow Sky in what was left of her bed. Wood burns hot and quick, but doesn't reach the temperature needed to reduce bones to ash. Jefferson gathered up the charred bones, placed them in white linen, and then carried them to his buggy.

"We picked out a spot to bury her, Doc," Emmet said.

Emmet, Blackbear, and Davies dug a grave under a tall oak tree that stood behind the corral and that would keep the grave well shaded.

"We'll mark the grave with a headstone as soon as we have one made," Emmet said.

After they covered up Yellow Sky's remains, Emmet placed a cross made of two sticks and a piece of rope into the soft earth.

"What about his horses?" Davies asked. "We can't leave them penned like that."

"No, we can't," Emmet said. "Tether them together and we'll take them to the livery in case Two Hawks returns."

"He won't return," Amy said as she shucked corn on the porch. "If he planned to return, he would not have burned his cabin and left five good horses behind."

"Who won't return?" Mary Louise asked as she opened the porch screen door and stepped on to the porch.

"This is grown-up talk, Mary," Amy said. "If I catch you snooping at the door again, I will tan your bottom."

"I wasn't snooping, Grandma," Mary Louise said. "I was

coming out and heard what you said, is all."

"Never you mind. Take this corn to the cook pot on the stove and be careful you don't burn yourself," Amy said.

"Yes, Grandma," Mary Louise said.

After Mary Louise toted the basket of corn into the house, Emmet said, "Maybe he plans to come back for his horses? Maybe he plans to never return? Who knows what's in a man's heart at a time like this. We'll talk to people at the service tomorrow. Maybe somebody saw him leave."

Amy looked at her son. "Nobody saw him, and he won't return," she said. "These may be what the newspapers call modern times, but in his heart Two Hawks is pure Comanche."

After supper, Emmet took his pipe and a cup of coffee to the porch to watch the sunset. Two Hawks was pure Comanche, his mother had said, but what did that mean anymore? The Comanche race was nearly as extinct as the buffalo had been ten years ago. The same could be said for the Kiowa, Sioux, Blackfoot, and every other native tribe.

It was ironic to Emmet that the tribes that fought so hard to defeat the American army were now almost completely dependent upon that same army for their very existence. Cattle companies made a fortune selling beef to the army that in turn delivered the beef to the reservations for the tribes to live on. Vast plains where buffalo once roamed free were now the sole domain of beef cattle.

Yet Emmet held no anger in his heart for the white man's ways. He himself was more than half white and would have no trouble living in a civilized city such as Boston or New York. His girls would receive a far better education there than on the reservation and would grow up to be socialites with promising futures. Here most of their friends at school were Comanche or Kiowa, and the only interaction they had with whites was when they went to Fort Smith with his mother and sometimes with him.

Amy joined him on the porch. She held a coffee cup and the pot and filled Emmet's empty cup, then took a seat next to him.

"Thank you, Mother," Emmet said.

"Why so heavy a heart?" Amy said.

"I was thinking about something you said earlier," Emmet said. "You called these modern times and I . . ."

"I said the newspapers called these modern times," Amy said.

"Do you believe it?" Emmet asked.

"I don't think there is any such thing," Amy said. "When I first met your father, he hunted with a Hawkins .50 caliber black-powder rifle. No one had dreamed of the railroad, the steam engine, the telegraph, and now the telephone and the electric light bulb, but people are still the same. Under the right circumstance, with their backs to the wall, people become savages. Does that answer your question?"

Emmet sipped coffee while he thought for a moment. "Do you think I am cheating the girls out of a proper education and upbringing?" he said.

"When you graduated law school in Boston, you returned and became a lawman on the reservation. Why?" Amy asked.

"That is what my heart told me to do," Emmet said.

"And what does your heart tell you to do about your girls?" Amy asked.

Emmet looked at the horizon and setting sun. "It's a beautiful night," he said.

"Yes it is," Amy said.

The preacher's name was Sam Hough, and he'd been a minister for close to fifty years. He first started converting the Sioux, Blackfoot, and Crow on the plains even before the war. Many times he'd come close to being killed by the very men he strived to convert. He was in his late sixties now and still as active as ever. During the week he taught bible study for two hours every day after school and held two services every Sunday, one at ten o'clock and the second at noon. The church held one hundred and twenty-five, and both services were standing room only. Every other Saturday, Hough hosted a church supper, outdoors in good weather, indoors in the church basement during winter.

Today Hough delivered a beautiful sermon and eulogy for Yellow Sky. Many of the women cried openly. When Hough served communion, every soul in attendance lined up to receive the sacred host.

What always amazed Emmet was how many Comanche, Sioux, and Kiowa had converted to Christianity. Nearly the entire population of the reservation wore the cross around their neck.

After the service, Hough hosted a special coffee and donuts session in the garden behind the church. While the girls played with other children and Amy chatted with her friends, Hough pulled Emmet aside.

"Where do you think Two Hawks will go?" Hough asked.

"I wish I knew, Reverend," Emmet said.

"Doc should have told me she was so close," Hough said. "Yellow Sky deserved last words."

"I don't think he knew himself until he showed up," Emmet said. "It was too late by then."

"If you hear anything about Two Hawks, please let me know," Hough said.

"I will," Emmet said.

"In the meantime, I will pray for him," Hough said.

Emmet didn't say it, but he thought Two Hawks was going to need all the prayers he could get.

CHAPTER TWO

Two Hawks rode through the night and into the new day and stopped only when the sun set again. Even then it was to rest his horse more than himself. He had tremendous strength and stamina and could ride very long distances without food and water if he had to.

The land appeared much as it always had, wide open and free, but he knew that wasn't true. Every road led to a town filled with whites. Even just twenty years ago, when Two Hawks was still a boy, that wasn't so. There were towns no doubt, but much of the land between them still belonged to the Comanche.

He should have been very hungry, but he wasn't. He ate a few hard biscuits with sticks of jerked beef and washed them down with sips of rye whiskey. The horse ate what horses were supposed to, tall sweet grass.

It was a warm night and he unrolled his blanket and slept on it, using his saddlebags as a pillow. He awoke an hour before sunrise and took the time to build a fire and make a pot of coffee. He had grown fond of coffee with sugar and condensed milk when he could get it. He made a pan of beans and bacon and dipped the hard biscuits into the gravy to soften them up a bit. As the sun broke dawn, Two Hawks finished his coffee and smoked his pipe.

He was traveling south, but to where, and for what purpose? It mattered not, he supposed, and saddled his horse and continued riding. He rode all morning and well into the

26

afternoon before he stopped to rest his horse.

He smoked a bowl of tobacco while the horse rested and grazed. He kept his mind clear of Yellow Sky. It served no purpose to cloud his mind with thoughts of her. Before mounting the saddle, he looked about and tried to figure out where he was. Oklahoma most likely; he hadn't ridden far enough south to reach Texas as yet. Where he was going seemed to have no purpose as well, so when he continued riding, it was at a much more leisurely pace.

Near sundown, Two Hawks was close to the mountains and looked for good cover to make camp for the night. As he removed the saddle from his horse, Two Hawks caught a faint scent in the air. Bacon and beans and something else, possibly beef. He removed the Winchester rifle from the sleeve and a box of ammunition. From the saddlebags, Two Hawks dug out his telescopic tomahawk and Bowie knife and attached both to his belt. Then he followed the scent, which came from the west.

He walked for about a quarter of a mile and paused to check the wind direction. The scent was much stronger and close. He waited for darkness to set in and the campfire to expose the campsite. Men were talking and laughing in front of the fire. They were white men, and Two Hawks could see a string of horses tethered together by rope.

Two Hawks's first thought was these men were outlaws and the horses were stolen, but as far as he was concerned, all white men were outlaws and thieves.

These men were also stupid. They sat on one side of the fire, and that blinded them to what was directly in front of them. He counted five men seated close together, and they were eating from tin plates.

There was no real reason for attacking these men. Two Hawks certainly didn't want their horses, and he could have avoided them altogether and let them be. He cocked the lever of his

Winchester and shot the first one in the chest. Before the remaining four could react, he shot two more. The other two jumped up and grabbed their sidearms but, blinded by the campfire, they didn't know where to shoot. Two Hawks simply shot them both.

He walked into their camp and checked the men. One was still alive, but barely. Two Hawks drew the Bowie knife, knelt before the man, and took his scalp. He went through the men's pockets and saddlebags and found several hundred dollars in gold coins and another hundred in folding money. He tossed the folding money into the fire. One of the men had a fine Peacemaker pistol and holster. Two Hawks took that and a box of ammunition. The men had ample supplies, including fresh pouches of tobacco. Two Hawks gathered what he wanted and wrapped them in a blanket. The horses were still tethered together, and he cut them loose. About to leave their camp, Two Hawks paused to take the scalps of the other four men, and then returned to his horse.

He built a fire and cooked bacon and beans. The men had a fresh loaf of cornbread and Two Hawks feasted on it. There were cans of condensed milk and he sweetened his coffee with it.

Afterward, his belly full, Two Hawks smoked his pipe and prayed to the great spirits for purpose. Although Yellow Sky was a devoted follower of the white man's Christian God, Two Hawks didn't believe. It seemed silly to believe in a god that existed in a country across the ocean, a god who allowed himself to be tortured and nailed to a cross.

As he settled in to sleep, the men he killed were already forgotten. As was his custom, Two Hawks awoke before sunrise. He took no food, just a few sips of water, then saddled his horse and continued riding in a southern direction.

He rode for hours without thinking or choosing a path. At a

crossroad there was a sign. Two Hawks read English just fine. The sign said *Texas Border Twenty Miles.* He stopped and rested his horse and ate what was left of the cornbread. He sipped rye whiskey while he ate and then smoked a bowl of tobacco.

Two Hawks rode ten more miles and came across a small farm. The farmer was growing corn. The stalks were young and needed months to reach maturity. At the edge of the field stood a cabin, barn, and corral.

He dismounted, took the Winchester, and walked to the corral. The farmer had four large plow horses and a mule. There were wagon tracks but no wagon. Smoke billowed up from a stone chimney.

Two Hawks removed his boots and walked up the steps to the porch and looked through a window. The farmer was eating at a table. He was alone. Two Hawks pushed in the door and entered the cabin with the Winchester aimed at the farmer.

The farmer wasn't afraid.

"Who are you?" the farmer asked.

"I am called Two Hawks."

"Where are your boots, Two Hawks?" the farmer asked.

"Outside. I took them off so they wouldn't squeak on the wood."

"No need to sneak up on me, Two Hawks. My door is open to white man, black, or red," the farmer said. "And you can rest easy with that Winchester unless you think I'm going to attack you with a bowl of stew."

Two Hawks lowered the Winchester. "Where is your woman? I saw wagon tracks but no wagon."

"My wife and daughter have gone to a neighbor's to help deliver a baby," the farmer said. "I don't expect them back for several days. Look, you can shoot me and rob my cabin or you can sit and share a meal. I have too much stew for one man to eat, and my wife baked fresh bread before she left this morning."

Two Hawks approached the table, set the Winchester aside, and took a chair opposite the farmer.

"I'll get another bowl," the farmer said.

He stood and reached for a bowl and spoon on the counter behind him and then filled the bowl with stew from the large pot hanging in the fireplace. He set the bowl and spoon in front of Two Hawks and then tore off a sizable hunk of crusty bread.

Two Hawks tasted the stew. It was full of beef with potatoes and carrots. He nodded his approval at the farmer.

"I saw a sign that said Texas was twenty miles away," Two Hawks said. "I plan to cross to Texas, how will I know the border?"

"Simple enough," the farmer said. "When you reach the Red River, you cross it and you're in Texas. I see you're an educated man and a Christian man."

"I had much schooling on the reservation," Two Hawks said.

"The Indian Nation in the Ozarks?" the farmer said.

As he ate, Two Hawks nodded.

"You set out by yourself?" the farmer asked.

"My wife died," Two Hawks said. "I had no reason to stay."

"I'm truly sorry to hear that," the farmer said. "Losing a wife is a terrible thing for a man to bear."

"She is with her God the Jesus Christ," Two Hawks said.

The farmer nodded. "I expect so," he said. "So what do you plan to do?"

"I won't go back to the reservation," Two Hawks said. "There is nothing there for me any longer."

"I expect not," the farmer said.

"In my youth, I left the reservation with Black Horse and took part in the war against the white man on the Llano," Two Hawks said. "When the army led us back to the reservation, we traveled through Fort Smith. There is a big general store on the main street. I saw in the window two small yellow birds living in a big golden cage. It was a beautiful cage for the birds to live in but still a cage. That's what a reservation is, a big cage."

"I understand," the farmer said. "Let's have us a cup of coffee and watch the sunset."

The farmer removed a coffee pot from the woodstove and filled two mugs with coffee. "I am partial to a little taste of bourbon with my evening coffee, Two Hawks. Would you like to try some?"

"Bourbon?" Two Hawks said.

"It's whiskey from Kentucky," the farmer said. "It has more flavor than rye and goes right nicely with coffee."

"I will try some," Two Hawks said.

The farmer added an ounce of bourbon to each mug.

"Let's watch the sunset," the farmer said.

Two Hawks and the farmer went to the porch, lit their pipes, and sipped coffee as the sun lowered to the horizon.

"This is fine whiskey," Two Hawks said.

"Every once in a while the white man does something right," the farmer said.

Two Hawks grinned at the farmer's joke. "Every once in a while," he said.

"It will be dark soon," the farmer said. "Let's have a few more cups of coffee and you can stay the night. Have breakfast in the morning and be on your way."

"You have no fear of me," Two Hawks said.

"If you meant harm, you'd a done it by now," the farmer said. "You're welcome to stay the night."

Two Hawks sipped his coffee. "What did you call this?"

The farmer grinned. "Bourbon," he said.

The famer prepared a hearty breakfast for Two Hawks. Afterward they had coffee and watched the sky brighten as the new day dawned.

"I have ample supplies to spare if you need some," the farmer said.

"I am well equipped," Two Hawks said.

"How about a bottle of bourbon then? To cut the dryness on the trail."

"I will pay you for it," Two Hawks said. "I have gold coin."

"Friends don't take money from friends," the farmer said.

Two Hawks rode south with an unopened bottle of bourbon in his saddlebags.

His horse was well-rested, and he pushed hard and reached the Red River before noon. The water was up, so he rode west a bit to find a good spot to cross. After about a mile, he reached a point where a large herd of cattle had crossed just a few days before. He waded the horse into the water and slowly crossed. The deepest point came to his boots, and the horse didn't need to swim to cross to the other side, although the horse did need to fight a strong undertow.

Once on the Texas side of the river, Two Hawks allowed his horse to rest. He sat in the sun to dry his pants and boots. After an hour, he mounted up and rode southwest for a while. He wasn't sure how far it was to the Llano Estacado, but he was in no particular hurry, so he traveled at a leisurely pace.

As a young man, when he traveled to the Llano with his father and Black Horse, the herds of buffalo covered the vast plains for as far as he could see. The buffalo hunters were there to kill as many buffalo as possible. The white government paid for the hides, and the hunters left the skinless animals to rot in the sun. Black Horse spoke the truth when he told those who followed him off the reservation that the white government paid the hunters to exterminate the buffalo, because to kill the buffalo was to kill all Comanche and every other native tribe.

Two Hawks witnessed with his own eyes the destruction caused by the hunters. Hundreds of skinless corpses spread across the plains with the coyote and buzzards and maggots feasting on the rotting meat.

The sight filled his heart with hatred and made it easy to follow his father and Black Horse into battle against the hunters. To kill so massive a beast as the buffalo required the most powerful of weapons, and the hunters were equipped with Sharps rifles. A Sharps could bring down a buffalo with one shot, but held just one round at a time and was slow to fire. A Comanche could fire five arrows in the time it took to fire and reload one Sharps bullet. Most of the hunters had just the Sharps rifle and a handgun. Very few had Winchesters. The hunters were also lazy men who ate and drank too much. They usually got drunk after dark, and many of their camps had whores they passed around. Their drunken behavior made it easy to attack at night and kill them where they slept.

Black Horse led raids on the hunters' camps. Many of them were killed and wounded, and scalps were taken. After several such raids, the Texas Rangers and army got involved. More soldiers than the young Two Hawks had ever seen before chased them across the Llano. His father was shot in the leg by a man named Dixon. Thirty-five Comanche were killed and a like amount wounded. Black Horse was sent to prison in Florida. The rest returned to the reservation in disgrace, escorted by soldiers and paraded through Fort Smith like beaten mongrel dogs.

The elevation slowly rose. The Llano was near. Two Hawks decided to make camp at a small stream that fed off the Red River. He filled his canteens with cool water and built a fire to make coffee. He had beans and bacon and while they cooked, he drank a cup of coffee with condensed milk.

The day his father was shot in the chest at the Adobe Walls, they were running from the soldiers and Texas Rangers. Two Hawks stopped to help his father, but it was no use. Moments from dying, his father said to him, "Never be afraid to fight and die. Fear is your only true enemy."

Two Hawks ate while watching the sunset. Afterward he enjoyed another cup of coffee sweetened with the farmer's bourbon. And for the first time in his entire life, Two Hawks felt real freedom in his heart and he knew that no matter what, he would never surrender that feeling again.

CHAPTER THREE

Emmet was chopping firewood when the message from Judge Isaac Parker in Fort Smith arrived. Parker sent a deputy marshal to deliver the message and the deputy said he would wait for Emmet to saddle his horse.

Amy and the girls were on the porch shucking corn and cracking snap peas.

"Judge Parker needs to see me," Emmet told them. "I'll be staying in town tonight and be back in the morning."

Amy looked at her son with that sixth sense she always seemed to have.

"I wouldn't worry, Mother," Emmet said. "Every time some new rules governing the reservation come down from Washington, Judge Parker sends for me."

Emmet changed his shirt, packed a small overnight bag, and rode to Fort Smith with the deputy.

Isaac Parker was not yet fifty years old, but had the look of a man twenty years older due to his snowy white hair and beard. He started graying when still in his twenties and it progressed quickly when he reached thirty. Some joked that his duties as a federal judge was what aged him, but Parker paid that kind of talk no mind.

A congressman in Missouri before being appointed a federal judge by President Grant, Parker gained notoriety quickly for his letter-of-the-law convictions and his quickness to hang folks.

35

He soon became known as the hanging judge, although the truth was he had no real desire to execute a man if the sentence wasn't dictated by the crime. On one September morning not long after he took office, six men were hanged at the same time; thus his fame as the hanging judge was born.

Parker also had complete jurisdiction over the Indian Nation as well and governed it as he did the court, with fairness and toughness and always within the law.

He stood at the window of his office on the second floor of the courthouse and watched the streets of Fort Smith. Arkansas was a wild and lawless place when he first took office a decade ago. Murder, rape, and robbery were daily occurrences. Decent citizens were afraid to walk the streets for fear of being killed. Parker increased the number of deputy marshals and slowly turned things around to the law's side. Arkansas still owned its share of outlaws, to be sure, but their days were quickly dwindling.

When he spotted his deputy and Emmet Youngblood riding to the courthouse, Parker returned to his desk to wait.

After a few minutes there was a knock on the door.

"Enter," Parker said.

The door opened and Emmet walked in. "You wanted to see me, Judge?" he said.

"I did, Emmet. Have a seat," Parker said.

Emmet took a comfortable chair facing the desk.

"I'll get right to the point, Emmet," Parker said. "Some settlers came across five dead two-bit horse thieves two days' ride south of here. They were scalped."

"Scalped?" Emmet said.

"Two Hawks went missing last week, didn't he?" Parker said.

"You think Two Hawks did that?" Emmet asked.

"I don't know, but it's entirely possible," Parker said. "I'm sending you to look for him."

"Judge, I'm no scout and tracker by any stretch," Emmet said.

"I know," Parker said. "You won't be alone. You'll leave as soon as I can arrange for a tracker. Are you staying in town tonight?"

"At the boarding house."

"Good. Report to me right after breakfast," Parker said.

"How is your mother?" the widow Stevens asked Emmet as he sat with her on the porch of her boarding house.

"Just fine," Emmet said.

"Your girls?"

"Also fine."

"You need a wife, Emmet."

"Mrs. Stevens, I don't need a . . ."

"My niece has just come of age," Stevens said. "Eighteen and pretty as can be. Good hips, too."

"How are her teeth?" Emmet asked.

"Her teeth?" Stevens said. "Oh, you're joking."

"Will you excuse me, Mrs. Stevens?" Emmet asked.

"Certainly."

Emmet left the porch and took a walk through town. The streets were crowded with pedestrians, men in suits, women in fashionable dresses. More people rode in buggies than on horseback. Electric wires for the telegraph were strung on poles on one side of Main Street.

He entered Greenly's General Store and Mercantile. Greenly was behind the counter. Most of the customers were women shopping for home goods.

"Emmet Youngblood, how are you, son?" Greenly said.

"Fine, Mr. Greenly. I'd like to get a couple of dolls for my girls. What do you have?"

"Follow me," Greenly said.

He led Emmet to a separate room filled with children's clothing and toys.

"That counter is dolls for girls," Greenly said. "I'll be at the counter when you're ready."

Emmet went through the array of dolls and selected two porcelain dolls that had real human hair and eyes that opened and closed. They came with tiny brushes, combs, and hair ribbons. He carried the two dolls to the counter.

"Can you wrap these for me?" he asked Greenly.

"I can."

"And what do you have in the way of candy?"

"Candy? Pretty near everything."

While Greenly wrapped the dolls, Emmet picked out licorice sticks, gumballs, and dark chocolate wrapped in paper that came from Switzerland.

"I'll take a fresh pouch of pipe tobacco," Emmet said. "What do I owe you?"

"Be eleven dollars," Greenly said.

"I'll take the tobacco with me and pick up the rest in the morning," Emmet said. "I'm staying in town tonight."

Emmet returned to the boarding house, sat on the porch, and smoked a bowl of fresh tobacco. He was still trying to wrap his mind around what Judge Parker told him about Two Hawks.

Emmet had known Two Hawks since he first went to work as a deputy on the reservation. Yellow Sky wasn't sick at the time, and she kept her brooding husband in line for the most part. Two Hawks was a powder keg searching for a lit match. Emmet was no head doctor, but it was possible Yellow Sky's death pushed him over the edge.

Emmet had no love for horse thieves to be sure, but to kill and scalp them in cold blood took a certain kind of attitude he couldn't understand. Emmet had never felt the hatred and prejudice many white men felt toward the Comanche and other natives. He was mostly white and easily passed for all white in college in Boston. He didn't hide his Sioux and Apache blood, but he didn't speak of it either. He went to college to get an education, not to discuss race relations.

The widow Stevens opened the porch door. "Supper is on the table," she said.

"Be right in," Emmet said.

Odd how, when he was at home and surrounded by the memories of his wife, he rarely went to sleep thinking of her and missing her. But when he was away from home, her loss always hit him like a punch to the heart.

Sometimes he could almost smell Sarah's scent on the pillow. She took great care of her hair and it always smelled of clean soap. Sometimes when she was asleep, he would bury his nose in her hair.

Sarah always went to sleep with a smile and awoke the same way, no matter how hard a day had been—and there were plenty of hard days.

Amy was right, of course, he should remarry.

But how do you commit to a woman when you still love your wife, heart and soul?

In the morning, Emmet ate a full breakfast prepared by Mrs. Stevens and then walked over to the courthouse to see Judge Parker.

"Emmet, I've sent for a tracker," Parker said. "Go home and pack your gear and be ready when I send for you. The court will supply you with expense money for as long as it takes to bring Two Hawks in to this court for questioning."

"It won't be easy smoking Two Hawks out, Judge," Emmet said. "He's pure Comanche, reservation raised or not."

"I didn't say it would be easy," Parker said. "But necessary."

"Okay, Judge, I'll be ready," Emmet said.

"How long will you be gone?" Amy asked as she watched Emmet pack his gear.

"I don't know," Emmet said. "Weeks, probably. Maybe even a month or more."

"The girls and I will ride with you to town when you leave," Amy said. "They would like to see you off since you might be gone a long time."

Emmet nodded. "All right, Mother," he said. "Mother, if something were to happen to me, the girls will be . . ."

"Do you need to even ask me such a question?" Amy said.

"No, I suppose not," Emmet said.

"Finish your packing," Amy said. "Supper is on the table."

CHAPTER FOUR

Whenever the prisoner wagon returned, it was as if the circus had come to town. Everybody in town lined both sides of Main Street to watch the wagon parade along to the courthouse.

When Parker heard the commotion in the streets, he went to his office window and spotted the prisoner wagon. He tossed on his coat and went down to the rear of the courthouse to greet his marshals.

Jack Youngblood, senior marshal, drove the wagon. His tall horse was tethered behind it. Five deputies rode alongside the wagon, which was filled with eleven prisoners. The wagon was really just a freight wagon fitted with a steel cage, but it did the job.

The wagon rolled to a stop, and Jack jumped down and walked to the rear of the wagon. He was what the newspapers and dime novels would call "larger than life." Six-foot-three in his stocking feet, broad at the shoulder, and narrow at the hip, he was every front cover of every dime novel ever written.

"Get this scum inside the jail," Jack told his men.

"Marshal Youngblood, a moment please," Parker said.

Jack turned and walked to Parker. "Hi, Judge," he said.

"I count eleven," Parker said. "You left with thirteen warrants."

"Two resisted arrest," Jack said. "I had to educate them on their folly."

"I can imagine how you did that," Parker said. "By God, you

41

smell worse than a hog giving birth."

"Been on the trail for a month, Judge," Jack said. "What do you expect?"

"I expect you to have a shave and a bath and to put on clean clothes and report to my office," Parker said. "Can you do that, Marshal Youngblood?"

"Sure, Judge," Jack said. "I can do that."

Jack soaked in a hot bath while Chao-xing Fong shaved him. She ran the Chinese bathhouse on the west side of town, and Jack was a frequent customer at the tubs and also his lover. She wasn't but thirty, but most of her male customers called her Mama.

"Hold still," she said as she scraped stubble off Jack's face.

"Can't help it," Jack said. "The way you're touching me has got me all excited."

"You are a bad man with bad thoughts," Chao-xing said.

"Come in here with me and I'll show you how bad," Jack said.

"Big talk for a man with a razor at his throat," she said. "Now hold still."

Jack held still while Chao-xing finished shaving him. "There," she said. "All pretty again. Want more hot water?"

"I do, and bring me a shot of whiskey," Jack said. "And mix a raw egg in it while you're at it."

Jack knocked on Judge Parker's door, opened it, and stepped inside. Parker was at his desk.

"I've been reading the reports," Parker said. "Your men all swear that you had no choice but to shoot those two men in self-defense."

Jack crossed the room to the woodstove where a coffee pot

rested. He grabbed a cup from the table and filled it with coffee.

"As your men think you walk on water, I expect them to say no less," Parker said.

"You send me after outlaws wanted dead or alive, and you're surprised some of them chose dead," Jack said as he took a chair. "Why is that?"

"They chose or you did?" Parker said.

"Tell you what, Judge. Next assignment, why don't you send me a babysitter," Jack said.

"Don't laugh, Jack," Parker said. "I might just do that."

"Make the babysitter about twenty-five with yellow hair," Jack said.

"Jack, I'm sending you out again," Parker said.

"Judge, I just got back after a month on the trail," Jack said.

"Can't be helped," Parker said. "This is an emergency situation."

"What about Witson and Reeves?" Jack said.

"They left last week after Blue Duck and his bunch."

"They won't catch Blue Duck," Jack said. "He's holed up somewhere with Belle and Sam Starr."

"Never mind about Blue Duck," Parker said. "What do you know about Two Hawks?"

"Two Hawks? Nothing. I've seen him in town a few times selling horses to the army," Jack said. "Why?"

"Last week his wife passed away," Parker said. "He burned down his cabin with her body in it and then took off for parts unknown."

"Left the reservation?"

"A few days ago some settlers on their way to Texas came across five dead horse thieves," Parker said. "They had papers posted on them so it was easy to make the identification. Jack, they were scalped."

43

"We haven't had a scalping around here in a decade," Jack said. "You think it was this Two Hawks?"

"I'm sorry to say I do," Parker said. "I'll draw a thousand dollars in expense money and supply ammunition and possibles from the general store. You'll leave in the morning after you pick up your expense money."

Jack sighed heavily and openly.

"Get drunk, get a woman, do whatever, but be here at ten tomorrow morning and be ready to ride," Parker said. "Or else turn in your badge."

"I'll be here," Jack said. "Although I don't know why."

"And Jack, be here sober," Parker said.

"You keep pulling on that bottle, Jack, and all you'll be able to do when we go to bed is sleep," Chao-xing said.

Jack and Chao-xing were in her small apartment above the bathhouse where she lived. They were eating Chinese noodles with chicken. Jack was sipping bourbon whiskey as they ate.

"Why don't you have some tea, Jack?" she said.

"No man drinks tea," Jack said.

"You said same thing about wearing a Chinese robe, and here you are wearing one," Chao-xing said.

"Damn judge," Jack said as he pulled on the bourbon.

"Is he sending you out again?"

"Tomorrow."

"You just got back."

"I know it," Jack said. "But it's my job."

"Get another job," Chao-xing said.

"Doing what? Clerking in a store? Hauling freight?"

"Nobody shoots at store clerks," Chao-xing said.

Jack pulled on the bourbon again and she snatched it from his hand. Even though Jack outweighed her by a hundred or more pounds and had the strength of a bull, he would never lay a finger on her. It was his nature never to strike a woman. That made it easy for her to bully him, which she did often.

"No more whiskey, Jack," Chao-xing said.

She stood and crossed the room and stood in front of her bed. She untied her robe and let it slip off her shoulders. "Come here," she said. "I'll show you some ancient Chinese love secrets."

"Oh, damn," Jack said.

Chao-xing toyed with Jack's thick chest hair. "Chinese men don't have chest hair," she said. "Did you know that?"

"I can't say I've paid much attention to the chests of Chinese men," Jack said.

"Well, they don't," Chao-xing said.

"I believe you," Jack said and closed his eyes. Between the bourbon and love-making, he was getting sleepy.

"Jack, what's my full name?" Chao-xing said.

"Your name?"

"Yes, what is it?"

"I don't rightly recall," Jack said. "I'm so used to calling you Chao I just forgot the rest."

"Well, it isn't Mama."

"I figured it wasn't, and I never call you that."

"It's Chao-xing."

"I remember now. That's a right pretty name," Jack said.

"It means morning star."

"Morning star, huh," Jack said.

"What does Jack mean?"

"Jack means John and John don't mean nothing."

"Do you know why people call me Mama?"

"No, I don't," Jack said.

"It's an insult, Jack," Chao-xing said. "The railroad workers used to call the wives of the Chinese workers mama-san. Even to our faces. When I came to Fort Smith that's what they called me, mama-san."

"Does it bother you?" Jack said.

"Of course it bothers me."

"When I get back, I'll see to it that it stops," Jack said.

"I didn't ask you to do that," Chao-xing said.

"If it bothers you, I'll . . ."

"They'll still do it behind my back and closed doors," Chao-xing said.

"What are you saying then?" Jack asked.

"Just to call me by my name. Okay?"

"I will never understand women," Jack said. "Of any race."

"Do you want to make love again or sleep?"

"Can I do both?"

"No."

"Hell," Jack said.

In the morning, Chao-xing prepared a full breakfast and they ate at her tiny table in the kitchen.

"How long will you be gone this time?" she asked.

"No idea," Jack said.

"Jack, I've been thinking of leaving Fort Smith," Chao-xing said.

"Why?"

"I see little future for me in Fort Smith."

"Well, hell, where is there a future anywhere?" Jack said.

"San Francisco."

"What's in San Francisco?"

"Thirty thousand Chinese, maybe more."

"That's no reason to pack up and move two thousand miles," Jack said.

"It's reason enough."

"We'll continue this conversation when I get back."

"I might be gone when you get back," Chao-xing said.

"If that's the case, write me a letter and let me know how you're faring," Jack said.

"That's all you have to say on the matter?"

"I ain't the one leaving," Jack said. "If you're still here when I return, we'll continue this conversation. Right now I have to meet the judge."

"You go to hell, Jack Youngblood," Chao-xing said.

Jack walked to the courthouse trying to figure out why Chao-xing was so mad at him. She tells him she's going to San Francisco and *she's* mad at *him*. White, black, red, or yellow, women just didn't make any sense.

At the courthouse, Jack checked in with the lobby deputy and then went to the second floor to Judge Parker's office.

Parker was behind his desk. His brother, Emmet, was seated in a chair. His mother stood at the window to the right of Parker.

"What is this?" Jack said.

"Before you say another word, Jack, I am pairing you with Emmet to pursue Two Hawks," Parker said.

"Like hell," Jack said.

Emmet stood up and looked at Jack.

"Emmet is the chief of reservation police and under my jurisdiction," Parker said. "Two Hawks is his responsibility and . . ."

"Then send him," Jack said and turned his back.

"Don't you turn your back on me," Parker said. "Or I'll have your badge."

Jack spun around and walked to Emmet. "I will not ride with a back-stabbing, woman-stealing pipsqueak like . . ."

Amy rushed forward and slapped Jack across the face. "The heart wants what it wants, and hers wanted him," she said.

"You can grow old and bitter or make peace with that fact and your brother. Now shake his hand or, so help me God, I will disown you as my son."

Jack looked at his mother.

"Don't think I don't mean it," Amy said.

Jack sighed and extended his right hand to Emmet. The brothers shook hands.

"I'll be downstairs with the girls waiting to say goodbye," Amy said. She looked at Parker and nodded. "Judge."

"Mrs. Youngblood," Parker said.

Jack and Emmet watched their mother stroll out of the office.

"Now to business," Parker said. "I've written a warrant for Two Hawks, but he is to be brought back alive if at all possible for questioning. Is that clear, Jack?"

"Yes," Jack said.

"I've drawn two thousand dollars for expense money," Parker said. "Emmet, I'll see to you to keep track of it. Your brother isn't fond of math. Draw your supplies, and good luck to you both."

Jack turned and walked to the door.

"Marshal," Parker said.

Jack paused and looked back.

"Alive, if at all possible," Parker said.

As Jack and Emmet walked down to the front of the courthouse, Jack said, "Did you know about this?"

"I did not," Emmet said. "It was as big a surprise to me as to you."

"Well, you can ride with me, but stay the hell out of my way," Jack said.

"Be nice, Jack, or I'll tell Ma," Emmet said with a grin. "She'd likely slap you again."

"She would, too," Jack said.

They reached the courthouse steps where in the street Amy, Mary Louise, and Sarah stood beside the buggy.

"Hello, Uncle Jack," Mary Louise said.

"Hello, sweetheart," Jack said.

Sarah looked at the ground.

"No hello for your uncle?" Jack said.

"You frighten me, sir," Sarah said.

"He frightens everybody," Emmet said. "Don't let it bother you none, honey."

"Yes, Pa," Sarah said.

"Well, we need to draw our supplies," Emmet said. "How about a kiss and hug for your pa?"

Mary Louise and Sarah gave Emmet warm hugs and kisses.

"You mind your grandmother while I'm gone," Emmet said.

"We will, Pa," Mary Louise said.

"We need to draw our supplies now," Emmet said. "You girls run along home and mind your grandmother."

"John, a moment please," Amy said.

She walked away, and Jack followed her.

"You brother is not the gunman you are, John," Amy said.

"I know that," Jack said.

"His daughters don't have a mother," Amy said. "They need their father. Promise me you will look after him."

"Ma, Emmet is a grown . . ."

"Promise me, damn you," Amy said.

Jack was always surprised with the ease his mother could toss a cuss word around.

"I promise," Jack said.

"Good," Amy said. "Now go do your job."

As they took the southwest road out of Fort Smith, Jack said, "I see you're still riding that skinny pinto. Be lucky to make twenty miles on that pony."

"That plow horse you're riding couldn't out run a jackrabbit," Emmet said.

"Want to see?" Jack said.

"No. We got a long way to go, and I don't fancy killing my horse before we get started," Emmet said. "It's going to take us two days just to reach the spot where Two Hawks killed those horse thieves."

"If I forget, remind me later when we make camp to beat your ass," Jack said.

"I'll put it on my social calendar," Emmet said.

Chao-xing watched from her bedroom window as Jack and Emmet took the west road out of town. They passed right by her window, and Jack didn't as much as glance her way. She waited until he was out of sight before turning away.

She sat at her table and drank tea.

Chao-xing came to America when she was just eight years old. Her father sought a better life for her and her mother, so they sailed to San Francisco on a four-mast schooner and arrived in America in 1863. Her father was an explosives expert and highly skilled in the handling of the very dangerous explosive called nitroglycerin. He went to work for the Central Pacific Railroad and was in charge of blasting through mountains and rocks. The work was dangerous, and he was well paid for his efforts. Most of the thousands of Chinese that worked on the railroad were backbreaking laborers who worked twelve hours a day busting rocks and laying track.

An entire tent-like city traveled with the railroad as it expanded west. Her mother, as did many of the wives of the Chinese workers, took in laundry. Her father had the idea of purchasing bathing tubs and a large service tent and expanded the laundry to a bathhouse. Her mother became skilled with a razor and scissors, and soon was barbering the men before they took their weekly baths. Chao-xing did laundry for her mother. When she reached the age of eleven, her mother taught her how to use a straight razor and scissors.

Many of the workers took delight in being shaved by tiny Chao-xing and she amassed a large following. By 1867, the railroad had switched to using dynamite, and her father's job became considerably safer. She was there when the transcontinental railroad was complete in Cheyenne.

Her father, growing wealthy by this time, stayed with the railroad to build tributaries that expanded routes to major cities and towns north and south. By 1873, when most of the expansion was completed, her father made plans to return to China as a wealthy man.

They were closer to New York at the time than California, and her father decided to visit relatives living in Manhattan. They traveled first by railroad to Little Rock in Arkansas and stayed overnight. Her father had amassed a fortune of fifteen-thousand dollars. He and her mother were murdered for the money by outlaws that had once worked for the railroad. The men responsible were never apprehended. Chao-xing, now eighteen, found herself alone for the first time in her life and with little money or resources.

There were some Chinese laundries in Little Rock, and she went to work at one just to stay alive. The hours were long, sometimes fourteen or more a day, but she had food and a place to stay while she saved her money. After four years she had amassed the tidy sum of one thousand dollars. Now twenty-two years old, Chao-xing was unaware of her beauty. She became aware of it one evening when a Chinese pimp came to visit her small room over the laundry and attempted to recruit her services. She declined his offer to work as one of his stable girls and he left. He returned two nights later with three thousand dollars in gold and promised her much, much more if she came to work for him. He explained to her that he had yellow-haired women, red-haired, Sioux, and black, but lacked an Asian, and that men would pay handsomely for sex with a beautiful Asian woman such as her.

Again, Chao-xing refused.

The pimp returned a few nights later with four of his men. They broke into her room and kidnapped her. They gagged her, tied her hands and feet with rope, and covered her head with a sack. It was the middle of the night, and the streets of Little Rock were deserted except for one man, a young marshal named Jack Youngblood. He was riding into Little Rock to pick up a prisoner from the sheriff to transport to Fort Smith for trial. Chao-xing wasn't going quietly as the pimp's men tried to stuff her into the back of a covered wagon.

Jack simply rode up to the pimp and his men and asked them what they were doing. Chao-xing couldn't see but she could hear what happened next. Three gunshots sounded in rapid succession, followed by the sounds of a scuffle. It was over in a matter of seconds, and when Jack removed the sack from her head, three men lay dead and two unconscious. One of the dead was the pimp.

It took some straightening out with the sheriff, but the two men who lived were prosecuted in Judge Parker's court in Fort Smith. Chao-xing had to testify at their trial. They swore vengeance on her, but she, like most Chinese, wasn't afraid to press charges.

After the trial, she returned to Little Rock and lived there for another two years. She worked hard, saved her money, and, after two years, had twenty-five-hundred dollars in the bank. She had many clients but few friends and decided to relocate to Fort Smith and open her own business. Part of her decision was business-oriented. Fort Smith was a growing community, and public bathhouses were few and far between. She was also an excellent barber.

Her other reason was personal. She was infatuated with Jack Youngblood and wanted to see him again, even if only as a client. She spent fifteen-hundred dollars on a location, tubs, and supplies and even a barber chair that came all the way from Chicago. For months, Chao-xing spotted Jack on the streets as he came and went from the courthouse. She even took to the streets to watch him ride into town with the prisoner's wagon, but never once did he glance her way.

Then one afternoon, filthy from a long trail ride, he entered her bathhouse. He didn't recognize her. "I need a shave, a hot bath, and a shot of whiskey with a raw egg in it," he said. "And stir the egg."

As she shaved him, he looked at her, and slowly recognition came into his eyes.

"You're that girl, the one they tried to kidnap in Little Rock," he said. "What in hell are you doing here?"

It didn't happen at first. Jack came in maybe once a week for a shave and a bath, sometimes not for a month. As it turned out, Jack was a bit of a dullard when it came to women and didn't even realize he was being seduced. Chao-xing finally had to take drastic measures to gain his attention.

After weeks on the trail, a filthy-looking Jack came in for a shave and a bath around closing time. There was hot water for just one more bath. She convinced Jack that the best way to shave him would be while he soaked in a hot tub because the heat and water softened his beard. It was night and the room was dark, as just a few candles were lit on a table. As she lathered his face, Jack didn't realize she was naked until her breasts brushed up against his shoulders.

As she sipped tea, Chao-xing slowly returned to the present, and the memories faded from her mind.

"Go ahead and ride away Jack Youngblood," she said aloud.

"You big dumb son of a bitch."

A few miles west of Fort Smith, Jack suddenly stopped his horse.

"What?" Emmet said.

"Here is as good a place as any to take your beating," Jack said.

"We both know you can whip me to a frazzle," Emmet said. "What good would that do?"

"It would make me feel a whole lot better," Jack said.

"You'll just have to wait until we make camp," Emmet said and rode on.

"Hey," Jack said as Emmet rode away from him. "You come back here and take what's coming to you."

Emmet ignored him and kept riding.

"Well, dammit," Jack said and tugged on the reins.

He caught up to Emmet and they rode side-by-side for a while.

"Anybody ever tell you that you have a serious problem with anger?" Emmet said.

"Anybody ever tell you kid brothers should mind their older brothers?" Jack said.

"Why do you think I didn't get a gun and shoot you after you beat the tar out of me that other time?" Emmet said.

"I figured Ma wouldn't like you shooting me, that's why," Jack said.

"Ma is the one who hit you over the head with a bottle, you dumb ox," Emmet said.

"I always wondered that," Jack said.

"You wondered?" Emmet said. "It amazes me that you can think at all. Come on, we need to make twenty miles before dark."

★ ★ ★ ★ ★

No stranger to hard work, Amy chopped firewood at the block in front of the house. Mary Louise and Sarah were on the porch cracking snap peas.

"Mary, come down here and bring some of this kindling into the house," Amy said.

Mary Louise carried an apple basket down to Amy and they filled it with kindling.

"Is Pa going to be all right, Grandma?" Mary Louise asked.

"Your Uncle Jack is with him," Amy said. "Heaven help any man stupid enough to get in his way."

CHAPTER FIVE

Two Hawks followed the Canadian River southwest for two days and nights. The land alongside the river was plush with life. He had no real destination in mind, and he didn't really want one. He was enjoying the idea of freedom without restraint for the first time in his life and decided to simply put no mark on where his horse could take him.

He made a temporary camp along the Canadian and fished and hunted wild chickens and hares. He was close to the Llano, and he decided in a few days he would travel south and explore the vast desert wasteland. He needed to prepare for the journey beforehand. His supplies would last a few weeks at best if he ate what he hunted for the time being, but the Llano was vast, and he didn't know what to expect in the way of game. There were sure to be towns along the Canadian River, but he couldn't venture close to one without being spotted.

For the moment, Two Hawks was content to roast the hare he caught earlier on the spit and drink bourbon-laced coffee while he watched the sunset. As soon as he ate and it was dark, he extinguished the fire. It was a warm night; he didn't need the fire for heat and the light could be seen from great distances.

Before he settled in to sleep, he noticed a red dot on the horizon to the west. It was several miles away, but he could tell it was a campfire. Two Hawks removed short pieces of rope and hobbled his horse so he wouldn't wander away or try to follow him. He removed the Peacemaker and holster from a saddlebag and put it around his waist. He carried the Winchester on one hand and the telescopic tomahawk in the other and then walked toward the red dot.

The campfire was several miles away and Two Hawks walked quickly to cover the ground. When he was several hundred yards away, he could hear men talking in hushed tones. He heard three distinct voices.

Two Hawks approached the campfire from the north and flanked the three men. He listened to their conversation for a while.

"Do you think they'll come after us?" one said.

"Course they'll come after us," a second man said. "We robbed their bank."

"It weren't much of a bank," a third voice said. "Or much of a town either."

"Maybe so, but it's all they had," the second man said. "They'll come. We'll head for Adobe Walls and hide out awhile. We got plenty of supplies to last."

"Can't say I ever been there," the third man said.

"Isn't far," the second man said. "Two days' ride to the southeast near the Canadian River. Good game, too."

Two Hawks knew of the Adobe Walls from the battle fought there between Quanah Parker and the civilians at the trading post and the army. Parker lost the battle and was returned to the reservation, but he spoke of it often.

Two Hawks removed his boots, stood, and drew the Colt from its holster. He cocked the hammer and silently approached the three men from the north. He was within ten feet of them before any of them noticed him.

The man closest to Two Hawks yelled, "Assassin!" and jumped up. Two Hawks shot him in the head. The second man reached for his sidearm and Two Hawks shot him in the right lung. The third man didn't have a gun. He made a grab for the second man's pistol. Two Hawks flicked the telescopic toma-hawk; it extended to its full length of two feet, and he clubbed the third man in the skull with it.

To make sure each man was dead, Two Hawks bashed in their skulls with the tomahawk and then he used his Bowie knife to take their scalps. He went through their pockets and gear and found eighty dollars in gold coins and the paper money they stole from the bank. He tossed the paper money into the fire and kept the coins. They had ample supplies, so he took what he wanted, including several bottles of rye whiskey and a large canteen, and wrapped them in one of their blankets. The three horses were hobbled with leather strips. He removed the hobbles and set the horses free.

The men had made a pot of coffee and he used it to extinguish the fire.

Aided by the bright moon, Two Hawks put on his boots and returned to his campsite.

In the morning he would ride to Adobe Walls.

Thirty minutes before sunset, Jack said, "We best make camp before dark."

The brothers dismounted, and as Jack started to remove the saddle from his horse, Emmet said, "Hey, Jack?"

Jack turned and Emmet punched Jack square in the jaw with all his weight behind the punch. Jack moved backward a few inches and looked at Emmet.

"What the hell did you do that for?" Jack asked.

"For making my girls grow up without their uncle," Emmet said.

"I can't be . . ." Jack said as Emmet punched him again.

"For making Ma worry all the time," Emmet said.

"Go ahead, punch me again and see what happens," Jack said.

58

"My hand hurts," Emmet said.

"Make a fire. I'll see to the horses," Jack said. "That is, if your hand don't hurt too badly."

Jack added a splash of whiskey to the fry pan to add flavor to the beans and bacon and stirred it a bit with a wood spoon.

"Be about ten minutes," he said.

Emmet smoked his pipe and drank coffee. Jack lifted the coffee pot and filled a cup, then rolled a cigarette.

"Let me ask you something," Jack said. "Did you deliberately try to steal Sarah away from me?"

"You know better than that," Emmet said. "Nothing was planned. It just happened. She wasn't a good fit for you, and we both know that."

"I reckon that's true," Jack said.

"So why did you spend all these years hating me for something you know is true?" Emmet said.

"A man needs to know he can trust his kin," Jack said. "That his kin ain't going to dry-gulch him when his back is turned."

"Is that what you think we did?"

"Well, didn't you?"

"I told you right to your face when you came back from your assignment," Emmet said. "You went crazy and would have beaten me to death if not for Ma. A man doesn't dry-gulch somebody by telling him something to his face."

"I reckon not," Jack said.

"Jack, what happened between me and Sarah just happened," Emmet said. "Nobody planned it, it just happened. The honest truth is if she really loved you, it would never have happened in the first place."

"I reckon not," Jack said.

"Now let's eat," Emmet said.

★ ★ ★ ★ ★

In his bedroll, Emmet watched the stars and waited for sleep to take him. Beside him, Jack puffed on a rolled cigarette.

"Let me ask you something," Jack said. "How did you know you was in love with Sarah?"

"You can't be this dumb," Emmet said.

"I'm going to give you back those two punches, and I promise you're going to hurt a lot worse than my hand."

Emmet sighed. "Sometimes, when she'd walk into a room and I'd look at her, I felt as if I couldn't breathe," he said. "And when we were apart for more than a day I'd feel a panic in my chest like there was a hole and only she could fill it."

"And you never felt like that about another woman?"

"Not even close," Emmet said. "Can I get some sleep now?"

Two Hawks awoke with a full heart. He built a fire, made a big breakfast, and watched the sunrise while he ate. Then he packed his gear and headed southeast toward Adobe Walls. The dead outlaws said it was a two days' ride, but they were lazy men on weak horses. He would do the ride in a day and a half or less.

After he saddled his horse and mounted up, Two Hawks rode at a steady pace toward Adobe Walls.

"Where do you figure Two Hawks is headed?" Emmet asked.

Jack was squatted beside a set of tracks that were about a week old. "I don't think he's headed anywhere in particular," he said. "He's just riding."

Jack returned to the saddle. "He's got a large head start on us. Let's hope something slows him down."

"Can we reach the place marked on the map by Judge Parker by sundown?" Emmet asked.

"If we push hard," Jack said.

They rode through the morning and into the afternoon. They

stopped once to rest the horses for thirty minutes and eat some jerked beef.

"We got six hours of daylight left," Jack said. "I suggest we ride right up until sunset."

Close to dusk, Jack noticed something in the distance. He stopped his horse and Emmet fell in line beside him.

"See it?" Jack said.

"I see it," Emmet said.

"No more than a half mile off," Jack said.

Emmet dug his binoculars out from a saddlebag and looked at the dust cloud.

"That's cavalry, Jack," he said. "Looks like they stopped to make camp."

"Let's go see," Jack said, then he turned his horse and took off riding.

"What for?" Emmet said. "Ah, hell."

Emmet caught up to Jack, and they rode to the squad of cavalry soldiers making camp. As they approached the campsite, a dozen Winchester rifles were suddenly pointed at them.

"United States Marshal Jack Youngblood," Jack said. "Who is in command here?"

"That would be me, Captain Roberts."

"We saw your dust and thought we'd check it out," Jack said.

Roberts looked at Emmet. "Who are you?"

"Emmet Youngblood, chief of police at the reservation in Arkansas," Emmet said.

"Well, what are you fellows doing out here?" Roberts said.

"We was going to ask you the same thing," Jack said.

"Make camp with us," Roberts said. "We'll talk."

As Jack ate a plate of beans, bacon, and a hunk of cornbread, he looked at the young man seated opposite him at the campfire.

He was maybe all of twenty, tall and rangy and with short, dark hair.

"Sam Starr and his gang stole a bunch of horses destined for the army," Roberts said. "Killed the cowboys leading the horses to the fort and took off with them. We've been on their tail the better part of a week."

"And?" Jack said.

"Ask our scout," Roberts said. "Young Tom Horn here."

Jack looked at the young man seated opposite him.

"No more than six hours ahead of us," Horn said. "I'll head out early and report back when I find them."

"Alone?" Jack said.

"I ride fastest when I'm alone," Horn said.

"What about Blue Duck?" Emmet said. "We heard he was riding with Starr."

"That is a possibility," Roberts said.

"Captain, we have two good marshals chasing Blue Duck and Starr," Jack said. "We have pressing business, but we'd like to ride along with you and find out what happened to them."

"What about your pressing business?" Roberts said.

"It's important, for sure, but the lives of two marshals come first," Jack said.

Roberts looked at Emmet. "What say you?"

"I agree with Jack," Emmet said.

"You can ride with us then," Roberts said. "But marshal or not, I give the orders."

"I best turn in if I'm to ride in a few hours," Horn said.

"Good night, Tom," Roberts said.

After Horn left the campfire, Roberts looked at Jack. "Exactly what is your pressing business, Marshal?"

"A buck named of Two Hawks left the reservation and killed five horse thieves not far from here," Jack said. "We're tracking him down, but a day or two won't matter much."

"A renegade buck Comanche on the plains is army business for sure, but I expect you two can handle him on your own later," Roberts said. "We'll leave to go after Blue Duck at first light right after breakfast."

"You army boys eat well," Jack said as he ate freshly scrambled eggs.

"Haven't you ever heard an army travels on its stomach?" Roberts said. "Sun's up, let's move out."

Roberts took the point while his dozen soldiers rode behind him in a column of twos. Jack and Emmet flanked Roberts. They rode until noon and stopped for thirty minutes to rest their horses. Those who were hungry ate a cold lunch of a can of beans or cornbread.

"This Tom Horn, is he any good?" Jack asked Roberts.

"Best damn tracker I've ever seen," Roberts said. "And right handy with his .45-60 Winchester."

Jack rolled a cigarette and stood beside Emmet.

"You think Blue Duck is with Starr and his bunch?" Emmet asked.

"It's a possibility," Jack said. "And I'd love to take a crack at that old bushwhacker."

"Mount up, men," Roberts said. "We have some riding to do."

They rode hard until five in the afternoon when Roberts spotted Horn in the distance. "Hold up, men, and dismount. I see young Tom Horn returning."

It took about ten minutes for Horn to reach them. He dismounted next to Roberts. Before he spoke, he removed his canteen from the saddle and took several long gulps of water.

"It's them all right," Horn said. "Sam Starr and about eight others. They have the horses and two prisoners. One of them is a black man."

"Was the other wearing an eyepatch?" Jack asked.

"Come to think of it, he was," Horn said.

Emmet looked at Jack.

"Are they your men?" Roberts asked.

"It's them," Jack said.

"How far?" Roberts said.

"Four hours," Horn said. "They're holed up in a little box canyon near the Canadian River. Looks like they plan to stay awhile."

"Make camp. Eat a good supper. We'll ride after we've all had a few hours sleep and the moon is up," Roberts said.

Riding point, Horn held up his right hand to stop the men riding behind him. He dismounted and waited for Roberts to dismount and walk to him.

"Canyon is just a few hundred yards from here, Captain," Horn said. "Best just a few walk in and hold the rest here."

"I'll go," Jack said.

"Horn, lead the way," Roberts said. "Marshal, you and Emmet come with us. The rest of you men dismount and rest your horses."

Horn led Roberts, Jack, and Emmet several hundred yards north to a cliff that overlooked a small box canyon. They got down on their stomachs and looked below at the camp. The three-quarter moon cast a strange white glow on the ground, and several large campfires provided enough light to see adequately.

Cal Witson and Bass Reeves were tied back-to-back near a campfire. They had been roughed up severely but were alive. Four of the men were at a blanket, gambling with dice. Two were asleep. Two were drinking whiskey.

Roberts gave the hand signal to pull back, and they returned to the rest of the men.

"That's our marshals all right," Jack said.

"They'll kill them if we ride in," Roberts said.

Jack looked at Horn. "I hear you're good with a .45-60," he said.

"I am," Horn said.

Jack looked at Roberts. "Let them get drunk for a while," he said. "They can't shoot straight when drunk."

"What's on your mind, Marshal?" Roberts asked.

"Got any horse soldiers in your ranks?" Jack asked.

"What are you thinking, Jack?" Emmet asked.

Jack, Roberts, Emmet, and Horn peered over the ledge at the box canyon below. Starr's men were still awake, but drunk and loud.

Jack motioned for them to pull back, and they retreated thirty feet to the soldiers.

"Emmet, give me that hogleg you carry," Jack said.

"You're not going to do what I think you are," Emmet said.

"Let me have it," Jack said.

Emmet pulled the Colt Dragoon from its holster and gave it to Jack.

Jack tucked it into his belt and turned to Horn. "Shoot straight, young Tom," Jack said. "I ain't fixing to get myself killed."

While Emmet, Roberts, and the soldiers watched on their stomachs, Horn took a seated position with his .45-60 Winchester. Jack mounted his horse, pulled his Colt revolver, and looked at Horn.

Horn nodded.

Jack yanked on the reins and rode his horse past Horn and over the edge of the cliff. It wasn't a steep angle, and the massive horse had little trouble riding down the sloping hill.

The drunk outlaws didn't even notice Jack until he was upon

them. He shot the two closest to him and, while the others reached for their guns, Horn picked off two. Atop his massive horse, Jack shot three more outlaws, and Horn got the last one, who was running away.

Jack dismounted and pulled his field knife and cut the ropes binding Witson and Reeves.

An outlaw still alive moved, and Jack shot him dead.

"Howdy Cal, Bass," Jack said. "How you faring?"

"We ain't had food or water for two days," Witson said.

"Eat your fill," Roberts said. "My men are on burial detail, and that's going to take a while."

"What happened to Blue Duck and Sam Starr?" Jack asked.

"Blue Duck left days ago," Reeves said. "Sam Starr lit out this morning. Probably back with Belle by now, the murderous bastard."

"Jack, this ain't got to go in no report, does it?" Witson asked.

"I ain't fond of paperwork," Jack said.

"What are you doing out here anyway?" Witson said. "Parker send you after us?"

"Chasing a renegade Comanche named Two Hawks," Jack said. "Me and my brother, Emmet."

"Emmet? Where is he?" Witson asked.

"Good question," Jack said.

"With the burial detail," Horn said. "I'm fixing to join them as soon as I finish my coffee."

"Young Tom Horn, each of those shots you made were a hundred yards and in the dark," Jack said. "Excellent shooting, son."

"I can do better," Horn said.

"I believe you," Jack said. "Captain Roberts, any objections to a man getting some sleep?"

★ ★ ★ ★ ★

"We'll ride with you a ways," Witson said to Jack.

"Marshal Youngblood, it was a pleasure having you and your brother ride with us," Roberts said.

Jack nodded and looked at Horn. "Young Tom Horn, stay on the right side of things," he said. "I'd hate to have to be chasing you."

"I will," Horn said. "And I'd hate to be chased by you."

"Let's go if we're going," Jack said.

Riding side-by-side with Jack, Emmet looked at him and said, "That was something, what you did back there, Jack."

"Shooting drunk outlaws ain't nothing, Emmet," Jack said.

"I couldn't have done it," Emmet said.

Riding behind Emmet, Witson said, "Jack has more hard bark on him than any man I ever met."

"Goes for me too," Reeves said.

Jack turned around in the saddle. "How'd you wind up captive like that?" he asked.

"Three nights ago I was woken up by Blue Duck's knife at my throat," Witson said. "Sam Starr held his knife to Bass. Next thing we know, we're captives."

"Why didn't they just kill you?" Emmet asked.

"We figure with the army on their tails, they wanted a hostage for leverage," Reeves said.

"Tell us about this Two Hawks," Witson said. "The name sounds familiar."

"There isn't much to tell, really," Emmet said. "Lived on the reservation most of his life. Raised and sold horses to the army outpost, so you probably saw him around town. Near ten days ago now, his wife died and he burned down his cabin with her body in and took off. They found five scalped horse thieves, and Judge Parker thinks he's responsible. We were tracking him when we came across Captain Roberts and tailed along."

"I, for one, am very glad you did," Witson said.

"Goes for me too," Reeves said.

"What are you going to do now, head back to Fort Smith?" Jack said.

"Reckon so, come morning," Witson said.

"Parker ain't going to be happy with you coming back empty-handed," Jack said.

"Well, Parker can come out from behind his desk and go chasing old Blue Duck himself if he don't like it," Witson said.

"We best rest our horses awhile," Emmet said.

They stopped for one hour to allow their horses to rest and graze. Emmet built a fire and boiled a pot of coffee. They ate hard biscuits while drinking coffee.

"This Two Hawks, have you known him to be violent?" Witson asked Emmet.

"The man has a marked temper for sure," Emmet said. "But killing and scalping is something I just don't know."

"Guess we'll find out when we catch up to him," Jack said.

They rode until sunset and made camp for the night. Supper consisted of beans, bacon, biscuits, and cornbread. They had cans of peaches in syrup given to them by Captain Roberts.

"Bass and me will head east back to Fort Smith at first light," Witson said. "Anything you want us to tell Judge Parker?"

"Just we'll telegraph him when we can," Jack said. "Put out the fire, Emmet. Let's get some sleep."

In the morning, after a quick breakfast, Bass Reeves and Cal Witson rode east back to Fort Smith.

"Mount up, little brother," Jack said as he sat atop his tall horse. "Let's see if we can track us a savage."

Emmet mounted his pinto and they rode west.

"Jack, Two Hawks is no more savage than you," Emmet said. "His people have been here a thousand years. Now they live where we tell them and eat food they don't want and live in white men's cabins."

"Are you saying that's my fault?" Jack asked.

"No, but before you call Two Hawks a savage, remember Ma has Sioux and Mexican Apache blood in her. That means we do, too."

"You got near yellow hair, Emmet," Jack said. "And blue eyes. No Indian has blue eyes."

"Doesn't matter," Emmet said. "Blood is blood."

"You spent too much time in college," Jack said.

"Some schooling might benefit you some, Jack," Emmet said.

"I had plenty of schooling," Jack said.

"Can you spell Mississippi?" Emmet asked.

"No, but I can find it without needing a map," Jack said. "Can you?"

"I doubt you can read a map," Emmet said.

"Be quiet and ride," Jack said.

By late afternoon, they reached the spot where they first met up with Captain Roberts.

"We got two hours of daylight left," Jack said. "We can keep riding or make camp. Which?"

"Let's give the horses a rest and get a fresh start in the morning," Emmet said. "We should reach the place marked on the map by midmorning."

"I'll see to the horses while you make a fire," Jack said.

"Ever think about the men you killed, Jack?" Emmet asked.

"Nope."

They were in their bedrolls under a clear sky filled with stars.

"Why is that?" Emmet asked.

"Every man I've killed was an outlaw," Jack said. "Murdering, thieving, rapist scum. I'll waste no time thinking about the likes of them."

"Mind a personal question?"

"If you must."

"I married Sarah eight years ago," Emmet said. "How come in all that time you never found another woman to marry?"

"I don't know," Jack said. "Maybe because I never had a woman take my breath away like you did."

"Ever give a woman a chance to try to?" Emmet asked.

"It never occurred to me to walk around breathless," Jack said. "Let me get some sleep, would you?"

"Jack?"

"What?"

"There are four s's in Mississippi," Emmet said.

CHAPTER SIX

The sun was in the noon position when Two Hawks rode into the abandoned trading post known as Adobe Walls. The post was much larger than he'd imagined, with many buildings. Since its abandonment, the roofs had all collapsed, and all that remained were the walls of the buildings.

He dismounted, explored the rundown structures, and selected one to camp in that had a partial roof. He removed the saddle from his horse and left him at his campsite so he could explore the structures more closely.

There were trinkets left in the ruins. An old tobacco tin, a watch chain without a watch, a box of women's buttons that he thought odd, a well-worn deck of playing cards, several old and yellowed newspapers. One of the newspapers was dated June 26, 1874.

Two Hawks gathered firewood and used the old newspapers to start a fire. He prepared a feast for the evening meal, including coffee flavored with the bourbon whiskey.

He passed a flowing stream nearby that was filled with fish and fresh drinking water. He could stay at the Adobe Walls for as long as he liked. As he ate, Two Hawks watched the sun lower to the horizon. The crumbling walls seemed to glow in yellow light.

As a boy, he would listen to the elders as they sat around a campfire and told of the first great battle at Adobe Walls twenty years ago. His people were many and strong back then. The

Civil War had drained the American troops. The Comanche and Sioux took advantage of that fact and conducted many raids along the Canadian River. The generals sent the great Colonel Kit Carson and four hundred men to end the raids. Supplied with Henry rifles, Colt revolvers, and howitzers, Carson marched his army through several Comanche and Kiowa villages, destroying them, until they reached the walls. At the walls, thousands of Comanche and Kiowa soldiers attacked, but were repelled by the powerful howitzers. Chief Iron Shirt was killed, and the battle was declared a victory by Carson.

Two Hawks had heard the story many times as a boy. The second battle at Adobe Walls was led by War Chief Quanah Parker, who launched the attack in 1874. Two Hawks no longer needed to be told this story around a campfire; he was there.

Several white businessmen returned to the abandoned Adobe Walls in 1873 and opened several stores and shops to accommodate the three hundred or more buffalo hunters living in the area. The two stores quickly grew, and the remaining free-range Comanche and Kiowa felt this threatened their very existence. Spirited by Quanah Parker, who had left the reservation with nearly two hundred men, including Two Hawks and his father, Parker declared war on Adobe Walls. Free-range Kiowa were recruited, and they joined the fight.

Three hundred warriors attacked the outpost protected by twenty-eight well-armed men. Many had buffalo guns, and all had Winchesters and Colt revolvers. The famous Bat Masterson and equally famous Billy Dixon took part in the battle. About thirty Comanche and Kiowa were killed, including Two Hawks's father. Quanah Parker was wounded.

The battle ended when Dixon shot and killed a Comanche warrior on his horse from a thousand or more feet away, using his famous Sharps .50-90 rifle.

Two Hawks could still see the battle raging in his mind, as if ten years hadn't passed. He could smell the gunpowder in his nose and hear the screams of the Comanche and Kiowa warriors as they were shot and killed. After his father was shot off his horse, he stood with tomahawk in hand and charged the walls, screaming a war cry. It took three more bullets to silence the war cry in his throat.

Ten years later, nothing remained to speak of the two battles. All that remained were crumbling walls and the memory locked away inside Two Hawks's mind.

"Those settlers did a good job burying those outlaws," Jack said as he and Emmet stood before five unmarked gravesites.

Jack inspected the ground.

"It's near noon," Jack said. "Why don't you get us some lunch going while I scout ahead for signs."

Jack rode south for a while until he picked up the tracks of a large, very heavy horse. What little evidence there had been of tracks on the grass was nearly gone now, but some tracks left in softer dirt were still easily readable.

He dismounted and took a closer look. Two Hawks's horse had shoes made on the reservation. They differed slightly in shape and size. He memorized the prints left by the horseshoes and then mounted his horse and rode back to Emmet.

"He went south from here and has a considerable head start," Jack said as he slid from the saddle.

"Stopping to help the army didn't help none," Emmet said.

"No, it did not," Jack said. "So we'll have to push hard to make up time."

"We need some fresh meat," Emmet said.

"I'll hunt us up some for supper later," Jack said.

"Where do you suppose he's headed?"

"We'll find out when we catch him."

"Are you sure we'll catch him?" Emmet asked.

Jack sampled the beans and bacon. "Only thing I'm sure of, is you are one lousy cook," he said.

An hour before sunset, they followed tracks leading to a farm. Smoke rose from a stone chimney at a cabin.

"He passed this way, no doubt," Jack said.

"We best stop," Emmet said.

They rode to the corral and dismounted.

"Hello in the house," Jack shouted. "United States Marshal Jack Youngblood."

The door opened, and the farmer stepped out onto the porch. He looked at Jack's marshal's badge and Emmet's reservation police badge and said, "You boys hungry? Supper's in the cook pot."

"Be four days . . . no, make that five days, he passed through here," the farmer said as he filled three bowls with beef stew.

"He said his name was Two Hawks?" Emmet asked.

"He did," the farmer said.

"And he wasn't violent with you?" Emmet said.

"Actually, he was right pleasant," the farmer said. "He sat right where you're sitting and shared supper with me. We talked some. He told me his wife died and he left the reservation. Afterward, I gave him a bottle of bourbon to take on his travels."

"Did he say where he was going?" Jack asked.

"Texas. He asked about Texas," the farmer said. "I told him to head south and cross the Red."

"I see many things in your cabin that tells me you aren't alone," Emmet said. "Women's things."

"My wife and daughter went to help a neighbor's wife with a baby delivery," the farmer said. "There were complications and they stayed on to help. Don't expect them back for at least a week. You fellows are welcome to stay the night,"

After supper, Jack and Emmet sat in chairs on the front porch of the farmer's cabin. Jack smoked a rolled cigarette while Emmet smoked his pipe. The farmer, carrying a tray holding three coffee cups, joined them.

"I sweetened it a bit with some sipping whiskey," the farmer said.

"You've a nice home here," Emmet said.

"We like it," the farmer said as he took a chair.

"Let me ask you something," Jack said. "Why do you suppose Two Hawks didn't try to harm you?"

"I thought of that very thing," the farmer said. "He's near as big as you and had a Winchester and a tomahawk. Near as I can figure, he saw me as no threat to him."

"Did he stay the night?" Jack asked.

"Slept in my barn even though I offered him a bed," the farmer said. "Now let me ask you something. You aim to take him back to the reservation?"

"We do," Emmet said.

"He will not go," the farmer said. "He so much as said so, and I believe him. I saw in his eyes he'd rather die than live by another man's rules."

"I hope you are wrong," Emmet said.

The farmer stood up. "I have to turn in," he said. "I need to tend my fields in the morning. You're welcome to stay for breakfast."

Bedded down in the barn, Emmet rolled over and looked at Jack.

"You think the farmer is right about Two Hawks, that he'd rather die than go back?" Emmet said.

"I've never seen it otherwise," Jack said.

Two Hawks stared at the fire as he smoked his pipe and pulled on a bottle of rye whiskey. It was difficult to remember the exact location of the Buffalo Hunters' War, but he knew it wasn't far from the Adobe Walls.

He killed his first white man during that war, and it seemed as if it happened just yesterday. A filthy buffalo skinner, his clothes smelling of blood and guts, had shot his father in the leg. The buffalo skinner had a Sharps rifle, which fired just one round at a time and was slow to reload. Before the skinner could chamber a round, Two Hawks rushed him and nearly took the skinner's head off with his tomahawk. The sensation of killing the skinner was like no other feeling Two Hawks had ever felt in his young life. It was as if he'd been blind his entire life and suddenly could see.

The Comanche lost the Buffalo Hunters' War, but that sensation had stayed with him ever since.

Two Hawks had never been able to describe the sensation or identify what he felt while killing that skinner. Until now, as he sat before a simple fire and smoked his pipe and sipped rye whiskey.

The feeling was freedom absolute.

As a boy, Two Hawks sat in the reservation schoolhouse and listened to the woman teacher talk about the Revolutionary War, about how the colonists were willing to fight and die for their freedom.

He never really understood any of that until this very moment.

What was it the doctor had told him?

"If a man is free in his heart, he is free in his mind."

CHAPTER SEVEN

Amy put the finishing touches on a shirt she had sewn for Emmet. It was dark blue with two pockets. She had sewn a small hole in the left pocket for him to pin his badge through so he wouldn't damage the material.

Mary Louise came out to the porch.

"Breakfast dishes are done, Grandma," she said.

"Mind that your sister is dressed properly," Amy said. "I don't want her looking raggedy in town."

"Yes, Grandma."

Sally Potts, who ran the whores over at the Big Oak Saloon, offered Chao-xing three thousand dollars for her store location. Chao-xing knew that Sally would use the bathhouse as an extension of her second-floor operation and have her girls administering the baths in private.

She had three thousand dollars in the First Bank of Fort Smith and could double that amount by accepting Sally's offer. Six thousand dollars would carry her a long way in San Francisco.

The fourth customer of the morning entered the shop, Marshal Cal Witson, a regular. He'd just come in from the field and was filthy. A bundle of clean clothing was under his right arm.

"Shave me close, honey," he said. "And draw a bath. I need to look presentable to see the judge."

Witson sat in a chair, and Chao-xing placed a steaming hot towel over his face to soften his beard. While Witson sat in the chair, she went to the back room to start a fire under a cauldron of water. When she returned to Witson, she removed the towel.

"Want your hair trimmed?" she asked.

"Probably could use it," Witson said. "Go ahead."

While she trimmed Witson's hair and shaved his face, Chao-xing caught sight of Amy Youngblood and her two grand-daughters as they rode past her shop in a buggy. She knew who Amy was, but had never spoken to her. She had seen Amy talking to Jack in front of the courthouse and on Main Street many times. She asked him once, and he told her Amy was his mother.

When she finished shaving Witson, Chao-xing went to the back room to fill a tub with boiling water. She set a bar of soap and clean towel on the table beside the tub and then returned to Witson.

"All ready, but wait a few minutes to let the water cool," she said. "There is a bucket of cold water beside the tub if you're in a hurry."

Witson paid the two dollars in coin and added a fifty-cent tip. While he was in back, Chao-xing went outside to the street. Amy's buggy was nowhere in sight. Chao-xing returned to her shop and placed the sign that read *Back in One Hour* on the door.

Chao-xing left the shop, walked to the end of the block, and looked both ways for the buggy. She spotted it parked outside Greenly's store one block away. She hurried to the store and entered. Greenly was behind the counter.

"Chao-xing, what brings you in this time of day?" Greenly asked.

"I'm low on supplies," Chao-xing said.

"What do you need?" Greenly asked.

"A dozen bars of soap, shaving soap, and talcum powder,"

Chao-xing said.

"Want it delivered?"

"I'll wait."

Chao-xing looked around and spotted Amy Youngblood looking at sewing materials. While Greenly filled her order, she
walked over to Amy.

"Mrs. Youngblood?" Chao-xing said.

"Yes?"

"My name is Chao-xing. I own the bathhouse. I wonder if I
may speak to you privately."

"What about?"

"Your son Jack."

"I see," Amy said.

"My shop is only one block from here," Chao-xing said. "I
can make tea if you'd like."

"Give me five minutes," Amy said.

Chao-xing returned to the counter, paid Greenly three dollars for her goods, and then hurried back to her shop.

Amy found the girls looking at dolls in the next room.

"Your father just bought you each a doll," Amy said.

"We're just looking," Mary Louise said.

"Come with me, girls," Amy said. She led them to the counter
and gave each a dime.

"Mr. Greenly, I have to run an errand," Amy said. "Can the
girls wait here for me?"

"Of course," Greenly said.

"I gave each of them a dime to buy candy," Amy said.

Amy sat at the tiny table in Chao-xing's cramped kitchen and
watched as Chao-xing poured tea and then sat.

"Are you pregnant?" Amy asked so suddenly, the question
caused Chao-xing to blush.

"No," Chao-xing said. "Of course not."

"Well, what can I help you with then?"

"I know of no other way to say this," Chao-xing said. "I love your son."

Amy sipped some tea. "Does my son love you?"

"I don't think so," Chao-xing said.

"Have you told him you love him?" Amy asked.

"Not in words," Chao-xing said.

"I see. Why not?"

Chao-xing shook her head. "I don't . . . I'm not sure," she said.

Amy sipped some more tea. "This is very good," she said.

"Thank you."

"I'll guess that you are like every other woman and wants to hear the man say it first," Amy said.

"Yes, I suppose so," Chao-xing said.

"If you are waiting for my son to say it first, you will be old and gray before that happens," Amy said.

"I know," Chao-xing said. "I am planning to sell my shop and move to San Francisco."

"Because my son doesn't love you?" Amy said. "Oh, honey, you have it bad, don't you?"

"I don't know what else to do," Chao-xing said. "I told him I was going to move to San Francisco, and he acted like he didn't even care."

Amy chuckled.

"What is funny?" Chao-xing asked.

"My son Jack is considered the best lawman Judge Parker ever appointed, and he's tough as a burnt nickel steak, but in many ways he's still a little boy," Amy said.

"I don't understand," Chao-xing said.

"I know my son," Amy said. "The things he pretends he doesn't care about are the things he cares about the most."

"That is very confusing," Chao-xing said.

"If my son acts like he doesn't care, it means he cares a great deal," Amy said. "You just have to make him see the error of his ways, my dear."

"How do I do that?" Chao-xing asked.

"I realize you are wearing those pants and shirt for working in your shop, but do you own any really pretty dresses?" Amy asked.

"Not what is considered pretty by western ways," Chao-xing said.

"Tomorrow is Sunday. Do you open on Sunday?"

"At noon."

"I'll be back in time for breakfast," Amy said.

Jack dismounted at the bank of the Red River and inspected the ground carefully.

"That farmer was right, no doubt," he said. "Two Hawks crossed the Red into Texas."

"Well he didn't cross here," Emmet said. "Water's too high to cross safely, even on a tall horse like yours."

Jack mounted his horse. "Ride downriver awhile," he said.

They rode west and followed the Red River for several miles until they came upon the spot where a large herd of cattle had crossed.

Jack dismounted and inspected the grass carefully. "He crossed here," he said.

"Are you sure?" Emmet asked.

"I am," Jack said and reached for his rope hooked to the left side of his saddle. He looped one end around Emmet's pinto at the neck, then mounted the saddle and tied the other end around the saddle horn.

"Keep her calm midstream, and she'll be fine," Jack said.

Jack walked his horse down the embankment and entered the river. Emmet followed close behind. The water rose quickly to

Jack's boots, but his horse had little trouble traversing the river. Emmet's pinto, considerably smaller than Jack's horse, panicked a bit when the water reached mid-chest. Jack turned, yanked on the rope to straighten out the pinto, and used his horse's strength to pull the pinto forward. Once past the midpoint, the water receded and the pinto calmed down enough to follow Jack's horse to the other side. Once safely on shore, Jack removed the rope from the pinto's neck and dismounted to inspect the ground for tracks.

"Can't be sure, but it looks like he started southwest to the Canadian," Jack said.

"Rest the horses awhile, Jack," Emmet said. "I'll make some coffee."

A while later they sat in the shade of a tall tree and drank coffee and ate hard biscuits.

"I have a hunch where he's going," Emmet said.

Jack, rolling a cigarette, paused. "We're not tracking a hunch," he said.

"It's a while ago, maybe ten years, but the raids on the buffalo hunters and the second battle at Adobe Walls, Two Hawks took part in both of them," Emmet said. "His father was killed at Adobe Walls ten years ago."

"You think he's chasing his memories?" Jack said.

"No, Jack. I think he's chasing his heritage," Emmet said.

Two Hawks stood naked in the stream that flowed near the Adobe Walls. He was fishing the way his father taught him to as a child. With his hands close to his knees, he waited for a large fish to swim by and then he scooped the fish out of the water and tossed it onto dry land.

After he scooped out the third fish, Two Hawks returned to shore and dressed. He tied the three fish to a stick, mounted his horse, and rode back to the walls.

He was well aware of the six riders that followed him from a distance of about a mile. They first appeared when he arrived at the stream. They came no closer as he stripped down and entered the water. They came no closer now as he rode to the walls.

Two Hawks smiled to himself as he pulled the Winchester rifle from the saddle sleeve and spun his horse around. He held the Winchester in his left hand high above his head and charged at the riders. Screaming a Comanche war cry, Two Hawks fired the Winchester at the riders. The riders turned their horses and ran.

Two Hawks stopped his horse.

"Dogs," he said aloud.

An hour before dark, Jack said, "We'll stop here and make camp. Get a fire going. I won't be long. I spotted some wild turkeys, and I'm sick of beans."

Emmet dismounted and gathered wood for a fire. Once he had the fire going, he saw to his horse. Jack was gone about forty-five minutes and returned with a turkey hanging from the saddle.

"I made coffee. Best let me pluck that bird, Jack. You'll make a mess out of it," Emmet said.

Two Hawks finished the last bit of fish in the fry pan and filled it with water from his canteen to soak overnight. He lifted the coffee pot from the fire, filled his cup with coffee, and added some bourbon for flavor. He stuffed and lit his pipe, grabbed the Winchester, and walked out of the crumbling building to watch the darkening horizon.

About a mile away, maybe a bit more, he could see the red dot of a campfire. The six riders were spending the night. They were too curious to leave and too afraid to approach him. They were probably Kiowa dogs or Mexican Apache who'd left a reservation somewhere and had nowhere to go and nothing to do except get drunk.

He could wait for full darkness and sneak up on them and kill them, but he decided to wait and see if they got their courage up.

"I can't eat another bite," Emmet said.

"I'm pretty well stuffed myself," Jack said.

"Want more coffee?"

"Sweeten it a bit," Jack said and tossed Emmet his flask of whiskey.

Emmet filled two cups with coffee and added a splash of whiskey from Jack's flask.

"What you said earlier today about Two Hawks chasing his heritage, what did you mean by that?" Jack asked.

"He's full-blood Comanche, Jack," Emmet said. "Reservation born or not, he's got warrior's blood, and he doesn't want to live like white men anymore."

"I get that part," Jack said. "But how do you chase your heritage?"

"It's his heritage to live free on the land of his ancestors," Emmet said. "To live the way they did, if even for just a short while."

"And he's willing to die for that?" Jack asked. "A way of life that's long gone."

"Like you said the other night, there is no other way to see it," Emmet said.

"I hate to kill a spirited man," Jack said. "It don't seem right."

"Nothing about this seems right," Emmet said.

"Mary, hand me those pins there on the table," Amy said. "Chao-xing, please hold still."

Mary Louise fetched the pin cushion from the table in Chao-xing's kitchen and handed it to Amy.

"Can we look at your dolls?" Mary Louise asked Chao-xing.

"Yes, of course," Chao-xing said. "They are in the bedroom."

"Mind you don't break anything," Amy said.

"We won't," Mary Louise said. She took Sarah's hand and led her to the bedroom.

"Step back a moment," Amy said.

Chao-xing took a few steps backward. She was wearing just her underwear.

"You've a fine figure," Amy said. "Let me take some measurements."

With a tape measure, Amy measured Chao-xing in several places.

"I think you would look very good in light blue," Amy said.

After riding most of the morning and into early afternoon, Emmet pointed to the sky in the distance.

"See it?" he said.

"Buzzards," Jack said.

"They're pretty far off," Emmet said. "Be close to dark before we reach them."

"Probably just a dead buffalo being feasted on by the buzzards," Jack said.

"Then why are they circling?" Emmet asked.

"Could be any number of reasons," Jack said. "Wolves or coyotes got there first and the buzzards are waiting their turn. Those stinking birds will eat rot off a week-old corpse."

"We're following Two Hawks, aren't we?" Emmet said.

"We are," Jack said.

"Let's pick up the pace," Emmet said.

★ ★ ★ ★ ★

"What do you think of the color, girls?" Amy asked.

Mary Louise and Sarah looked at the pale-blue material draped over Chao-xing's shoulders.

"Is that a Sunday church dress?" Mary Louise asked.

"Not exactly," Amy said.

"It's very pretty, Grandma," Mary Louise said.

Amy looked at Sarah, who was holding a small Chinese doll dressed in traditional robes.

"You should put that back before you break it," Amy said.

"It's pretty," Sarah said.

"She can keep it," Chao-xing said.

"Are you sure?" Amy asked.

"I have many," Chao-xing said. "Both girls can have one."

"Can we, Grandma?" Mary Louise asked.

"I suppose," Amy said.

Chao-xing removed the material from her shoulders. "Come. We'll pick out a doll for each of you," she said.

"Hold up, Jack," Emmet said.

They stopped their horses, and Emmet dug out his binoculars from a saddlebag. He trained them on a spot about a mile away where the buzzards were still circling.

"Oh, my God," Emmet said.

"What?" Jack asked.

Emmet passed the binoculars to Jack.

"Those are women digging graves," Jack said.

"No, Jack, those are nuns digging graves," Emmet said.

"We best see what they're up to," Jack said.

They rode hard for about a mile until they approached a covered wagon. Not far from the wagon, five nuns in full garb were digging three graves.

"Ladies, I'm Marshal Jack Youngblood," Jack said. "What's

happened here?"

"I'm Sister Katherine, head of the order from Chicago. The sisters and I are traveling to Yellow House Canyon in Lubbock County where a church and hospital are being built," Sister Katherine said. "We are also trained nurses, you see."

Jack and Emmet dismounted.

"You mean to tell me you're five women traveling alone across the Llano?" Jack said.

"Not all the way," Sister Katherine said. "Just from Tulsa."

"Just from . . . ladies, this is bad country you're crossing," Jack said. "Full of cutthroats, rapists, murderers, and thieves."

"We are in no fear, Marshal," Sister Katherine said.

"Maybe so, but why don't you ladies go sit and rest, and we'll finish the digging," Jack said.

"We will prepare an evening meal," Sister Katherine said. "You will join us?"

"Certainly, Sister," Emmet said.

Jack removed the linen clothes the nuns had placed over the three dead men.

"Emmet?" Jack said softly.

Emmet looked at the bodies.

"Scalped," Emmet said.

"And one was killed with a tomahawk," Jack said.

"Best finish these graves," Emmet said.

It was well after dark when the last grave was covered with dirt and stones. The nuns had fastened three crucifixes from sticks, and they placed one on each grave. Sister Katherine said a prayer for the souls of each man.

"Please join us for the evening meal," Sister Katherine said.

The sisters had five little folding chairs and a small folding table.

"I'm afraid we don't have any additional chairs," Sister Katherine said.

"We brung our own," Jack said and sat on his saddle.

Emmet did the same.

"Tell me what happened here," Jack said.

"As I said, we are traveling to Yellow House Canyon and came across three dead men," Sister Katherine said. "We stopped to bury them. It would have taken us much longer if you hadn't come along, and we are grateful that you did. Please, don't be shy. Eat."

There were seven wood bowls full of beef stew on the table. Each bowl had a wood spoon in it.

"Don't be shy," Sister Katherine said. "We have plenty for seconds, and you must be hungry after all that digging."

Jack dug in, as did Emmet. Then Jack said, "This is delicious, Sister. You ladies sure can cook."

"Thank you, Marshal," Sister Katherine said.

"Can these other ladies speak?" Jack asked.

"Of course they can speak," Sister Katherine said. "They are in the final year of taking their vows, and they are not allowed to unless it's to each other or to me. And to pray, of course."

"I see," Jack said.

"Sister, you've come all the way from Tulsa in this covered wagon?" Emmet said.

"We have," Sister Katherine said.

"It's a good forty miles or more to where you're going," Jack said. "And this is bad country."

"My brother is right, Sister. This is no country for five women to be traveling alone," Emmet said.

"We will manage the journey," Sister Katherine said.

"There are three men we just buried who didn't survive the journey, and they looked a lot tougher than you," Emmet said. "My brother and I will ride along with you to Yellow House Canyon."

Spooning beef stew into his mouth, Jack paused and looked at Emmet.

"Perhaps you are right," Sister Katherine said. "It would be safer traveling with two lawmen. We accept your kind offer."

Two Hawks hunted wild prairie chickens on the plains, killed two of them, and found a nest of fresh eggs. He plucked the birds, roasted them on spits, ate one for lunch, and saved the other for supper. While the chickens cooked, he cracked three eggs into his cup and filled it with rye whiskey and stirred it with his finger. He swallowed the concoction in one long swallow.

When the chickens were done, he took one to the front of the Walls and searched the plains while he ate. There was no sign of the six dogs that were hanging around yesterday. They were probably away hunting or fishing.

After dark, Two Hawks decided to do some hunting of his own.

The nuns slept inside the covered wagon while Jack and Emmet set up their bedrolls near the fire.

Jack smoked a rolled cigarette and looked at Emmet. "Forty or more miles is a long delay," he said.

"What choice do we have?" Emmet said. "Those women are helpless out here, and those men were killed by Two Hawks. What if he's still about somewhere and spotted their covered wagon?"

"I know that," Jack said. "All I said was forty miles is a long delay, and it is. Best put out the fire and get some sleep."

Holding her new doll, the one Chao-xing gave her, Mary Louise rocked in Amy's rocking chair and watched Amy stitch material.

"Why are you making a dress for . . . ?" Mary Louise asked.

"Chao-xing," Amy said.

"She has a funny name," Mary Louise said.

"Not to her," Amy said. "She is from China."

"Is that why her eyes look funny?"

"To her our eyes look funny," Amy said. "In China everybody has eyes just like hers."

"Don't they wear dresses in China?" Mary Louise asked.

"Of course they do, just different. Like the doll you are holding," Amy said.

"Where is China?" Mary Louise asked.

"Very far away," Amy said. "Halfway around the world. I'll show you in a book tomorrow. Right now it's time for bed. Your sister is already asleep."

"She's a baby. Can't I watch you sew for a while longer?"

"All right, but just for a little while," Amy said.

Two Hawks stood beside his horse and ate the second chicken as he watched the horizon. If the six dogs were out there, they didn't make a fire, or he would see the red dot he was looking for. Perhaps they'd moved on to another location? Perhaps they'd decided it was wiser not to interfere with him.

It didn't matter.

In the morning he would hunt them down and kill them all.

CHAPTER EIGHT

In the morning, while the nuns prepared breakfast, Jack and Emmet went through the saddlebags of the three men they buried. There was little in them of any use. Two Hawks took everything of value except the saddles. They could track the three horses, but for what reason?

"Hey Jack, look at this," Emmet said as he held up an empty money sack with the words *First Bank of Yellow House Canyon*.

"Best tuck that in your bags," Jack said.

"What do we do with the saddles?" Emmet asked.

"Leave them on their graves," Jack said. "They're cheap saddles anyway."

Two Hawks made a small hole in an egg and drank the contents while he watched the sunrise. He drank a cup of coffee and smoked his pipe and prayed to the spirits for strength and guidance.

As the new dawn broke, the harsh desert ground seemed to glow yellow, as if the new sun cast a spell on the land.

When Two Hawks mounted the saddle, it was with a heart filled with determination. He rode to the campsite the dogs occupied several nights ago and dismounted to inspect the site. The ashes and bits of charred wood were cold. Bones from prairie chickens had been tossed into the fire and were singed black. An empty bottle of mescal had been left behind, and ants had crawled inside to eat the sugar.

Tracks led to the east.

He followed the tracks for several miles until he reached another campsite. The ashes here were from last night. The remains of prairie chickens were scattered about. Two empty mescal bottles were filled with ants.

Two Hawks continued to follow the tracks, and they took a sudden turn to the north. He followed and rode about ten miles to the Canadian River. He stopped and dismounted when, a half mile away, he spotted six skinny horses grazing on sweet grass on the banks of the river.

The six riders were gathered around a campfire, eating fish and drinking mescal.

Two Hawks sat in the sun and waited. The six riders finished eating the fish and continued drinking mescal. Soon enough they were drunk and laughing. One of them tossed the bottle and tried to shoot it with his pistol and missed. The others laughed drunkenly. Another bottle of mescal was opened and it wasn't long before the six riders were passed out drunk.

Two Hawks didn't even bother to ride to their camp. He held the reins and walked his horse beside him to the six drunken riders. He stood over them and inspected the men. Two appeared to be Kiowa. The remaining four were Mexican Apache. He could kill them all right where they slept, but what was the gain?

Instead, Two Hawks sat against a tree and smoked his pipe. It took a while, but slowly they woke up. Two Hawks stood and looked at the drunken riders, who disgraced themselves with their weak behavior.

One of them looked at Two Hawks. "Who are you?" he said in Apache.

Two Hawks kicked the man in the face, knocking him over.

"I am Two Hawks, son of the Comanche Nation and I could kill you all right now," Two Hawks said. "You can die right here like the drunken dogs you are, or you can sober up and join me at Adobe Walls. The choice is yours. If you are not at Adobe Walls by sunset, I will hunt you down and kill you all."

Two Hawks mounted his horse, yanked on the reins, and rode away in a fury.

Jack drove the covered wagon while Sister Katherine sat beside him. Jack's horse was tethered behind the wagon, while Emmet rode his pinto to the left of Sister Katherine.

"We covered some ground today, Sister," Jack said. "I'd like to make another five miles before dark."

"May I ask you a question?" Sister Katherine said.

"Certainly."

"Have you killed many men in the line of duty?"

"Yes, Sister, I have," Jack said.

"I see," Sister Katherine said.

"My job is to bring outlaws to justice," Jack said. "Sometimes they don't want to go and put up a fight."

"Doesn't this dangerous life worry your wife and family?" Sister Katherine asked.

"I'm not married, Sister," Jack said. "All I have is my mother and my brother, Emmet, there."

"You never married? Why is that?"

"A lot of reasons," Jack said. "Mostly because I never found the right woman, I suppose."

"Your brother wears a wedding band," Sister Katherine said.

"His wife died five years ago in childbirth," Jack said. "He has two daughters. Our mother is watching over them."

"We will pray for his wife tonight before evening meal," Sister Katherine said.

"That's kind of you, Sister, but right now we need to pick up the pace," Jack said. "It wouldn't surprise me none to see old

Sam Starr or Blue Duck come riding across the plains with an army of men."

Two Hawks roasted the large wild turkey he caught over a large fire. Boiling in the fire was the coffee pot. He removed it and filled a cup. He didn't bother to get up when he heard the six riders approach and dismount.

They filed into his adobe and looked at him.

"Why are you living like drunken dogs on the plains?" Two Hawks said in Apache.

"Who are you to insult us?" one of them said.

"What is your name?" Two Hawks asked him.

"I am called Little Buffalo of the Kiowa Nation."

"Little Buffalo, if your tongue moves again without me asking, I will cut it off and stuff my turkey with it," Two Hawks said. "All of you sit and eat. We have many things to talk about."

Little Buffalo had been in charge, but he knew the moment he entered the adobe that Two Hawks had assumed command.

The men were Big Tooth, a Kiowa like Little Buffalo, and Red Crow, Kuruk, Diablo, and Taza, all Mexican Apache. Each cut off a sizable piece of turkey and ate while Two Hawks smoked his pipe and talked.

"None of us here will live to become old men," Two Hawks said. "The whites have taken the land that was ours for five hundred years. They killed the buffalo to starve us out and moved us to reserved land once we were conquered. Their iron horse fouls the air with its black smoke. My wife died of a white man's disease. I will not die of a white man's disease. I will die in battle the way my father and his father did in the Great War on Austin fifty years ago."

"What war?" Little Buffalo said. "There are no more wars to fight. What people we have left live a reservation life or as stray mongrel dogs as we do."

"How we live is up to us, not the white man," Two Hawks said. "I would rather die tomorrow fighting than live a hundred more years as the white's pet on a leash."

"What are you suggesting we do?" Little Buffalo asked.

"Fight," Two Hawks said. "And die as men."

"I couldn't eat another bite, Sister. Thank you," Emmet said.

"Where is the marshal?" Sister Katherine asked.

"Jack has excellent night vision," Emmet said. "He went for a walk to make sure we haven't been followed."

"Followed? Out here?"

"Many a bandit or renegade Apache would consider that wagon of yours quite a prize," Emmet said. "Not to mention you and the other ladies."

"Your brother is a brave man," Sister Katherine said.

"As brave as they come and equally tough," Emmet said. "By the way, thank you for the prayer. I am sure my wife heard it."

"If we are to be up before dawn, I best turn in," Sister Katherine said.

"Good night, Sister," Emmet said. "I'll put the fire out once my brother has returned."

After Sister Katherine was inside the wagon, Emmet filled his cup with coffee, stuffed and lit his pipe, and kept his Winchester at arm's reach.

Before supper, Sister Katherine led them in the Lord's Prayer for his wife. It was an odd feeling, but Emmet felt Sarah actually did hear the prayer. It made him feel lonely. He knew the right thing to do was remarry so the girls would have a mother. A new wife would also ease some of the burden he placed on Amy. The damned thing of it was he couldn't marry a woman he didn't love, and he still loved Sarah heart and soul.

He heard Jack returning to camp.

"Coffee is still hot," Emmet said when Jack arrived and sat

next to him.

Jack grabbed his cup and filled it from the pot.

"Quiet," Jack said. "I don't like it none."

"Think we should stand watch?"

"I do," Jack said. "Grab some sleep, and I'll wake you in three hours."

Emmet nodded and went to his bedroll.

Jack rolled a cigarette, lit it with a wood match, and sipped his coffee. The moon was but a tiny sliver in the night sky and cast very little light. He extinguished the fire and set the coffee pot in the hot ashes to keep it warm. There was nobody out there; he was sure of that, but the odd feeling of being watched stayed with him. He was gifted with excellent eyesight, even in the dark, and if something or someone was nearby he would have seen it or them.

As he smoked and sipped, Jack's thoughts turned to something Sister Katherine said earlier in the day when she asked if he was married. It never occurred to him to settle down and marry after Sarah married Emmet. It was a foolish notion to be sure that a man couldn't love more than one woman, especially after the woman loved and married another, but that's how he felt all those years.

Something odd happened when he was patrolling around the campsite in the dark. His thoughts turned to Chao-xing. Would she really move to San Francisco as she said, just to be around more Chinese? In the course of a week she must shave a hundred men and prepare baths for the like amount, and he never gave that a thought. While he was patrolling in the dark, an idea entered his mind. What if he wasn't the only one to share her bed? What if, when he was out of town, she shared her bed with another?

The idea didn't sit well with him. He thought of talking to Emmet about the subject, but he was afraid his kid brother would just laugh at his silly schoolboy crush.

Jack rolled a fresh cigarette and kept a keen eye on the dark prairie.

"We need more warriors," Two Hawks said. "At least another dozen or more."

"There are others living on the plains such as we," Little Buffalo said.

"Are they drunken dogs like you, or do they have the warrior spirit?" Two Hawks said.

"We are warriors and we will fight," Little Buffalo said.

"We shall see," Two Hawks said. He reached into his saddlebags for the last unopened bottle of rye whiskey. "No more drinking mescal," he said. "The one thing the white man does well is make good whiskey."

Two Hawks handed the bottle to Little Buffalo.

"Tomorrow you will take me to the others," Two Hawks said. "Enjoy yourselves tonight, but tomorrow be ready for blood."

CHAPTER NINE

"I'm glad we got an early start, Sister," Emmet said. "We should reach the mission in Yellow House Canyon by early afternoon."

Emmet was driving the wagon while Jack went ahead to scout the trail. Sister Katherine sat beside Emmet and pointed to Jack in the distance as he rode toward them.

When Jack arrived, he said, "No more than five miles at best. They're building a church and hospital all right, and from the looks of it, an entire town around them."

"Did you see Father Ramon?" Sister Katherine. "He's a large man with white hair."

"I didn't stop, Sister," Jack said. "But maybe it would be a good idea to give your horses thirty minutes rest."

Two Hawks followed Little Buffalo, and the others followed him. They rode north to the Canadian River, turned west, and rode into the hills. Mountains loomed in the background.

Little Buffalo led them through a narrow box canyon where the hills were higher on each side. An Apache warrior watched them from atop a hill. As they rode past, the warrior disappeared.

A mile or so later, they arrived at the camp of a dozen Apache and Kiowa warriors. The camp was protected on three sides by tall hills. Two warriors stood guard on top of the hills.

Two Hawks dismounted.

"I am Two Hawks of the Comanche Nation," he said. "Who

is the leader of the sorry looking bunch of mongrel dogs?"

"I am called Eagle's Nest. I am the war chief of these warriors."

Two Hawks looked at Eagle's Nest.

"War chief?" Two Hawks said. "I see a bunch of drunken mongrel dogs that drink too much mescal and rot their brains in the sun."

"Who are you to speak such words to me?" Eagle's Nest said.

Two Hawks pulled his Bowie knife and shoved it into Eagle's Nest's stomach to the handle, twisted, and sliced across the abdomen. When he pulled out the knife, Eagle's Nest slumped to his knees with most of his guts hanging out.

"Useless dog," Two Hawks said, placed a foot on Eagle's Nest, and shoved him to the ground.

The dozen or so warriors stared at Two Hawks.

Two Hawks held the blood-stained Bowie knife above his head.

"Listen to me, you drunken dogs," he shouted. "You can live like cowards in these hills, or you can follow me and be a whole people again. Which do you choose?"

Emmet stopped the wagon in front of the partially constructed hospital. Sister Katherine could barely contain her excitement and stuck her head inside the covered wagon.

"We are here, Sisters," she said. "Everybody out."

Jack dismounted and tied his horse to the front wagon wheel. Emmet hopped down from the wagon and helped Sister Katherine to step down.

"I see a man coming fits your description, Sister," Jack said.

Father Ramon was tall, with broad shoulders and white hair. He wore work clothes and carried a hammer.

"Sisters, I see that you arrived in one piece," he said. "I was a bit worried when I was informed you set out alone from Tulsa."

"As you can see, Father, we are not alone," Sister Katherine said.

Father Ramon looked up at Jack. "A United States marshal as an escort and a chief of police. How did you manage that, Sister?"

"I'm afraid they managed us, Father," Sister Katherine said.

"We just happened by," Jack said. "We couldn't very well let the sisters fend for themselves on the Llano."

"We are most grateful that you did," Father Ramon said. "We will have a feast tonight to celebrate the occasion. I wish you two lawmen to stay as our guests."

"Be happy to, Father," Jack said. "But is it possible for us to have a shave and a bath?"

"Of course," Father Ramon said.

"There is another matter, Father. An important one," Jack said. "Lubbock is how far from the mission?"

"An hour on a fast horse," Father Ramon said.

Jack looked at Emmet. "We can ride there and see the sheriff and be back in time for the doings," he said.

"I'll show you where you can freshen up," Father Ramon said.

After a shave and a bath, and wearing clean shirts, Jack and Emmet rode toward Lubbock. It was just a few miles to the west, and they traveled the distance in thirty minutes.

Lubbock wasn't officially a town, but more like a village in the heart of Lubbock County. It was a dry, dusty place that served as a way station for cowboys on a drive north and as a place to let off steam on the return trip south. There were twenty buildings, of which one was a saloon. A small office for a county deputy sheriff was the last building on one side of the street. A storefront served as the First Bank of Yellow Canyon.

A few cowboys hung around outside of the storefronts, but

mostly the entire village appeared deserted.

"Let's see if anyone is home," Jack said as they dismounted in front of the deputy sheriff's office.

Emmet removed the money bag they recovered from the dead men they buried and held it in his right hand.

An old man was sleeping at a desk when Jack and Emmet entered the office. Jack slammed the door, and the old man woke up.

"What the hell is wrong with you?" the old man said.

"To hear some tell it, a great deal," Jack said. "You're too old to be a deputy. What are you?"

"Duly appointed constable responsible for keeping the peace in the absence of the deputy," the old man said.

"From the looks of this place, a dead chicken could keep the peace around here," Jack said.

"Well, what do you want?" the old man said.

"I'm United States Marshal Jack Youngblood and this is Chief of Reservation Police for the reservation in Arkansas, Emmet Youngblood, and what we want is the deputy sheriff," Jack said.

"The deputy is with the county sheriff on a posse," the old man said.

"No doubt about the bank robbery," Jack said.

"How do you know about that?" the old man said.

"We came across the three men who robbed the bank. They were dead, and we buried them," Jack said.

"Dead?" the old man said.

"Unless they were sleeping and we buried them by mistake," Jack said.

Emmet placed the money sack on the desk. "From your bank?" he asked.

The old man nodded.

"Tell the deputy upon his arrival that he can wire me in Fort Smith, Arkansas, in care of Judge Parker for details," Jack said.

"Is your saloon open?"

"Hold on, and I'll go with you," the old man said. "I could use an afternoon whiskey."

"Well, come on then, old-timer," Jack said. "We got better things to do than hang around this town full of tumbleweed."

Jack, Emmet, and the constable left the office, crossed the street, and walked to the saloon. Some dusty cowboys waiting on work were loitering on the street in front of the saloon doors.

One of the cowboys looked at the badge pinned to Emmet's shirt as he entered the saloon. As saloons go, this one was basic. A long bar, some tables, a bartender, rows of bottles of whiskey, and a mirror on the wall.

"Barkeep, three whiskeys if you please," Jack said.

"Bourbon or rye?" the bartender asked.

"Bourbon will do," Jack said.

The bartender set up three glasses and filled them with bourbon.

The cowboys on the street entered the saloon and walked to the bar.

"Hey, buck, you're not going to drink that in here," one of the cowboys said. "This bar is for white men only. Indians that can't hold their liquor have to drink outside by the outhouse."

"Now, fellows, before you go causing a ruckus, you should know the man standing behind me is a United States marshal," the constable said.

"I ain't talking to the marshal," the cowboy said. "I'm talking to this here savage."

"Hold on a second, boys," Jack said. "Three on one ain't exactly fair."

"Boys, why don't you . . ." the constable said.

Jack stepped around the constable, grabbed one of the cowboys and smashed his face into the bar, grabbed his Colt pistol, and clubbed the other cowboy over the head with it, leaving just the one cowboy facing Emmet.

"There. Nice and even," Jack said.

Emmet stared at the cowboy. "You're right about one thing," Emmet said. "I am a savage. It's my job to keep the other savages in line."

Emmet pulled the field knife from his belt. "I'm going to cut your nose off and eat it like it was candy," he said. "Then I'm going to scalp you and peel back your head and eat your brains raw like my ancestors did to give them strength."

"Mister, you're plumb crazy," the cowboy said.

Jack cocked his Colt and aimed it at the cowboy. "If he don't kill you, I will," he said. "That is, unless you offer to pay for our drinks."

The cowboy stared at Emmet.

"You can say the words," Jack said. "If you value your life."

"Can I buy you a drink?" the cowboy said.

Emmet smiled and replaced the knife into its sheath. "I appreciate that, I surely do," he said.

The cowboy placed three one-dollar coins on the bar.

"Get your friends up, and get out of here while I'm still in a good mood," Jack said.

The cowboy helped his two friends stand up, and they slowly walked out of the saloon.

Jack lifted his glass and tossed back his shot. "Well, best be going," he said.

Riding back to the mission, Emmet was silent, almost brooding.

"What's eating you, little brother?" Jack asked.

"That cowboy," Emmet said.

"Don't let it bother you none," Jack said. "Idiots are everywhere."

"Maybe so," Emmet said. He turned his horse suddenly and galloped to a large tree, dismounted, and sat in the shade.

"What the hell?" Jack said and followed. He dismounted and stood by Emmet.

"I think I've been living in Fort Smith too long," Emmet said.

"What do you mean?" Jack asked.

"You know damn well what I mean," Emmet said. "If I wasn't wearing this badge, that cowboy back there would have no cause to think I'm anything other than just another white man in a white country. But everybody knows only an Indian can be police on a reservation."

Jack sat beside his brother and rolled a cigarette.

"Even when I was in college studying law, I never went out of my way to let folks know I have Indian blood in me," Emmet said. "Because I have fair hair and blue eyes, it just didn't occur to people I might be anything other than white. That little bit of Kiowa and Apache blood we got in us is enough to make people change how they feel about us."

"So?" Jack said as he struck a wood match and lit the cigarette.

"That's your opinion on the matter? So?" Emmet said.

"I may not be a college-educated squirt like you, but the truth is I don't give a damn what folks think about me," Jack said. "People are going to think what they want, and I'll think what I want, and that's all there is to it. I have one rule. I won't be wronged and I won't allow a hand to be laid on me. Otherwise people can talk and think what they want about whatever they want."

"That's two rules, Jack," Emmet said.

"What?"

"You said you had one rule and then you stated two," Emmet said.

"Little brother, do you want to find out how hard I can punch?" Jack said.

Emmet stood up. "I already know," he said. "Let's get going."

Two Hawks sat before a roaring campfire while Little Buffalo and the other twenty or so warriors sat in a circle around him. When he was a little boy, his father and grandfather sat at council fires not much different than this one.

"We have nothing to live for," Two Hawks said. "We have no land, no hunting grounds, no wife and children. Everything we once had has been stripped away from us. Our people live as slaves on reserved land subject to the white man's will. We will never have what we once had as a people. I ask you now to follow me into battle and die a great death as our ancestors did, or continue to live like beaten old women on the plains. It is your choice, but I will ask only once."

Three long tables had been placed together and two dozen mission workers were seated in place. Jack sat on one side of Father Ramon and Emmet on the other. Father Ramon led the group in prayer and then the sisters served fried chicken with all the trimmings.

In the background, one man played the fiddle and another strummed on a banjo. Assisting the nuns serve the food was a dark-haired, very pretty woman of about twenty-five years old. As she served Emmet, she smiled at him and they made eye contact and held it for a moment.

For a tiny fraction of a second, Emmet felt as if he'd been shot through the heart.

The woman moved on down the line, and Emmet sat and stared at her.

"Tell me, Marshal, where do you go from here?" Father Ramon asked.

"I am sorry to say that we're chasing a renegade Comanche

who has already murdered more than a half-dozen men," Jack said.

"Including the three men the sisters were burying when you came upon them?" Father Ramon said.

"Yes."

"That was your pressing business in Lubbock?"

"It was, Father," Jack said.

Emmet stared at the dark-haired woman. As she moved down the table, she glanced back at Emmet and when she caught him looking at her, she smiled coyly.

"The sisters and I will pray tonight for your safety," Father Ramon said.

"Thank you kindly, Father," Jack said.

When the dark-haired woman reached the end of the table, she turned and walked to the partially constructed mission building. Just before she entered, she turned and looked back at Emmet.

Emmet stared at her until she was inside the building.

"You are welcome to stay the night with us," Father Ramon said. "The roof isn't finished as yet, but there is no rain this time of year and we have extra cots."

"To tell you the truth, Father, I could use a good night's sleep," Jack said.

"We will follow you," Little Buffalo said. "All of us. I feel as you do, that the whites have taken all we had. I lost my wife and son to the whites. We have all lost something to the whites. It is time we made them answer for it."

Two Hawks looked around the circle.

"We will all die a glorious death, one that our ancestors will be proud of," he said.

★ ★ ★ ★ ★

The sun was down and torches were lit. Jack sat with Father Ramon at the table and drank coffee. The fiddle player and banjo player made softer, sweeter music in the background.

"Tell me something, Marshal," Father Ramon said. "Have you ever thought of doing something else besides wearing a badge?"

"I can't say as I have, Father," Jack said. "I always figured a man should stick to what he's good at."

"Does your brother feel the same as you?" Father Ramon said.

"Ask him, but if you ask me, I would have to say he doesn't," Jack said. "And speaking of which, where is my brother?"

"I saw him enter the mission building a little while ago," Father Ramon said.

Emmet entered the mission building and found the dark-haired woman rinsing dishes. He stood beside her and said, "My name is Emmet Youngblood and I'm . . ."

"I know who you are," she said in English accented with Spanish. "I asked Sister Katherine."

"Why?"

"Because I wanted to know."

Emmet started to help rinse the dishes.

"What are you doing?"

"Helping."

"Men do not help with women's work."

"Said who? Anyway, what's your name?"

"Maria della casa Lopez."

"Mexican girl," Emmet said. "Native-born to Texas?"

"Yes," Maria said. "Twenty miles north of the Grande, but we moved to Austin when I was a child."

"You work for the mission?"

"I'm finished with the dishes," Maria said. "There is some coffee left. Let us have some and go outside and listen to the music."

Emmet filled two cups with coffee from the pot that rested on top of a woodstove, and they went outside. There was a small bench next to the wall, and they sat.

"Why did you ask about my name?" Emmet asked.

Maria looked at him, and it was as if she could see clear through his soul. "Do you believe in love, Emmet?" she asked.

"Yes, I do," Emmet asked.

Maria became an orphan fifteen years ago when she was just ten, after Comanches raided her parents' farm outside of Austin. She hid in the fields and was spared. The wars had been over for years, but many natives refused to surrender, and they raided farms, homesteads, and ranches. She lived on the streets of Austin after that and begged for food and money to feed herself. Father Ramon spotted her one afternoon and brought her to his mission. He fed and clothed her and saw to it she received a proper education. She had been with the mission ever since.

"We have built missions in San Antonio, Dallas, Houston, and now here," Maria said.

"And after here?" Emmet asked.

"Wherever we are needed next," Maria said.

"That doesn't sound like much of a life," Emmet said.

"Father Ramon serves the church, and I serve him," Maria said. "We have helped many people. It is a good life, Emmet."

"No husband, no children. It seems a waste of a beautiful woman, if you ask me," Emmet said.

"Do you think I am beautiful?" Maria asked.

"Yes. As beautiful as my wife once was," Emmet said.

"Tell me about her," Maria said.

Emmet spoke for a good thirty minutes, and Maria listened

without interrupting or asking questions.

"It sounds to me like she was a wonderful woman," Maria said.

"She was."

"And you never remarried?"

"No."

"It seems like a waste of a handsome man, if you ask me," Maria said.

"I have to leave in the morning," Emmet said.

"I know."

"Would it . . . I mean . . . do you think it would be all right with you if I came back when my job is done?" Emmet asked.

"It is all right with me," Maria said. "If that is what you want to do."

"It probably won't be for a month," Emmet said.

"A month is not so long," Maria said. "Will I see you in the morning?"

"If you are up."

"I will be up. Who do you think makes breakfast for all these hungry men?"

"I'll see you in the morning then," Emmet said.

Maria smiled. "Good night."

"How many farmers, ranchers, and homesteaders do you think there are along the Canadian River?" Two Hawks asked.

"Many," Little Buffalo said.

"We need more rifles and ammunition, but we will take what we need along the way," Two Hawks said. "Starting tomorrow."

"More will follow us," Little Buffalo said.

Two Hawks stood up and looked at the twenty warriors. "If any one of you is not willing to die in battle, you are free to leave tonight," he said. "But if you are here in the morning and show any act of cowardice, I will kill you myself. Are there any cowards here tonight?"

Nobody moved.

"Put out the fire," Two Hawks said. "And get some sleep."

Sleep wouldn't come. Emmet was in a cot beside Jack in a room that housed twenty other cots. Men were snoring. Others made bathroom noises. Jack had been asleep the moment his head hit the pillow, something he'd always been able to do for as long as Emmet could remember.

Emmet looked up through the partially completed roof at the stars. Thousands of them were visible. From the corner of his eye he saw a figure. He turned on the cot and stared down the long interior of the building to the open frame of a doorway.

The figure was Maria.

Emmet sat up in the cot and looked at her. She nodded once and then appeared to float away. He stood, didn't bother with his boots, and walked to the open door. Maria was walking toward an open field of wildflowers. He followed her. The sliver of a moon provided little light, and he had difficulty keeping her in sight.

Suddenly, Maria was gone.

Emmet stood still and allowed his night vision to scan the darkness. He walked through a thicket of tall wildflowers for about a hundred feet and paused. Maybe he had been asleep and dreamed that he saw her? Maybe it was just his heart and eyes playing tricks on him?

Emmet took a step and he felt his legs being pulled out from under him and he fell to the thick grass with Maria on top of him.

"What are you . . . ?" Emmet whispered.

"Don't talk," Maria said and kissed him.

★ ★ ★ ★ ★

Maria rested her face against Emmet's bare chest.

"I have waited my whole life to do that," she said.

"I must confess it's been more than seven years myself," Emmet said.

"Was I worth it?"

"I can't remember feeling this happy," Emmet said.

"Me too," Maria said. "Emmet, will you really come back?"

"I doubt that anything could keep me away," Emmet said.

"I have to get back before I'm missed," Maria said.

"I know."

She kissed him sweetly, stood up, and dashed away in the darkness.

Emmet waited a few minutes and gazed up at the stars. His nose was filled with the scent of the wildflowers and Maria, and he felt almost drunk on the aroma.

Finally, Emmet stood up and returned to the mission and got into his cot.

Beside him, Jack said, "Well, it appears that somebody had himself a good time."

Chapter Ten

"Girls, get a move on. I want to finish Chao's dress today," Amy said.

"Coming, Grandma," Mary Louise said.

Amy sat in the buggy as Mary Louise led Sarah out of the cabin.

"Close the door," Amy said.

Mary Louise closed the door, and then she and Sarah went to the buggy and sat beside Amy.

Amy cracked the reins and the buggy rolled forward.

Jack shook hands with Father Ramon and then mounted his horse.

Sister Katherine said, "We will pray for you both."

"Thank you kindly, Sister. Emmet, let's go," Jack said.

Maria was in the doorway of the mission, watching them ride off. All Emmet could do was nod to her. He saw her lip quiver, and then she turned away.

They rode east several miles in silence.

Jack spoke first. "Want to tell me about it?" he said.

"Nope."

"Suit yourself."

"I never thought I would ever again feel about a woman like I feel about Maria," Emmet said.

"We lost a lot of time," Jack said. "I suggest we ride straight to Adobe Walls and try to pick up his tracks."

"Out of nowhere," Emmet said.

"Maybe old Two Hawks stayed put long enough for us to pick up his trail," Jack said.

"Like being hit by a bolt of lightning," Emmet said.

"Although I strongly suspect Two Hawks ain't done with his traveling just yet," Jack said.

"I know nothing about her and I don't really care," Emmet said. "I only know what I feel."

"Are we talking about the same thing?" Jack asked.

"Turn and let me check the back," Amy said.

"It's too long, Grandma," Mary Louise said.

"She isn't wearing proper shoes," Amy said.

"Stand on your toes," Mary Louise said to Chao-xing.

"Yes, stand on your toes," Amy said.

Chao-xing stood on her toes.

"Turn," Amy said.

Still on her toes, Chao-xing spun completely around.

"Lovely," Amy said. "What do you think, girls?"

"Very pretty," Mary Louise said.

"Can I have another doll?" Sarah asked.

"Yes, a pretty one," Chao-xing said. "One as pretty as you, but after I fix us lunch."

"I have an idea," Amy said. "Why don't we all go to the restaurant at the hotel and have lunch there. My treat."

"Oh, Grandmother, let's do," Mary Louise said.

"We got four hours of daylight left," Jack said. "I suggest we ride three and give our horses a good rest. We need to ride thirty miles tomorrow if we're to make Adobe Walls the day after."

Brushing his pinto, Emmet said, "We'll need to send a wire to Judge Parker on our progress."

"What progress, and from where?" Jack said. "We'd have to ride north to Amarillo to find a telegraph station, and that would take us a week out of our way."

"Not if we continued east to Wichita Falls," Emmet said. "I heard they're on the line as of a year ago."

"Thank goodness for the modern times we live in," Jack said.

"Don't be a horse's ass, Jack. There may be some news on Two Hawks we're unaware of," Emmet said.

"I was thinking more of the Wichita Falls Metropole Saloon," Jack said. "I ain't sure how, but they got two electrified lights over the bar that they turn on at night. They got what they call red lampshades."

"No kidding?"

"And they got a chorus line of a dozen girls that dances on the hour," Jack said. "You can set your watch by it. I was there just a few months ago picking up some *hombres* on a warrant."

Emmet finished brushing his pinto and replaced the saddle.

"Ever think about what you'd do when you're done being a lawman?" Emmet said as he mounted up.

"Sit in a rocking chair on the porch and sip whiskey," Jack said as they rode east.

"I'm serious, Jack."

"I know you are," Jack said. "I ain't college educated like you, Emmet. Only thing I'm good at is lawman. I'm not cut out for clerking in a store or mending fences on some ranch somewhere. Why?"

"I'm tired of doing this, Jack," Emmet said. "Lately I've been thinking of putting my law degree to good use."

"Lately, or since last night?" Jack said.

"The past several months at least," Emmet said. "But I will admit the notion got expedited some after last night."

"You don't pick them often, but when you do, you pick the

good ones," Jack said. "She's a stargazer, all right. I'll give you that."

"I didn't think you noticed."

"I noticed her looking at you," Jack said. "I noticed you run off to the kitchen to help her with the dishes."

"I didn't run," Emmet said.

"So what do you figure to do, hang a shingle outside an office somewhere?" Jack said. "*Emmet Youngblood, Attorney-at-law.* Get a little yellow house with flowerpots in the windows?"

"I owe it to my children, Jack," Emmet said. "And Ma. And you."

"Me?"

"I know you paid for most of my tuition, Jack," Emmet said. "I know you made her promise not to tell me, but I'm not stupid. I know she could never pay the tuition on what a teacher makes."

"Ma always was a bucket mouth," Jack said.

Two Hawks and his warriors hid in a tall field of wheat and watched the farmhouse in the distance. They determined that, besides the farmer, there was a wife and two children. A large corral with six horses faced the house; a tall barn sat to the left.

Among the twenty of them, they had just six rifles and several boxes of ammunition, and Two Hawks was the only one with a Colt pistol, but that didn't matter. The farmer and his family would pose little problem, armed or not.

They would wait for nightfall, for the lanterns in the windows to go out. As darkness set in, lights shone in the windows. After a while the lights went out. Two Hawks gave the hand signal, and the twenty warriors followed him from the wheat field to the front porch of the farmhouse. The windows were open, as it was a warm night. Two Hawks walked silently onto the porch and took hold of the knob on the front door. The door was unlocked.

Two Hawks drew the Bowie knife and held it in his left hand. He removed the tomahawk from his belt and flicked his wrist to extend it to full length. Then he burst through the door with a war cry, and his warriors followed.

The farmer had a revolver on a table beside the bed, but he never got to use it. When Two Hawks crashed through the bedroom door, the farmer reached for the revolver and Two Hawks split open the farmer's skull with the tomahawk. The farmer's wife sat up in bed and screamed, and Two Hawks nearly cut her head off with the Bowie knife.

There came screams from the children, but they lasted only a few moments. Then Little Buffalo was behind Two Hawks.

"Take all weapons and ammunition you can find and any supplies we can carry," Two Hawks said.

"What about the horses?" Little Buffalo asked.

"Plow horses are useless in open country," Two Hawks said.

Little Buffalo nodded and turned away.

"And take their scalps," Two Hawks said. "All of them."

After a later afternoon lunch, Amy took Mary Louise and Sarah to the boarding house near the courthouse where she made arrangements to spend the night. Then she returned to Chao-xing's shop to finish the dress.

As she stitched up the laces on the back, Amy said, "Not much longer, but it's getting dark. Maybe you could light a few lanterns."

Chao-xing lit two lanterns on the table and was about to return to Amy when the door opened and a man entered the shop. He stood in shadows and Chao-xing couldn't see his face, but she could certainly smell him. He stank of horse sweat and liquor.

"We are closed," Chao-xing said.

"All I want is some grub money," the man said.

Chao-xing backed up a few feet as Amy stood up from her chair.

"There is a mission at the church," Amy said. "They will give you all the food you need."

"Is that right," the man said.

Chao-xing had immediate thoughts of the men who tried to rape her years ago. This time Jack wasn't around to stop them.

"Please leave immediately," Amy said.

The man stepped into the light of the lanterns. He was a filthy specimen, with greasy hair and beard and yellow teeth.

"I'll leave as soon as you give me grub money," the man said.

"Chao-xing, come over here," Amy said.

The man reached inside his belt for a long knife. "I don't wish to harm you women, but know that I will if you don't give me the money," he said.

Chao-xing looked at the knife, then turned and ran to Amy. The man lurched forward, grabbed Chao-xing by her hair, and yanked her backward. Chao-xing screamed. Amy grabbed the coffee pot from the table and hit the man in the face with it.

"Why you stinking old bitch," the man yelled. He released Chao-xing's hair and punched Amy in the face. Amy flew backward and Chao-xing jumped on the man. The man tossed her over his shoulder to the floor. Amy stood up, the man punched her twice more, she hit the floor, and he kicked her a half-dozen times.

The man turned to Chao-xing and picked her up. "Let's see what you got under that dress," he said. He grabbed the front of the dress and ripped it open. Chao-xing slapped at the man. He punched her, and she fell onto the table. He grabbed the ripped material and tore it away, exposing Chao-xing's underwear. "Right pretty," the man said as he loosened his belt.

Chao-xing reached for something, anything, that she could use as a weapon and her right hand found Amy's knitting scissors. They were long and razor sharp. She grabbed the handle, and as the man leaned forward, Chao-xing shoved the scissors into his left lung to the handle.

The man gasped loudly as blood squirted onto Chao-xing. She pushed upward and spun away from him as he took hold of the knife and said, "You slant-eyed little yellow bitch."

Chao-xing picked up a razor from the counter near the barber chair and held it at arm's length.

The man staggered to the door. "Killed by a slant-eyed yellow bitch," he said. He opened the door, staggered to the wood sidewalk, and fell dead.

Chao-zing ran outside and screamed as loud as she could.

Chao-xing sat in the waiting room while Doctor Long treated Amy in one of his patient's rooms.

Sheriff Kyle, the sheriff of Fort Smith, entered the waiting room. "How is she?" he asked.

"I don't know. She's still in with Doctor Long," Chao-xing said.

"Well, that drifter won't be robbing or harming anybody anymore," Kyle said.

"He's dead?"

"As yesterday's fish."

Chao-xing placed her face in her hands and started to cry.

"You had no choice," Kyle said. "Who knows what he would have done to you and Amy if you hadn't fought back."

"I know," Chao-xing said.

Mary Louise and Sarah rushed into the waiting room with one of Kyle's deputies.

"Grandmother," Mary Louise cried.

"She's in with the doctor," Kyle said.

Mary Louise rushed forward and Chao-xing grabbed her. "The doctor will come out when he is ready. Stay here with me," she said.

Mary Louise took a chair next to Chao-xing. Sarah sat on Chao-xing's lap and started to cry.

"It will be all right," Chao-xing said.

Kyle turned when Judge Parker entered the waiting room. "How is she?" he asked.

"Doc's still in with her," Kyle said.

"The man who did this?" Parker asked.

"He's with the undertaker," Kyle said.

"I see," Parker said.

"I did it," Chao-xing said. "He left me no choice. I only meant to get him off of me. I never intended to kill him."

"You did what you had to do," Parker said.

The door to the patient's room opened. Doctor Long walked out and closed the door.

"Her right arm is broken and she has a concussion, but she is a strong woman and will recover," Long said.

Chao-xing and Mary Louise started to cry with relief.

"She'll have to stay here for a few days before she can be moved home," Long said. "Sheriff, can you send word to Doctor Jefferson on the reservation?"

"First thing in the morning," Kyle said.

"There is nothing more to do tonight," Long said. "I will stay with her, so all of you can go home tonight."

Chao-xing looked at Mary Louise and Sarah.

"Do you wish to return to the boarding house or go home with me?" Chao-xing asked.

"With you," Mary Louise said.

"Ladies, if you don't mind an escort, I'll walk you back," Kyle said.

★ ★ ★ ★ ★

The bed was large enough to hold the three of them, and Chao-xing slept in the middle. Mary Louise slept to her left and Sarah on her right. Sarah started to cry and Chao-xing turned to hold the child. After a while, the crying stopped and they fell asleep.

CHAPTER ELEVEN

"We should reach Adobe Walls by this afternoon," Jack said. "I guess we'll know if you were right about your hunch."

"From the Walls, how far to Wichita Falls?" Emmet asked.

"Three days southeast," Jack said. "Amarillo is far closer, but they're not on the line as yet."

"We have no choice if we want to contact the judge," Emmet said.

"You want to contact the judge," Jack said. "I want to find Two Hawks."

"And what if there is some new information that could lead us to him and we don't bother to find out what it is?" Emmet said.

"Well, I could do with a shot of whiskey and a line of dancing girls," Jack said.

Doctor Long and Chao-xing held Amy by the arms as they escorted her to the street where Doctor Jefferson waited in a large buggy. Amy's right arm was in a white cast made of plaster. Mary Louise and Sarah sat on the buckboard with Jefferson.

Chao-xing opened the buggy door and helped Amy inside, and then she climbed in and sat next to her.

"What are you doing?" Amy asked.

"Going with you," Chao-xing said.

"But you have your shop to . . ." Amy said.

"I made arrangements," Chao-xing said.

"I feel like an infant," Amy said.

"No arguments, Amy," Long said. "That concussion will lay you up for a week or more, and that arm needs to heal for at least six weeks."

Long closed the door and walked to Jefferson.

"She's your patient now, Doctor," Long said.

"I'll take good care of her," Jefferson said and yanked on the reins.

After a quick look around Adobe Walls, Jack said, "He's been here, all right, and it appears he's made some friends. At least six of them."

"Kiowa ponies," Emmet said. "I recognize the horseshoes from the reservation."

"Six rode in. Seven rode out," Jack said. "Appears we need to wire the judge after all. Best make camp, and we'll get an early start in the morning."

Emmet built a fire in the abandoned adobe Two Hawks had used because of the partial roof and because the air smelled of rain. They built a fire and cooked a supper of beans, bacon, and fresh cornbread baked by the sisters. They had several cans of condensed milk, thanks to Father Ramon, and opened one for their coffee.

"Odd to get rain this time of year on the plains," Jack said. "Best hobble the horses under the roof and build a lean-to out of our ponchos for us."

The rain held off long enough for them to eat and build a lean-to. The rain came suddenly and without warning. One moment the sky was a veil of black, and the next it lit up with a flash of lightning followed by a boom of thunder, and the rain fell in hard sheets.

"Well," Jack said. "Any chance we had at following his tracks will be washed away by morning for sure."

Amy fell asleep with her head on Chao-xing's shoulder for the better part of the long ride to the cabin. She awoke a mile before they arrived. Her arm was in considerable pain, and Chao-xing saw Amy wince.

"Doctor Long gave me medicine for your pain, but I can't give you any until we reach your home," Chao-xing said.

"Will you stay the night?" Amy asked. "It will be dark soon and . . ."

"I talked it over with your grandchildren. I'll stay until your arm is healed," Chao-xing said.

"I can't ask you to do that," Amy said.

"You didn't ask," Chao-xing said. "I volunteered, and that's the end of it."

"All right," Amy said. She closed her eyes. When she opened them again, the buggy was in front of the cabin.

Jefferson got down from the buckboard, helped Mary Louise and Sarah down, and then opened the door.

"It's getting dark," he said. "Let's get inside and I'll build a fire."

With assistance from Chao-xing and Jefferson, Amy made it into the house and sat in her chair by the fireplace. Jefferson built a fire in the fireplace.

"I'm going to give you something for the pain so you can sleep tonight," Jefferson said. "Doctor Long and I have instructed Chao-xing on how to prepare this medicine, but you are to take it only when the pain is severe."

"Girls, show me the kitchen," Chao-xing said. "We'll fix us all something to eat."

Mary Louise and Sarah took Chao-xing to the kitchen.

"I'll be back in the morning to check on you," Jefferson said. "There are a lot of supplies in the back of the buggy I best bring inside."

"Damn this rain," Jack said. "If I get any wetter, I'll be sleeping in my next bath."

"His tracks will be washed away for sure," Emmet said. "We have no choice now but to ride to Wichita Falls, send a wire to the judge, and check with the local sheriff for information."

The sky lit up from lightning, and the nervous horses snorted and bucked a bit.

"If we don't get struck down by lighting first," Jack said.

"How do you figure Two Hawks met up with six others?" Emmet asked.

"I've been all over the Llano, Oklahoma, New Mexico, and Arkansas in the line of duty the past ten years and there are hundreds, maybe even thousands by now, who have left the reservations to risk living as renegades," Jack said. "It isn't all that difficult for water to seek its own level if you give it a chance."

"I didn't think it was so widespread a problem," Emmet said.

"Since you returned from college, how many times have you left Fort Smith?" Jack asked.

"Not many."

"For all we know, old Two Hawks may have doubled the number of those following him by now," Jack said.

"A band that large can do a lot of damage," Emmet said.

"And for a very long time," Jack said. "They know this land better than any white man and can hide out for years."

The rain seemed to fall harder, and they huddled closer under the lean-to.

"Still got that flask of bourbon?" Emmet said.

"Good idea," Jack said and removed the silver flask from his inside vest pocket. He took a sip and handed the flask to Emmet, who took a sip and passed it back to Jack.

Jack held the flask up to the rain and said, "To the exciting life of a lawman."

"I feel so sleepy," Amy said.

Chao-xing adjusted the covers over Amy. "That's the medicine. You'll sleep until morning," she said.

"My son Emmet is away with his brother, Jack. You can sleep in his bed," Amy said.

"Thank you," Chao-xing said. "I'm afraid the beautiful dress you made for me is ruined."

"I'll make another when my arm is healed, don't worry," Amy said.

A few moments later, Amy was sound asleep.

Chao-xing left her and went to the living room, where Mary Louise and Sarah were in their nightclothes and seated on the sofa. Sarah held her tiny Chinese doll.

"There is a bag of cookies in the supplies Doctor Jefferson brought in. Who would like some cookies and milk before bed?" Chao-xing asked.

Two Hawks and his warriors feasted on the meat of a wild deer they killed on the plains. The farmer they killed had a well-stocked liquor cabinet, and the warriors passed around bottles of rye and bourbon. As the festive mood reached its pinnacle, Two Hawks suddenly stood up and the warriors quieted down.

"I have studied the white man's ways my entire life," he said. "When they are an army, they are powerful and can't be stopped. But as people, they are weak. Especially when it comes to their women and children. I have read many of the white man's books and learned a great deal about their behavior. The white man will pay in gold and rifles for their women and children. They call it kidnapping, and what they pay is called ransom. For some reason, they pay more and quicker for their girls. We need a camp the white man doesn't know about and won't find. Who knows of such a place?"

"On the Oklahoma side of the Ozark Mountains, there is a canyon south of the border of Missouri where many hide without fear of the white man," Little Buffalo said. "I have been there. Good hunting and water, even in winter."

"We will begin the journey there in the morning," Two Hawks said. "We will take no captives until we are a day's ride from this camp, but we will take weapons, food, and gold to supply ourselves."

Two Hawks turned suddenly as five riders raced into the camp. Even in the dark, Two Hawks could see they were Kiowa and Apache. One of them dismounted and looked at Two Hawks.

"I am called Running Bear," he said. "And we have come to join you."

Chao-xing wasn't in bed five minutes before Sarah came tiptoeing into the bedroom and got into bed beside her, still holding her Chinese doll.

"I can't sleep," Sarah said.

"No wonder," Chao-xing said. "You weren't in bed long enough to close your eyes."

"I want to sleep with you," Sarah said.

"All right," Chao-xing said. "Hop in."

Mary Louise appeared in the dark doorway. "Can I . . . ?" she said.

"Yes," Chao-xing said. "But no snoring."

"Looks like it's a cold breakfast for us," Jack said in the morning when all the available firewood was wet.

"We got cornbread, hard biscuits, jerked beef, and water," Emmet said. "What's your poison?"

"I'll take a biscuit and a stick of beef," Jack said.

Emmet had the same. Afterward they saddled their horses and rode away from Adobe Walls.

"South to Wichita Falls it is," Jack said.

Chapter Twelve

Chao-xing proved handy with an ax, having chopped wood for many years working for her father on the railroad and even now to chop kindling for hot water at her barbershop.

On the porch, Amy sat in her rocking chair and watched Mary Louise and Sarah shuck corn.

"Girls, you are making a terrible mess," Amy said. "Please try to get the husks into the basket instead of the porch."

"Yes, Grandma," Mary Louise said.

Chao-xing set the ax aside, lifted the kindling basket, and carried it to the porch.

"Chao-xing, would you put on a pot of coffee?" Amy said. "I see two coffee drinkers approaching."

She couldn't see down the road from the ground, but on the higher elevation on the porch Chao-xing could see two buggies heading toward the house.

"Come on, girls, let's get all this into the kitchen," Chao-xing said.

At Sunrise, Two Hawks gathered his twenty-six warriors into a tight circle around a campfire.

"We must ride to the north and to the east to reach the camp in the Ozarks Little Buffalo spoke about," he said. "We will ride along the Canadian River for as long as possible and raid as many settlers and farms as we come across. This is a long journey. Some of you are riding nags and won't make it. Take whatever good horses you can find as we raid."

The first attack was on a small farm ten miles northeast along the Canadian River. Two unmarried brothers were making a go of one hundred sixty acres of fertile topsoil. The brothers were having a breakfast of porridge and biscuits when Two Hawks and his warriors burst through the front door of their cabin and killed them where they sat. The raid produced two fine Winchester rifles, two excellent Colt revolvers, ammunition for both, good supplies, and two horses. When they left, they put two of the nags in the corral.

The second raid was a bit confusing at first. Two Hawks and his warriors came upon two men using plow horses to turn a field. They didn't have a house, but a large tent near the field. It occurred to Two Hawks that the men hadn't yet built a cabin and lived in the tent. The raid was over in a matter of seconds as Two Hawks and his warriors rode down upon the men and killed them as they ran to the tents for their weapons. Inside the tent they found two Henry rifles and ammunition, one revolver and ammunition, a cash box with paper and gold coins, and supplies. They took the men's horses and left their nags behind.

"We will raid one more time before we cross the Canadian River and ride to Oklahoma," Two Hawks told his warriors as they rode away.

Judge Parker drove his own buggy while Sheriff Kyle drove the buggy belonging to Amy. Amy's buggy was loaded with supplies, and Kyle carried them into the house and to the kitchen.

"Chao-xing, would you get my purse so I can pay for the . . ." Amy said.

"No need," Parker said. "Seeing as how both of your sons are away on my behalf, the least I can do is pay for some supplies."

Chao-xing had a coffee pot and four cups ready, filled them all, then took the chair to Amy's left. Kyle and Parker also sat, and there was an awkward moment of silence.

"Judge Parker, you have the look of a man who has something on his mind he does not want to say out loud," Amy said.

"I guess we've known each other too long for me to fool you much," Parker said.

"Say what you came to say," Amy said.

"I should wait inside with the girls," Chao-xing said.

"Stay right where you are," Amy said. "You've earned the right to hear what the judge has to say."

Parker sighed. "I expect to hear from your boys any day now with a report," he said. "I am torn between telling them what happened and not telling them. I thought I would ask your opinion on the matter."

Amy used her left hand to take a sip of coffee. Then she said, "My sons are men, and both are officers of the court. They have a job to do. You can't expect them to put aside their duty because their mother has met with an accident. Besides, I am healing quite well and my nurse, Chao-xing here, is more than up to the task of taking care of the girls and me. You tell my sons nothing."

Parker nodded. "About what I expected you to say," he said. He looked at Sheriff Kyle. "Go ahead," he said.

"Sally Potts has met your offer of four thousand dollars for the barbershop," Kyle said. "The money has been deposited into your account in the bank. She also said she will have all of your personal belongings packed and held at the courthouse for you to pick up at your convenience."

Kyle reached into his vest pocket and produced a bank statement and handed it to Chao-xing. Her account had slightly more than seven thousand dollars in it.

"Thank you," Chao-xing said.

"Well, Sheriff, if we're to get back before dark, we best get moving," Parker said.

After Parker and Kyle left in Parker's buggy, Amy and Chao-xing sat in silence for many minutes.

"You sold your shop," Amy said. "Why?"

"When your son returns, if he doesn't want me, I will go to San Francisco," Chao-xing said.

Amy took Chao-xing's hand in her left hand. "When my son returns, if he doesn't want you, I will have the judge lock him up and charged with extreme stupidity," she said.

Two Hawks and his warriors waited in a circle around a campfire for Little Buffalo and Running Bear to return from their scouting mission. Two Hawks smoked his pipe as he waited, allowing his thoughts to take shape. His warriors were spirited and willing to die in battle for their beliefs, but they lacked vision. The raids weren't just to inflict pain upon small pockets of white men, but as a bridge to something larger.

Little Buffalo and Running Bear returned, dismounted, and sat beside Two Hawks.

"About eight miles along the Canadian is a farm with two men and their women," Little Buffalo said. "A few miles beyond that to the east is Oklahoma."

"Soon, if not already, the army and lawmen will be searching for us," Two Hawks said. "We will need to ride quickly to the Ozarks to your hidden campsite, but along the way we can't grow careless."

"I know the country well," Running Buffalo said. "There are many places to hide along the way."

Two Hawks stood up.

"Let us ride," he said.

"We should reach Wichita Falls sometime late tomorrow afternoon," Jack said.

Emmet added wood to the fire and stirred the pan full of

beans and bacon. "After we wire the judge, I'm going to have a shave, a hot bath, and the biggest steak I can find," he said.

Jack, seated against his saddle, was rolling a cigarette. He paused to look at the horizon. "Company," he said.

Emmet reached into his saddlebags for his binoculars and scanned the horizon. "It's an army patrol, Jack," he said. "They should be here before dusk."

"Maybe they got a couple of extra steaks on them," Jack said.

Two Hawks and his warriors waited in a field of corn for night to fall. The cabin was large, and light shone in every window. Smoke billowed up from the chimney. He turned to Little Buffalo.

"How many rifles do we now have?" Two Hawks asked.

"Thirteen and ammunition for each," Little Buffalo said.

"We will use tomahawks and knives only," Two Hawks said. "We must save the rifles and ammunition until we have many more of them. When the last light in the windows goes out, we will strike."

They waited in the field for about ninety minutes until all lights inside the cabin were extinguished. Two Hawks used the time to make a dozen torches from cornstalks that he soaked in rye whiskey. The night was moonless, and Two Hawks had to rely upon his night vision to guide his warriors across the field to the cabin. Two of his warriors waited a mile away with the horses so that the raid could be conducted in silence. When they reached the porch, Two Hawks nodded to Little Buffalo, and he walked up the steps, tried the door, and found it locked.

Little Buffalo tried the front window and found it unlocked. He gently moved the window up until there was enough room for him to crawl through. Once he was inside, Two Hawks lit his torch with a wood match and it instantly burst into flames. The others lit their torches as well, and when Little Buffalo opened the door from the inside, Two Hawks let out with his war cry and led the charge into the cabin.

"I'm Captain Grimes. We spotted your fire from a ways off and thought we'd camp with you tonight, Marshal."

Jack looked at Grimes and his dozen men. They were dust-covered from hard riding.

"You appear to be on some pressing business," Jack said.

Emmet handed Grimes a cup of coffee.

"Thank you," Grimes said. "To answer your question, Marshal, units have been dispatched from several locations to the Canadian River. It's been reported that Indian attacks on farmers and settlers have started up out of nowhere. We need to find out what's going on."

Emmet exchanged a glance with Jack.

"What's going on is, a renegade Comanche named Two Hawks has got himself a following and he's raiding along the river," Jack said. "That's what's going on, Captain."

"Do you know this for a fact?" Grimes asked.

"We do," Emmet said. "We tracked him to Adobe Walls, where he was joined by six others. We're headed to Wichita Falls to . . ."

"That's south of here," Grimes said. "The Canadian is north."

"He's long gone, Captain," Jack said. "By the time you reach the Canadian, you might find his handiwork, but you won't find him. We need to wire Judge Parker over in Fort Smith, and Wichita Falls is the closest telegraph."

Grimes sighed and then turned to his sergeant. "Have the men make camp. See to the horses and then break out the supplies."

The raid was successful. Two Hawks and his warriors picked up two more Winchester rifles and two Colt revolvers, ammunition for both, and a pouch of gold coins. They used the white man's pillowcases to carry supplies from the pantry, including several bottles of rye and bourbon whiskey. The horses were plow horses and useless so they left them behind.

Two Hawks and his warriors stood in the field and watched as the cabin burned to the ground. When they finally left the field, Two Hawks used his torch to set fire to the cornstalks.

Grimes ate a plate of canned beef stew. His squad had ample supplies, so they opened a can of the stew for Jack and one for Emmet.

"It wouldn't surprise me none if Two Hawks recruited more warriors since we lost his trail during a hard rain," Jack said.

"I hope not," Grimes said. "We'd have to dispatch additional squads to hunt him down if that's the case."

"Captain, I'd get my mind around that fact right now," Jack said.

Grimes nodded. "I suspect you might be correct, Marshal."

"Two Hawks left the reservation in a lot of pain, Captain," Emmet said. "His wife died, and he hated reservation life. He's trained in the old Comanche ways and is willing to die for what he believes. Don't sell him short, Captain."

"You know him?" Grimes said.

Emmet tapped the badge on his shirt.

Grimes nodded. "Do me a favor and send a wire to my commanding officer advising him of the situation," he said.

"We will," Emmet said.

Chao-xing and Amy were having a cup of tea at the kitchen table when Mary Louise and Sarah, each holding a Chinese doll, sneaked past them and entered Emmet's bedroom.

"It appears you won't get a good night's sleep around here," Amy said.

"I don't mind," Chao-xing said. "Your son has a fine big bed, and there is plenty of room."

"My son needs a wife," Amy said. "Both of them do."

Chao-xing blushed slightly.

"Emmet is a steady, stable man, and unless something or someone comes along that rocks him off his feet, he won't look to marry until the girls are grown. By then he'll be so set in his ways, I'm afraid he won't want to," Amy said. "But Jack, he's a wild one, as I'm sure you know. He's a good man, but a wife will make him a better man."

Chao-xing nodded. "I think I will turn in. Do you need the medicine?"

"No, dear," Amy said. "Go to bed and get some rest. God knows, we all need it."

"Tomorrow we ride to the hidden camp in the Ozarks," Two Hawks said to his warriors, who were gathered around a campfire. "When we have enough weapons and gold, we will take hostages and make the white man pay for their crimes."

Little Buffalo stood up suddenly and scanned the darkness past the fire. "Riders coming," he said.

"I see them," Two Hawks said. "Let them come."

The riders came closer until they reached the camp. They were four Apache renegades.

One of them said, "We have come to join with you."

CHAPTER THIRTEEN

Maria was grinding corn at the grist wheel when she happened to glance up at the hills behind the mission and spotted the two Apaches she'd seen a week earlier. They sat atop their horses and simply looked down upon the mission. They made no attempt to come closer.

Maria turned and went to look for Father Ramon. She found him on a tall ladder with the men building the roof.

"Father Ramon," she called up to him.

He looked down. "Yes?"

"They have returned, the two Apaches."

"Be right down," Father Ramon said.

He climbed down the ladder and reached for his robes resting on the back of a saw table.

"Where?" he asked.

"On the hill, the same place," Maria said.

They walked to the grist mill and looked at the two Apache riders.

"They haven't moved," Maria said.

"I think they are curious," Father Ramon said. "Get me a bowl, please."

Maria rushed into the kitchen and returned quickly with a large wood bowl, which she gave to Father Ramon.

He held the bowl up with his left hand and waved to the two Apaches with his right. They stared at him for a few moments and then slowly started to ride down the hill.

"They are coming down," Maria said.

"They are hungry," Father Ramon said. "Is there enough stew from breakfast for two bowls?"

"Yes, and bread," Maria said.

"Good," Father Ramon said.

The two Apaches stopped before Father Ramon and Maria. Most of the workers stopped what they were doing to watch.

"Do you speak English?" Father Ramon asked.

"English, French, and Spanish. I am called Uday," one of the Apaches said. "This is Natan."

"I am Father Ramon. Would you like to share food with us?"

Uday nodded, and he and Natan dismounted.

"Maria, bring food to the dining hall for our guests," Father Ramon said.

"Yes, Father," Maria said and went into the dining hall.

"Rest and water your horses," Father Ramon said to Uday and Natan. "We have much grain for them if you wish."

Uday nodded.

Father Ramon waved to several of the workers, and they walked to him.

"Please see to our guests' horses," Father Ramon said. "We will be in the dining room."

The men approached Uday and Natan.

"It's all right," Father Ramon said. "They will care for your horses."

Uday and Natan handed the reins to the workers.

"Good. Come, let's go inside and share food," Father Ramon said.

Uday and Natan walked with Father Ramon into the dining hall, where Maria was filling up two bowls with stew. A half loaf of bread, two glasses, and a bottle of wine also sat on the table.

"Please sit and eat," Father Ramon said.

Uday and Natan took chairs.

Father Ramon poured the wine. "The wine is made from the red grape. It is very sweet and warm," he said.

Uday looked at the gold crucifix around Father Ramon's neck. "What are you building here?" he asked.

"A hospital, a church, and a mission for the poor," Father Ramon said.

Uday nodded and lifted a wood spoon to taste the stew. He nodded his approval at Father Ramon.

"That Captain Grimes seems a decent enough officer, but if he and his twelve soldiers come across Two Hawks and his bunch, I wouldn't bet on Grimes or his soldiers making it out alive," Jack said as he and Emmet rode down Main Street in Wichita Falls.

"I can't say as I disagree with you," Emmet said.

Named for the Wichita River waterfalls, Wichita Falls was hot and humid, with a population of nearly two thousand citizens.

"We best check in with the sheriff first," Jack said.

They dismounted in front of the sheriff's office and tied the horses to the hitching post. Sheriff Matt Hogan was at his desk when Jack and Emmet entered the office.

"Let me guess," Hogan said. "You're here about the Indian attacks."

"A fine meal," Uday said.

"You are welcome to take supplies with you for your journey," Father Ramon said.

"You are building a church?" Natan asked.

"Yes. Would you care to see it?" Father Ramon said.

"Yes. We had teaching of your Jesus Christ from the French missionaries and also the Spanish," Uday said.

"Come," Father Ramon said.

He led Uday and Natan outside and across the complex to

the nearly completed church. The door wasn't in place as yet, and they simply went up the stone steps to the church interior. Uday and Natan looked at the fine stained-glass windows, the marble altar and cabinet where the gold cups were stored.

"It is a fine church," Uday said.

At the restaurant across the street from the sheriff's office, Jack cut into his thick steak and said, "Those reports of yours are a week old."

"That's right," Hogan said.

"So there are probably more than three raids by now," Emmet said.

"I haven't had word as yet, but that's my guess as well," Hogan said.

"The army has sent units to track down Two Hawks, but they won't find him," Emmet said.

"How can you be sure of that?" Hogan asked. "A dozen squads of soldiers. He can't evade them forever."

"Sheriff, what you and the army are failing to realize is that Two Hawks doesn't want to evade the army forever," Jack said. "Just long enough for him to amass a large enough following to declare war."

Hogan stared at Jack.

"My God," Hogan said.

"Sheriff, we have to wire Fort Smith," Emmet said. "I suggest you wire the army and the Texas Rangers with this new information."

Father Ramon and Maria watched Uday and Natan ride back up the hill and disappear over the other side.

"Where do you think they will go?" Maria asked.

"Maybe to a reservation?" Father Ramon said. "Wherever

they go, I pray they are safe from harm."

Jack sat in a chair outside the telegraph office and waited for Emmet. He rolled and smoked a cigarette and watched the horse and pedestrian traffic on Main Street. Citizens seemed uneasy. Most were probably aware of the attacks on settlers along the Canadian River, and were probably worried Two Hawks would continue to raid along the nearby Red River.

To guess what Two Hawks would do next was a foolish waste of time. Jack was sure Two Hawks had a plan, but what it was he had no idea. It was a wait-and-see game at the moment. He hoped they didn't have to wait too long for Two Hawks to make his move.

Emmet exited the telegraph office and Jack stood up.

"I told the operator to have the reply brought over to the hotel," Emmet said.

"Let's get us a shave and a bath, get our dirty laundry cleaned, and then have a drink at the Metropole," Jack said. "No reason why we can't enjoy ourselves while we wait for the judge's reply."

"Where did the sheriff go?" Emmet asked.

"His office. Why?"

"I expect he'll want to hear what Judge Parker has to say."

"I expect so," Jack said.

Two Hawks sat in front of the campfire and took stock of his warriors, which now numbered thirty. The rifles numbered nineteen, the revolvers eight. He needed more warriors and weapons, at least twice those numbers and more.

He stood up, and the warriors grew silent before the fire.

"I am willing to die in battle rather than live as a dog being fed the white man's scraps," Two Hawks said. "Every one of you feels the same way or you would not have followed me.

When we reach the hidden site in the mountains, we must increase our numbers and weapons. The whites value their children, and they value their gold. We will use one to get the other, and when we are strong enough, we will attack in force and destroy as many whites and their property as possible. Maybe some of us will survive in the end, but don't count on that. The white army is powerful, and they have weapons that kill in large numbers. If you have wives and children, recognize the fact that you will never see them again. Every man here will die the glorious death of our ancestors. We will be dogs being fed scraps no longer."

The thirty warriors stared at Two Hawks.

"More will join us in the mountains," Little Buffalo said.

"I hope some of them are women," Running Bear said.

Little Buffalo grinned and then laughed. "Yes. Nice big fat women to keep a man warm at night," he said.

The Metropole Saloon was a large and prosperous establishment. The bar was sixty feet long. The mirror behind it was nearly as long. Mounted on the wall on each side of the bar was an electric light bulb covered with a reddish glass shade that came all the way from Denver. There were sixty tables centered on the floor. To the left and right against the walls were gambling tables. Directly in front of the bar was a large dance floor.

Jack carried two shots of whiskey from the bar to the table where Emmet sat. Emmet was smoking his pipe. Jack set the shot glasses down and took a seat.

"This is quite a saloon," Emmet said.

Jack rolled a cigarette and said, "In about five minutes, keep an eye on those two electric lights at the bar."

Emmet took a sip of his whiskey and looked at the two lamps. "I'm more interested in Judge Parker's reply at the moment than lights at the bar."

"Trying to have fun with you is as useless as a pointless pencil," Jack said.

"We're not here to have fun," Emmet said.

"I'll remember you said that the next time you run into that Mexican girl you left behind at the mission," Jack said.

Before Emmet could reply, the two electric lamps started to glow softly.

"See there," Jack said.

The lamps slowly glowed brighter until they were brighter than any dozen candles combined.

"That is something," Emmet said.

"I told you," Jack said.

When the two lamps reached maximum brightness, a dozen dancing girls raced onto the dance floor and immediately the piano player in the corner played a quickstep dance tune.

Most patrons clapped to the music as the dozen girls danced around the floor. Even Emmet appeared to enjoy the music and dancing girls. Clapping along with everyone else, Jack stopped suddenly when he noticed that one of the girls was Chinese. She was slight and pretty, with fine features, and she reminded Jack very much of Chao-xing.

He hadn't thought much about her since leaving Fort Smith; partly because there wasn't time, but mostly because he knew thinking about her would lead to missing her. Watching the Chinese dancer, Jack wondered if Chao-xing had made good on her threat to move to San Francisco. He was bothered by that idea a great deal more than he anticipated.

"Well, that was something," Emmet said when the music ended and the girls left the stage.

Jack tossed back what was left of his whiskey and said, "Let's go see if the judge sent us a reply yet."

★ ★ ★ ★ ★

Summoned to Judge Parker's courthouse chambers, Bass Reeves and Cal Witson read Emmet's telegram.

While they read the telegram, Parker filled three glasses with whiskey.

"There hasn't been a problem like this since Custer," Witson said when he set the telegram on the desk.

"At least," Reeves said. "Is Jack still out there?"

"Along with Emmet," Parker said. "I want you men to ride over to the fort and ask the commanding officer to meet me here in my office first thing in the morning. Tell him the problem is severe."

They waited in the hotel lobby with cups of coffee. Emmet smoked his pipe, and Jack a rolled cigarette.

"I read in a newspaper that they're planning to sell cigarettes already rolled in a box, or separate for a penny apiece in New York and Boston," Emmet said.

"Already rolled?" Jack said.

"By machines."

"A man should roll his own," Jack said.

"It's progress, Jack."

"It's lazy is what it is," Jack said. "I doubt that fad will catch on."

The telegraph operator came through the lobby door, holding a sheet of paper. "Got the reply you fellows are waiting on," he said.

Emmet took the paper and read aloud. "Stay in Wichita Falls until I contact you with instructions. Judge Parker."

Emmet lowered the paper. "He must be planning something," he said.

"Me, too," Jack said. "A good night's sleep."

"We need to inform the sheriff," Emmet said.

"Go ahead then," Jack said. "Just don't wake me when you come in."

Hogan was at his desk when Emmet entered the office and showed him Judge Parker's reply.

"What do you suppose Parker is up to?" Hogan asked.

Emmet took a chair opposite the desk. "My guess is he wants to consult with the commanding officer at Fort Smith and send a team of marshals along with a patrol," he said. "I'd advise wiring the Texas Rangers of the situation."

"I already have," Hogan said. "I'm waiting on a reply from Austin. It might not come until morning."

"I guess there is nothing to do now but wait," Emmet said.

Hogan stood and went to the woodstove where a pot of coffee was being kept warm. He filled two tin cups, returned to the desk, and gave one cup to Emmet.

"It isn't good, but it's hot," Hogan said as he sat.

Emmet took a sip and nodded.

"Mind a personal question?" Hogan said.

"My mother is a quarter Sioux and Apache," Emmet said. "Also French and Irish. My father was Scottish and Irish."

"That accounts for the sandy hair and blue eyes," Hogan said.

"I expect so," Emmet said.

Hogan sighed. "I hate waiting. Fancy a game of chess?"

"How do you know I play?" Emmet asked.

"During the war I spent a lot of time in Boston with the 54th," Hogan said. "Some of your words sound like you went to school there. Any man goes to school in Boston knows the game."

"Law degree," Emmet said.

"I'll get the board," Hogan said.

Jack usually fell asleep within a few seconds of closing his eyes. Tonight was an exception. No matter how hard he tried not to think of Chao-xing and see her face, she was plastered there in his mind.

After tossing and turning, Jack gave it up and got out of bed. He lit the oil lamp on the table and dug out his flask of whiskey. He sat in a chair and rolled a cigarette, smoked, and sipped from the flask.

Jack wasn't a man who usually examined his emotions. Generally he just ignored them and went by instinct. Seeing that Chinese dancer at the saloon triggered something in his gut he didn't like or understand.

He sipped and smoked and rolled thoughts around for a while. He denied it for as long as possible, but finally had to admit, if even just to himself, that jealousy was eating away at him. The idea of another man sharing Chao-xing's bed made Jack sick to his stomach. She had a way of blushing that could drive a man to madness, and the soft noises she made when they were in bed drove him to lust. Sometimes she whispered in Chinese, and even though he had no notion what she was saying, it made him want her even more.

The realization hit him like the kick of a mule.

What he was feeling was love.

"Ah, Jesus Christ," Jack said aloud.

He sipped from the flask and rolled another cigarette. As he lit the cigarette with a wood match, the hotel room door opened and Emmet walked in.

As he removed his holster, Emmet said, "Figured you'd be asleep by now."

"I guess I was worried about my little brother," Jack said.

CHAPTER FOURTEEN

Colonel Henry Tate took the mug of coffee from Judge Parker, sipped, and nodded his approval.

"I am sure you've seen the same dire reports I have," Parker said. "Two Hawks has proven to be far more resourceful and dangerous than I would have imagined."

"I learned a long time ago to never underestimate a Comanche," Tate said.

Parker sat behind his desk and Tate took the chair opposite it.

"Units are being dispatched to the field from half a dozen forts as we speak," Tate said. "I am sending a patrol of twenty-four men, two officers, and two scouts this afternoon."

"I would like to add two of my marshals to your patrol," Parker said. "After all, the reservation is my jurisdiction."

"Of course," Take said.

"What is the army's plan, Colonel?" Parker said.

"The attacks have all taken place along the Canadian River so far," Tate said. "Army patrols are already scouting the river for signs of Two Hawks and his followers. We will join them and divide up to cover more territory. Our scouts are Comanche and Apache and know this area well. Hopefully we can bring a close to this campaign rather quickly."

"How many dead so far?" Parker asked.

"A dozen, maybe more. Could be as high as twenty."

146

"Dear God," Parker said. "What's Washington's position on this?"

"End it quickly with as little bloodshed as possible," Tate said. "And speak to no newspapers and reporters. Nobody wants a repeat of Little Bighorn."

"I'll have my officers report to you at the fort," Parker said.

"We plan to ride at one," Tate said. "Have them there an hour early."

Jack and Emmet were having breakfast at the restaurant in the hotel when Sheriff Hogan entered with a telegram.

"Join us for breakfast, Sheriff?" Emmet asked.

"Already ate, but I'll take coffee," Hogan said. He sat, and the waitress brought him a fresh cup of coffee. "Got a telegram for you," Hogan said.

Emmet took the telegram and read it. "Judge Parker wants us to ride north to the Canadian River and join up with one of the army details scouting for Two Hawks. Reeves and Witson have joined the patrol from Fort Smith."

"What are we supposed to do, ride around until Two Hawks decides to find us?" Jack said.

"A company of Texas Rangers has been dispatched," Hogan said.

"Austin to the Canadian will take them a week," Jack said.

"We best draw supplies after breakfast and head north," Emmet said.

"Good luck to you both," Hogan said.

Little Buffalo led the way through a narrow notch in the Ozark Mountains in Oklahoma. The ride had taken several days and nights to cross the state undetected. Once through the notch, Little Buffalo took them to higher ground and finally through a narrow canyon that elevated to a mountain.

"On the other side of that ridge is the campsite," Little Buffalo told Two Hawks. "We should reach it by nightfall."

"This is a dumb idea," Jack said.

"Orders are orders, Jack," Emmet said.

"It will take us a week to reach the Canadian in Oklahoma, ten days or more if we travel through the panhandle," Jack said.

"What do you suggest?" Emmet asked.

"Turn around and ride south to Dallas," Jack said. "We can make it in eighteen hours; maybe less if we push hard. We can get the railroad in Dallas and be in Tulsa in ten hours without killing our horses."

"That would save us five or six days," Emmet said.

"Well, let's turn around then," Jack said.

"The arm is looking fine," Jefferson said after he removed the plaster cast. "Are you in any pain?"

"Mild at most," Amy said. "I haven't needed the pain medicine in days."

"Good," Jefferson said.

They were at the kitchen table. Chao-xing brought a pot of coffee and a cup to the table and filled the cup.

"Have you had lunch, Doctor?" Chao-xing said.

"Haven't had time," Jefferson said.

"Please stay," Chao-xing said.

"I have patients to see," Jefferson said.

"It will do you no good to argue with her, Doctor," Amy said.

"Well, all right," Jefferson said.

"Girls, come to the kitchen," Chao-xing said. "We're making lunch."

Mary Louise and Sarah came running into the kitchen.

"Before she came along, I couldn't get them to slice a carrot," Amy told Jefferson.

"Jack, hold up," Emmet said. "My horse needs rest and grain."

They dismounted and found shade under a tree.

"Give them an hour," Jack said.

They removed the saddles and brushed the horses, then gave them grain for strength to continue the ride to Dallas.

Jack checked his pocket watch. "We should reach Dallas by midnight," he said.

Emmet dug out sticks of jerked beef and gave one to Jack. "That's Dad's old pocket watch, isn't it?"

"It is," Jack said. "I got the watch, you got his Dragoon," Jack said. "Still have it?"

"I do," Emmet said. "Every once in a while I dig it out, load it up, and take target practice with it. How Dad used such a heavy weapon all those years is a mystery to me. It kicks like a mule and is accurate no more than ten feet."

"Is that why you carry that hogleg, because Dad carried one?" Jack asked.

Emmet withdrew his Dragoon from the holster and tossed it to Jack. "I'm not the gunman you are, Jack," he said. "If it comes down to it, I need to put a man down with one shot because I probably wouldn't get a second."

Jack looked down the barrel of the Dragoon. "Well, this surely will do it," he said and tossed it back to Emmet. "If you can find a fence post to balance it on."

"Let me see your Colt," Emmet said.

Jack drew the Colt and tossed it to Emmet. The revolver was black with black ivory grips that had a raised gold crucifix on the thumb side. "I've never seen a gun quite like this," he said.

"And you won't," Jack said. "That was a special order for me from Colt. You won't find a faster cock anywhere, and the trigger pull is one pound of pressure. That gun cost me an entire month's pay."

Emmet returned the Colt to Jack.

Rolling a cigarette, Jack paused. "Let me ask you something, brother. Do you really plan to see that Mexican gal again?" he said.

"Not just see, Jack. I plan to make her my wife," Emmet said. "As soon as we're done with this assignment, I'm going back to the mission and bring her home. And that's not all I've decided. I'm going to take the bar examination and practice law. Maybe I can get appointed to Judge Parker's court? My girls deserve a real home, and so does Ma, and so will Maria."

"Got it all figured out, huh?" Jack said.

"As long as we don't get killed on this assignment." Emmet grinned.

"Right," Jack said.

"I can't honestly say I've used chopsticks before," Jefferson said.

"It's easy once you get the hang of it," Mary Louise said.

"I'm afraid I got more on my shirt than in my mouth," Jefferson said. "But the lunch was delicious. Amy, don't move around too much until that new cast fully hardens. Chao-xing, you see to that."

"Don't worry, Doctor," Chao-xing said.

After Jefferson left to make his rounds, Amy and Chao-xing took tea to the porch while the girls did the dishes.

"I need to chop more wood for tonight," Chao-xing said.

"We have plenty," Amy said. "Why not do something fun with the girls this afternoon?"

Chao-xing nodded.

"What?" Amy asked.

"I feel like something . . . bad is going to happen," Chao-xing said.

Amy smiled. "That's how it feels to be married to a lawman," she said.

"Those lights you see there, that's Dallas," Jack said. "We should be there in about an hour."

"Good, because my horse is as tired as my back hurts," Emmet said.

"You and your horse can sleep on the train," Jack said.

They rode in silence for a few minutes until Jack said, "Do you feel about this Mexican gal the way you felt about Sarah?"

"I believe so, yes."

"But how do you know?"

"Jack, only loving a woman can make a man feel sick to his stomach," Emmet said. "Like he has a great big pain in the center of his gut."

"Sounds more like an illness to me," Jack said.

"Are we talking about me or are we talking about you?" Emmet asked.

"We're just talking," Jack said.

"It's okay to admit you have feelings, Jack," Emmet said.

"Nobody is talking about no feelings," Jack said, irritated.

"Not a few weeks ago I watched you ride down on a passel of outlaws and shoot them all, and it didn't unnerve you in the least," Emmet said. "Talk about your feelings for a woman and you turn into . . ."

"Nobody said nothing about no woman," Jack snapped.

"All I said was . . ."

"No more talk," Jack said.

They rode in silence for a while and then Emmet said, "Jack, just about everybody in Fort Smith knows you see that Chinese girl who runs the bathhouse. Hell, you practically live there."

"Say one more word and I'll drag you off that nag pony and beat you senseless," Jack said. "And this time Ma ain't around to save you with no bottle."

Emmet grinned and looked straight ahead.

"That's better," Jack said.

There were a dozen tipis erected in a circle around a large campfire. A few stray dogs slept by the fire. Two dozen horses were tethered to a long rail, and they whinnied nervously as Little Buffalo led Two Hawks and the warriors into the secret camp.

Two Hawks turned to Little Buffalo.

"Wake them," Two Hawks said.

The railroad station sat a hundred yards outside the border of Dallas. At one in the morning, the streets were dark, although the wood sidewalks were well lit by lanterns elevated on posts. Dallas had many saloons, and they too were well lit and loud with piano music.

The ticket office was closed. A chalkboard had a schedule written in white. The first train was scheduled to leave at six in the morning. The office opened at five-thirty.

"I'm going to sit here and close my eyes until the clerk shows up and we can buy tickets," Jack said as he sat on a bench.

"You don't want to get a drink at a saloon?" Emmet asked.

"No, I don't."

Emmet sat on the bench next to Jack.

"Want to talk about it?"

"No, I don't."

"All right," Emmet said and placed his hat over his eyes.

A few moments of silence passed and then Jack said, "Damn you, Emmet, you don't give a man no room."

"I didn't say . . ." Emmet said, removing his hat.

"I love her, okay? Is that what you want to hear?"

"I didn't ask . . ."

"I don't know what it amounts to, if you ask me," Jack said.

"I didn't ask," Emmet said.

"Now just shut up about it," Jack said.

"No problem," Emmet said.

Jack placed his hat over his eyes and another silent moment passed. Then he removed his hat and said, "I think I may have sent her away, if you must know."

"How? Why?" Emmet said.

"Before we left, she was acting all strange," Jack said. "She said she was thinking of moving to San Francisco because there was nothing for her in Fort Smith."

"And you said?"

"I told her to go ahead and go," Jack said.

"It's impossible for you to be this stupid about women," Emmet said. "She was testing you to find out if you care for her, you big dope."

"How am I supposed to know that?" Jack said. "Why can't she just say what she means?"

"Women don't operate that way, Jack," Emmet said. "They need romance. They need to know their men care for them. They need tenderness."

"Tenderness? You make them sound like a steak," Jack said.

"Oh, for God's sake."

"It doesn't matter, anyway," Jack said. "She's probably in San Francisco by now."

"More than likely she's right there in Fort Smith," Emmet said. "You have to learn, Jack, that women have a mind of their own and rarely can a man change it once it's made up. You should have learned that from Ma by now."

"You think she's still in Fort Smith?" Jack said.

"I do," Emmet said as he placed his hat back over his eyes. "It's nice to know my big brother is just as stupid as the rest of us when it comes to women."

Two Hawks looked at the dozen men and seven women who vacated the tipis. They weren't warriors. They had the look of a beaten people about them. A people made foolish and drunk, a people who had lost everything in life worth keeping.

"Who leads you?" Two Hawks asked.

"He is away," one of the men said.

"I asked who he is," Two Hawks said. "Not where he is."

"He is called Uday," the man said.

Two Hawks turned to Little Buffalo. "We will hold council in the morning," he said.

Little Buffalo nodded. He looked at the warriors. "See to your horses and spread your blankets," he said.

"Which tipi belongs to Uday?" Two Hawks asked.

One of the women pointed to a tipi.

Two Hawks entered the tipi and closed the flap.

CHAPTER FIFTEEN

Jack removed his hat from his eyes when a buggy arrived at the railroad station. He nudged Emmet and said, "Wake up, little brother."

"Morning gents," the station manager said.

"We need two tickets on the first train to Tulsa," Jack said.

"Horses, too?"

"Unless you want to buy them," Jack said.

"Come in the office and get the tickets," the manager said. "The train leaves at six, give or take a few minutes."

Jack stood up. "I'll get the tickets," he said. "And we'll be in Tulsa in time for a steak dinner."

Two Hawks awoke first and walked away from the tipi to sit and wait for the sunrise. As darkness slowly faded to light and the new sun hit his face, Two Hawks closed his eyes to meditate.

He could feel the spirits of his ancestors in his heart. He asked them for strength and prayed for guidance. He wasn't afraid to die in battle, but he wanted his death to have a higher purpose and meaning than simply death.

As he prayed, Two Hawks felt everything else block out, and there was just his spirit and the heat of the sun on his skin.

Little Buffalo emerged from a tipi he shared with five others. He looked at Two Hawks and then went to build a fire in the fire pit. Little Buffalo knew from experience never to disturb Two Hawks in the morning. Once the fire was going, Little

Buffalo sat before it and waited. One by one, the others awoke, and soon they were all seated around the fire in a circle. Supplies were plentiful and the women prepared breakfast.

Two Hawks inhaled until his lungs were swollen and then opened his eyes as he exhaled. He stood and sat next to Little Buffalo at the fire. A woman offered Two Hawks a wooden bowl of food.

Everyone stopped eating and waited for Two Hawks to use the wood spoon to sample the food. Two Hawks nodded his approval, and everyone continued eating.

Jack nudged Emmet awake.

"The dining car is open," Jack said. "Let's get some breakfast."

They walked through several cars to the dining car, which was quickly filling up. They found a table for two by a window. A waiter wearing a suit, tie, and white gloves came to the table.

"Eggs, fried, steak, bloody, and potatoes," Jack said. "And bring a pot of coffee."

"Make that two," Emmet said.

"I reserved a sleeping car with two bunks," Jack said.

"Good. Sleeping in a chair doesn't agree with me," Emmet said.

"Ever been to Tulsa?" Jack asked.

"Can't say as I have," Emmet said.

"Borders what they call the Indian Territory in the Ozarks," Jack said. "We can wire the judge and then head west along the Arkansas River and pick up the Canadian in a day or two depending upon the army sightings of Two Hawks."

"Do you think the army has a chance of sighting him?" Emmet asked.

"No, I don't," Jack said.

"I agree," Emmet said. "It is my opinion of what I know of

the man that he has some higher purpose in mind."

"Like what?" Jack asked.

"War."

Two Hawks stood and looked at the forty-five warriors and seven women seated in a circle around the fire.

"Who stands against me?" Two Hawks asked. "Rise up and tell me to my face like men. If you talk against me behind my back, I will cut your tongue out and feed it to these mongrel dogs."

Nobody moved.

"Are there more like us on this mountain?" Two Hawks said.

"I am called Coyote and there are others," the warrior beside Little Buffalo said.

"Stand up, Coyote," Two Hawks said.

Coyote stood.

"Will they join us?" Two Hawks asked.

"Not for me," Coyote said. "They will for you."

"We will ride to speak to them," Two Hawks said. "Do you have enough skins to build more tipis?"

"Yes," Coyote said.

"Some of you build new tipis," Two Hawks said. "The women will make arrows."

"Arrows?" Coyote said. "But you have rifles and revolvers."

"When you go down the mountain to hunt deer for meat, what do you use?" Two Hawks asked.

"Arrows," Coyote said.

"Because they are silent and swift," Two Hawks said. "It is no different than hunting a man."

Jack was sprawled out in one of the bunks in a sleeping car. His massive size took up all of the room, and it was impossible for him to get comfortable.

In the other bunk, Emmet was sound asleep.

Jack took out his father's watch and looked at it. His name was inscribed on the back with the date he was appointed a US marshal. The memories of his father were distant and faint. The man was nearly as large as Jack and had a relaxed way about him that put people at ease. When they would go to church on Sunday, his face and hair smelled of lilac water. Men tipped their hats to him. Women admired him from afar, and children called him sir.

Amy took his death hard. She was still in her twenties at the time and figured on a full and long life with John Youngblood. Emmet was but two years old at the time, and Amy had to make many sacrifices to support her sons and keep the family together. She taught school during the day and took in laundry at night to make ends meet. Jack remembered stirring the cauldron of boiling hot water with dirty clothes in it and hanging them on the line in the backyard of their home on the edge of town.

When the need for a teacher arose on the reservation, Amy took the position. She moved the family to the cabin, but she kept the home in Fort Smith. She rented it out for many years. When Jack was appointed a marshal, he went to live in the tiny home where he still resided. After Chao-xing entered his life, he found he spent more time with her than at the home, but with some fixing up and repairs, the home could be a comfortable place to live.

If, as Emmet had said, she was still in Fort Smith.

That was a mighty big if.

He treated her poorly, he knew that. He used her for sex and she never rejected him or complained. She cooked for him and did his laundry, and never once did he say that he cared for her.

Who could blame her for leaving?

When he returned home, he had a lot to make up for.

If, as Emmet said, she was still in Fort Smith.

Two Hawks, Little Buffalo, Coyote, and a dozen warriors rode into the camp composed of a dozen tipis. Fifteen men and eight women looked at them as they dismounted.

"Who leads you?" Two Hawks said.

"I am Little Wolf, and I lead," a warrior said as he came forward.

Two Hawks studied Little Wolf for a moment. "I know you from the reservation," he said.

"And I know you," Little Wolf said.

"Answer carefully," Two Hawks said. "Do you wish to die in battle like our great ancestors, or right here in the dirt like a stray dog? If you choose battle, pack up your tipis and follow me."

"Let's get our horses," Jack said when he and Emmet stepped down from the train to the platform.

They retrieved the horses from the boxcar and walked them along Main Street to the center of town. Tulsa was a cowboy destination stop on cattle drives, which brought the railroad and growth as a town. The population grew from three hundred to nearly two thousand since the railroad first laid tracks at its door.

"Let's find the sheriff and check in," Jack said. "Then we'll wire the judge."

Tulsa had quite a large sheriff's department that included the sheriff and six deputies. Along with the growth of the town came a dozen saloons and thirsty cowboys off the trail. Saturday night usually meant a dozen cowboys sleeping it off in the large jail.

Sheriff James Hanten was behind his desk when Jack and Emmet entered the office.

"Marshal Jack Youngblood," Hanten said. "Haven't seen you in a year, not since you picked up two of the Dalton boys for trial."

"This is my brother, Emmet, chief of reservation police at the reservation," Jack said.

"Nice to meet you, Emmet," Hanten said.

"I guess you know why we're here," Jack said.

"A squad of soldiers rode through yesterday from Fort Scot," Hanten said. "They headed out for the Canadian."

"We have to send a wire to Judge Parker," Jack said. "Why don't you join us for supper in about thirty minutes?"

Two Hawks watched as Little Wolf's people put together their tipis after following Two Hawks back to camp.

Afterward, they sat around the campfire and ate a fine meal of fresh deer meat.

"We have sixty warriors," Two Hawks said. "It is not enough. We need more followers willing to die for the cause."

"There are more camps along the mountain," Little Wolf said. "Others from the reservation who have chosen to leave as we have."

"We will seek them out tomorrow," Two Hawks said. "When our numbers are greater, we will form small raiding parties and strike where the white man won't expect us to. They value gold, their women, and their children. We will take all three from them and make them pay for what they have done to our people."

The Tulsa House was a six-story hotel on Main Street that had a first-rate restaurant in the lobby.

Hanten met Jack and Emmet at a table for dinner.

"Would I be wrong in assuming that you know this Two Hawks?" Hanten said to Emmet.

"I know him," Emmet said.

"What started this?" Hanten asked.

"Hatred, despair, hopelessness," Emmet said. "All of those and more."

"I suppose if I was in his shoes I might feel the same way," Hanten said.

"Have you had any new reports?" Jack asked.

"Nothing," Hanten said. "It's been weeks since he's been sighted."

"He's holed up, is my guess," Jack said.

"Why?" Hanten asked.

"He's building an army," Jack said.

"My God," Hanten said.

"I am of the opinion that God has little to do with this," Jack said.

"Why do we need their women and children?" Coyote asked. "Their women are weak and their children are useless things."

"There is a word the whites have called ransom," Two Hawks said. "I have read this word in many books written by them. They will pay handsomely for the return of their women and children. In gold."

"What do we need with their gold?" Little Wolf asked. "It is of no real use to us."

"You must learn to think like the whites do," Two Hawks said. "They value gold above all else. If you take it from them, it weakens them. If we take their women and children, they will pay great amounts to get them back. And they won't attack for fear we would kill their women and children."

Little Wolf nodded and then smiled.

"What of their army?" Coyote asked.

"I have seen the might of their army in two battles that we lost," Two Hawks said. "They have powerful weapons like the

Gatling gun and mortars, but they won't use them if they fear for their women and children."

"When do we attack and where?" Coyote said.

"When our numbers are larger, when we have made thousands of arrows and hundreds of tomahawks," Two Hawks said. "When we have taken more rifles and revolvers, then we will attack in small numbers in places the whites won't expect, and our tomahawks will run red like those of our ancestors. Only then will we be a whole people again."

The telegraph operator found Jack and Emmet on the porch of the Tulsa Hotel.

"Got the reply you're waiting on," the operator said.

Emmet took the folded paper, and after the operator left, he read it aloud.

"No new activity or attacks reported. Contact the army outpost in Tulsa and join the closest patrol. Report progress when able. Judge Parker," Emmet said.

Jack sighed. "Guess we'll see the army in the morning," he said.

"As long as we're here, I'm going to send a telegram to Ma and let her know we're all right and we'll be a while longer," Emmet said.

"Could you ask . . . ?" Jack said.

"About Chao-xing? I reckon so," Emmet said with a grin.

CHAPTER SIXTEEN

Two Hawks watched the process of arrows being made. It was a complicated and tedious task. Some of the men cut branches thirty inches long from trees to create the shafts. They trimmed off any bumps and shoots before removing the bark. Rough stones were used to smooth the shaved shafts and then passed along to another group that dried and straightened them over a fire.

Women gathered tree pitch in bowls and softened the pitch over a fire. They also gathered feathers for the arrows.

Another group of men made arrowheads from deer bones and antlers. This was time-consuming and required great skill to sharpen the bones and antlers as well as polish them.

The last group assembled all the components into completed arrows. This task required skill and a steady hand, as notches needed to be cut in the shaft and the feathers attached. Even a slight mistake ruined the arrow.

Two Hawks found Little Buffalo carving arrowheads.

"I haven't done this since I was practically a boy," Little Buffalo said.

"We have a dozen good bows," Two Hawks said. "We need many more. Send three men to cut branches five feet long and as thick around as a fist for bows. Have them cut three-foot-long branches for the women. You and I will lead a hunting party for mule deer for the antlers and bones. We will make tomahawks and knives from the larger bones. Get your horse and rifle."

Major Richard Beal was the outpost commander. He met with Jack and Emmet in his office and had an orderly serve coffee.

"I have eighty men, four officers, and four Navajo scouts assigned to me, gentlemen," Beal said. "Two patrols comprised of sixteen men, one officer, and one scout left two days ago to patrol the Arkansas and Canadian rivers. I need every man in the post to defend Tulsa and the territory."

"Understood, Major," Emmet said. "Have your patrols reported any activity?"

"Nothing," Beal said. "He's killed a dozen or more people, and then simply vanished like a ghost. I tell you I don't like it one bit, gentlemen."

"I guess we'll head west along the Arkansas and pick up a patrol," Jack said. "Thank you for your time, Major."

Two Hawks and Little Buffalo canvassed one side of the mountain while Coyote, Little Wolf, and several others patrolled the other.

Their primary target was large mule deer. On the slope, Two Hawks spotted a bull elk that had an antler spread of four feet or more. The elk saw them and ran upward and around a turn. Two Hawks and Little Buffalo gave chase and picked up the trail after about a half mile. The elk weighed about five hundred pounds and was winded from running up the mountain.

Two Hawks cocked the lever of his Winchester rifle, knelt, and took careful aim. He estimated the distance at three hundred yards. There was a slight easterly wind. He held his breath and slowly squeezed the trigger. The elk went down from a head shot.

By the time Two Hawks and Little Buffalo reached the elk, Coyote and Little Wolf had raced to their side.

Two Hawks used his Bowie knife to slice open the elk from neck to lower abdomen. Then he removed the massive gut sack, reducing the weight of the elk by over a hundred pounds.

"Carry it to the horses, and we will bleed it out at camp," Two Hawks said.

Emmet left the general store with forty pounds of supplies and carried them to the hotel. Jack and Sheriff Hanten were in chairs on the porch, drinking coffee. Emmet packed the supplies into the saddlebags of his and Jack's horse at the hitching post.

Jack stood up. "Well, Jim, see you the next time I'm in town," he said.

"You boys be careful," Hanten said.

Jack and Emmet took the road west out of town and headed to the Arkansas River.

"I think we're wasting our time, if you ask me," Jack said. "We ain't going to find Two Hawks until he's damn good and ready to be found."

"I think it's more than that," Emmet said.

"How do you mean?" Jack asked.

"What I said before. I believe he's preparing for war," Emmet said.

"Then he'll get slaughtered, him and those who follow him," Jack said.

"He knows that, and so do his followers," Emmet said.

"He's deliberately starting a war he knows he can't win? What's the point?" Jack said.

"Freedom," Emmet said.

"Dead ain't much of a freedom," Jack said. "Dead is just dead."

"Well, that's his reason," Emmet said. "And I'll tell you something else. Two Hawks is skilled in the old ways. He knows how and where to fight. He'll do a lot of damage before this is over."

"If he's expecting another Bighorn, it ain't going to happen," Jack said.

"No, it's not," Emmet said. "That's not his game. Two Hawks learned guerrilla warfare from his father and great war chiefs like Parker. He fought in the Buffalo Hunters War and the second war at Adobe Walls. He knows how to fight and, more important, when to fight."

"Like I said, when he's good and damn ready," Jack said.

The elk hung from a tree near a campfire to keep the carcass warm and the blood dripping freely. Two Hawks sat on a log in front of the fire and a woman handed him a wood bowl of stewed vegetables and meat.

"May I sit with you?" the woman asked.

"Sit," Two Hawks said.

The woman took a seat to Two Hawks's left.

"I am called Doli," she said.

"The bluebird," Two Hawks said.

"Yes, the bluebird."

"What can I do for the bluebird?" Two Hawks asked.

"You have no woman," Doli said.

"I do not," Two Hawks said. "She died."

"I would be your woman," Doli said. "I can give you sons so that when you die in battle, your seed won't be lost."

Two Hawks looked at Doli. She was a well-built, pretty woman about thirty years old.

"Show me your teeth," Two Hawks said.

"My teeth? Am I a horse?"

"I don't like bad teeth on a woman," Two Hawks said. "It is a sign of illness."

Doli grinned, exposing her white, perfectly straight teeth.

"Move your things into my tipi and make your mark on the flap," Two Hawks said.

Doli stood up. "I will give you much good loving and many sons," she said and went to gather her belongings.

Jack stirred a hot can of beans and tasted them with a spoon.

"Want a biscuit?" Emmet asked. "We got a bunch."

"Toss me two," Jack said.

Emmet grabbed the bag of biscuits from a saddlebag and sat next to Jack.

"We'll make the Canadian in about two hours," Jack said. "Maybe we'll get lucky and meet up with some army boys."

"I've been thinking on that," Emmet said. "I don't fancy riding around with a patrol of soldiers looking for a man who's holed up and won't show himself until he's good and ready."

"That's our orders, waste of time or not," Jack said.

"I know, but it sticks in my craw," Emmet said.

"The judge won't like us disobeying orders," Jack said. "It might not speak well if you decide to take up being a lawyer for the court."

"I know that," Emmet said. "The judge said to find a patrol of soldiers; he didn't say we needed to stick with them."

"No. No, he did not," Jack said.

"We can find a patrol and offer to scout ahead on our own," Emmet said. "Two Hawks is holed up somewhere, and patrolling the area to keep farmers and settlers safe isn't the way to smoke him out."

"I agree," Jack said. "But first we need to find a patrol."

Chao-xing, Mary Louise, and Sarah were tending to the vegetable garden behind the house when Jefferson arrived in his buggy and found Amy on the porch.

"Good afternoon, Doctor," Amy said. "I wasn't expecting

167

you until next week."

"I had to go to town yesterday to pick up supplies," Jefferson said as he carried his bag to the porch. "The post office asked me to deliver this telegram to you. Well, as long as I'm here, let me have a look at that arm."

Jefferson examined the cast and determined he would return in one week to remove and replace it with a soft sling.

"My guess is in a few months you won't even remember the bone was broken at all," Jefferson said. "I'll see you in a week."

"Doctor, the telegram," Amy said.

"Of course," Jefferson said and dug it out from his bag.

After Jefferson left, Amy called Chao-xing and the girls to the porch.

"News," Amy said and tore open the envelope.

She read the telegram aloud. "Jack and I are still in pursuit of Two Hawks, although we have no idea where he is. We will join up with the army and continue pursuit. I love you all and miss you terribly. Girls, you mind your grandmother. Ma, this is for you only. Jack asked about Chao-xing. He pretends he doesn't care, but he loves her a great deal and told me so. Will telegram again soon. Your sons."

Amy lowered the paper and looked at Chao-xing.

"Well, there you go," Amy said.

Chao-xing lowered her face into her hands and started to cry.

"Ma, she's crying," Mary Louise said. "What's wrong?"

"Nothing's wrong, honey," Amy said. "She's happy."

Jack stirred the pan full of bacon and beans and then sat back against his saddle and rolled a cigarette.

"Well, we made the Canadian and then some and haven't crossed paths with one army patrol," Jack said. "I take that as a poor sign."

"I can't say as I disagree," Emmet said. "Do you want biscuits or cornbread?"

"Cornbread."

After eating, they spread out their bedrolls and settled in to watch the stars until sleep came.

"Dammit, Jack, I should be on my way to see Maria, and you should be with your Chao-xing instead of sleeping on hard ground in the middle of nowhere," Emmet said.

"Welcome to the life of a lawman, little brother," Jack said. "I expect right about now you wish you were a lawyer."

In late summer, the night air is chilled in the mountains. Two Hawks built a fire in his tipi. He went for more firewood and when he returned, Doli was naked and giving herself a wet bath from a bowl of hot water.

He stared at her. She was a very healthy woman indeed.

"Get under the blankets," Doli said. "I will be there in a moment."

Two Hawks removed all of his clothing and got under a blanket. Thick buffalo and elk hides served as a mattress.

Doli turned away from the fire and got under the blanket next to Two Hawks. He turned to get on top, but Doli slipped away and sat on his legs. Two Hawks looked at her in confusion.

"Did your wife never get on top?" Doli asked.

Two Hawks shook his head.

"Then you are about to learn something new," Doli said.

Chao-xing waited for Amy and the girls to go to bed, and then she sat at the kitchen table and read the telegram several more times.

Jack told his brother that he loved her.

She felt happiness in her heart that she had never felt before. She was almost giddy, like a young schoolgirl.

She took the telegram with her to bed and placed it under

her pillow. Then she turned toward Mary Louise, and the girl surprised her by opening her eyes.

"I'm glad that my Uncle Jack loves you," Mary Louise said. "Then you'll never have to leave us."

CHAPTER SEVENTEEN

Shortly after sunrise, Two Hawks led a hunting party consisting of Little Buffalo, Coyote, Little Wolf, and several other warriors around the mountain to hunt deer. Each had a bow and six arrows, a tomahawk, and a knife.

They left their horses and walked and climbed for at least a mile until they spotted a large mule deer with a three-foot rack.

"Little Buffalo and I will pursue the deer and chase him to the other side, where you will be waiting for him," Two Hawks said. "We will wait until you get into position. Go."

Coyote, Little Wolf, and the others left Two Hawks and Little Buffalo. Once they were out of sight, Two Hawks motioned to Little Buffalo and they took off up the side of the mountain. The deer spotted them and gracefully raced away.

The deer was strong and swift. The chase went on for about a mile. The men lost sight of the deer several times, but then, as the deer turned a corner, arrows flew at him. One struck him in the right upper leg.

Wounded, but not down, the deer continued running and more arrows followed. All missed. The men followed the trail, and after several hundred yards they spotted the deer limping badly.

"Take him," Two Hawks said to Little Buffalo.

Little Buffalo placed an arrow in his bow and drew the string. He took careful aim and released the arrow. It flew straight, striking the deer in the neck; it went down, struggled for a few seconds, and then went still.

"Jack, do you see what I see?" Emmet asked.

"Sure enough," Jack said. "Captain Roberts and his squad."

They were riding west along the Canadian River near the border of the Texas Panhandle. The army patrol was camped about a quarter-mile away, and they rode into camp and dismounted.

"Howdy, Captain. I see you're still out here," Jack said. "I doubt you're still after Blue Duck, though."

"Two Hawks, as are you. We returned once for fresh horses and supplies," Roberts said. "We rode half a day and decided to rest our horses until morning."

"From the looks of your nags, they need it," Jack said.

"Want some coffee?" Roberts asked.

A soldier brought coffee for Jack and Emmet.

"Where's young Tom Horn?" Jack asked.

"Scouting," Roberts said. "I expect him before dark."

"Our orders are to find an army patrol and join them," Emmet said.

"You're welcome to join us for as long as we stay out," Roberts said. "We have orders to return to the fort in two weeks if we have no progress to report."

"Do you?" Emmet asked.

"We patrolled the Red River, hundreds of miles along the Canadian and most of the Arkansas, and haven't so much as seen a sign of him," Roberts said.

"My belief is you won't," Jack said. "Not until he's good and ready to show himself."

"I can't say as I disagree with you, Marshal," Roberts said.

"Captain, have other patrols reported such inactivity?" Emmet asked.

"I'm afraid so," Roberts said.

Emmet and Jack exchanged glances.

"What?" Roberts said.

"My brother is of the opinion that Two Hawks is holed up somewhere preparing for war," Jack said.

"I can't say as I disagree with that assessment," Roberts said.

Two Hawks carried the deer across his shoulders to the horses and then placed it across his saddle. Then he and the others rode back to camp and found Uday and Natan standing in front of Two Hawks's tipi.

Two Hawks dismounted and walked to Uday. The entire camp went still as Two Hawks approached Uday and the two warriors looked at each other.

"It has been a long time, old friend," Uday said.

Two Hawks nodded. "Since you left the reservation."

The two warriors embraced.

"Come into my tipi and talk," Two Hawks said.

"Captain, rider coming," a soldier said.

Roberts stood up. "That would be Horn," he said.

The entire squad, Emmet, and Jack stood and watched as Tom Horn raced his horse against the backdrop of the darkening sky into camp.

Horn arrived and dismounted by Captain Roberts. "Twenty miles west, Captain, I picked up the tracks of two Apache riders headed northeast," he said.

"Just two?" Roberts asked.

"Yes, sir," Horn said and looked at Jack and Emmet.

"Young Tom Horn," Jack said.

"Howdy, Marshal, Emmet," Horn said. "I didn't figure to see you again."

"We've been dispatched to ride along with you," Jack said.

"What about the Apache riders?" Emmet asked.

"Came from the south and are headed north," Horn said. "That's all I can tell you."

"As it is our first sign of any activity in weeks, we will pursue in the morning," Roberts said. "Grab some hot food and sleep, Tom. You can probably use it."

"I will join you, Two Hawks," Uday said. "My rifle and bow are yours."

The entire group was seated around a large council fire.

"Our numbers have grown," Two Hawks said. "When we reach one hundred strong, we will begin to raid in small groups from all directions. The army will be confused and unable to follow us. We will kill the whites, take their children and gold, and when we are powerful enough, the whites will listen to our terms."

"I know of a place that has much gold, women, and the men carry no weapons," Uday said.

"Where?" Two Hawks said.

"The Christians are building a mission to the southwest on the Llano," Uday said. "Natan and I were there just a week ago. The church is filled with gold and the men carry no guns."

"Did you see the army on your journey here?" Two Hawks asked.

"They are easily avoided," Uday said. "They patrol the rivers to protect the farmers. If we ride south and then west, we can avoid them all with no problem."

"We will take ten warriors on the best horses and ride to this mission in the morning," Two Hawks said. "Uday and I will lead the charge."

"I am proud to ride with you," Uday said.

Two Hawks lit a long pipe and passed it to Uday.

"It is good to know that warriors such as us will die in battle instead of rotting away from white man's disease like my wife did," Two Hawks said.

"I am sorry to hear about Yellow Sky," Uday said. "She was a good woman."

Two Hawks took back the pipe and inhaled on it.

"There is something else," Uday said. "I saw the reservation policeman Emmet Youngblood and a lawman at the Christian mission. They arrived with five Christian holy women. They stayed the night and left in the morning."

"Emmet must have been sent to track me," Two Hawks said. "The lawman with him must be his brother. Did you see them on your journey here?"

"No."

"That is a matter for another time," Two Hawks said. "Prepare tonight. We leave right after sunrise."

As she ate her evening meal in the dining hall, Maria wondered if Emmet would ever return to her. It was many weeks since he and his brother left to pursue the renegade Comanche Two Hawks. During that time two patrols of soldiers stopped by, and the roof was completed on the dining hall and hospital.

She wanted to ask the soldiers if they had seen Emmet, but she held her tongue. Tonight, as she did every night since Emmet left, she prayed for his safety and for his return.

"Is something wrong?" Sister Katherine asked. "You've hardly touched your dinner."

"No, Sister, nothing is wrong," Maria said. "I feel a bit tired tonight. It was a very long day."

"The day after tomorrow I will take a wagon to town for supplies," Sister Katherine said. "Why not come with me? It will do you good to get away for a day."

"Thank you, Sister, I will," Maria said.

★ ★ ★ ★ ★

Two Hawks entered his tipi to find Doli under the blankets. She had made a fire, and the interior was warm. Light from the fire flickered off her face. She sat up and her bare breasts glowed yellow.

"It is my time to conceive," Doli said.

"Are you sure?" Two Hawks said.

"A woman knows," Doli said. "Come under the blankets and let us make a son."

Two Hawks removed his clothing and got under the blanket.

"Do you want to get on top?" he asked.

Doli shook her head.

Two Hawks reached for her.

"Don't be gentle," Doli said. "We don't want a girl."

CHAPTER EIGHTEEN

"Little Buffalo, Coyote, I expect our numbers to be greater when I return," Two Hawks said.

"They will be," Little Buffalo said.

Two Hawks mounted his horse and led Uday, Natan, and nine other warriors away from camp. All watched, including Doli, who seemed to take great pride in watching Two Hawks lead the party.

They rode south through the Ozarks. Two Hawks kept them riding at an incredible pace. Their horses were strong, with great stamina, and were equal to the demands put upon them. Late in the day they reached flat ground and turned west. They avoided the Red River and the white man's towns. They rode into the sunset and continued riding for many more miles and hours.

When the new moon reached the point of midnight, Two Hawks signaled to stop, and they rested until sunrise.

Before the sun fully rose, they were riding west into Texas toward the Llano. The late summer heat wasn't as bad as it had been months ago, and the horses were able to keep the pace. They rode into the afternoon, stopped once to eat and water the horses at a small stream, and then rode into the night. At midnight, they stopped to rest for two hours.

"We will reach the mission just after sunrise," Uday said.

★　★　★　★　★

Jack and Tom Horn rode their horses in a shallow stream where the tracks of the two Apaches disappeared.

"We followed them for two days now, and this looks like the end of the line," Jack said. "This stream comes from the Canadian, and they could have followed it for miles before coming out."

"Better report back to the captain," Horn said.

They rode the ten miles back to where Roberts had made camp.

"We lost the trail in a stream, Captain," Horn said. "East, but they could have backtracked. I'll try to pick it up in the morning."

"All right, men. Grab some hot food and get some rest," Roberts said. "We'll try to pick it up tomorrow."

Jack sat next to Emmet at the campfire.

"Old Apache trick of losing your tracks in a stream," Jack said. "They could be on their way to Canada by now for all we know."

"The captain said he has orders to return to his fort in ten days," Emmet said. "We'll give it until then and wire the judge for orders."

"Suits me," Jack said.

It was odd how she kept feeling as if something terrible was about to happen. As she tossed and turned and tried to fall asleep, the pending feeling of doom kept Maria awake.

It was silly to have these feelings. The mission and hospital would be complete within the month. There was no word from Emmet, but she would try to find out what she could in town in the morning.

When sleep wouldn't come, Maria got out of bed, put on her robe and slippers, and went outside where the air was cooler.

She sat at one of the tables and looked up at the new moon. It illuminated the hills and mountains in the background. Passing clouds glowed white.

She stared at the hills and felt the doom in her heart again. A noise sounded, and she turned to look at Father Ramon as he exited the church and walked toward his quarters. He noticed her and walked to the table.

"Maria, is something wrong?" he asked.

"No, Father. It's hot and I couldn't sleep," Maria said.

Father Ramon sat next to her and looked up at the hills.

"It's a beautiful night," he said.

"Yes."

"I must get some sleep, and I advise you to do the same," Father Ramon said.

"I will, Father," Maria said. "Don't worry."

"Good night, child," Father Ramon said.

Two Hawks and Uday peered over the hills at the mission. The sun had just risen, and activity was taking place inside the buildings.

"It is a good day," Uday said. "They will probably take breakfast at the tables outdoors."

After a while, Maria and the nuns came out with plates and bowls and set the tables.

"We will give them time to get settled at the table," Two Hawks said.

Two Hawks and Uday returned to their warriors.

"Tomahawks, bows, and arrows," Two Hawks said. "A rifle will sound for a great distance in the hills. Mount up and follow me."

Father Ramon led the morning prayer before breakfast. All heads were bowed except his. Midway through the prayer, he noticed movement in the distance. A cloud of dust arose.

He stopped praying and focused on the dust cloud. Others noticed his silence and looked up at the priest. Some turned to see what he was looking at. Then, out of the cloud of dust rode Two Hawks, his face a mask of fury, a tomahawk high above his head.

There was a moment of disbelief.

A man at the table yelled, "Indian attack!" Panic set in, and people started to run.

Two Hawks arrived first, jumped from the saddle, and immediately killed a man with his tomahawk.

"Take the holy man and that woman hostage," Two Hawks said and pointed to Maria. "Kill everybody else."

Weaponless, the men and woman at the mission were defenseless and easy prey for the highly trained warriors. The bloodletting was over in minutes. Only Father Ramon and Maria survived. The warriors tied their hands and feet.

"This is a place of God," Father Ramon shouted.

Two Hawks smacked the priest. "Not my god," Two Hawks said.

"That is the church," Uday said.

Two Hawks looked at Natan. "Take the two best horses from their corral and saddles."

Two Hawks and Uday entered the church. They found two large cups made of gold, several large gold crosses, and many gold ornaments. They loaded everything into a sack and went outside.

Father Ramon and Maria were atop two large horses with their hands tied to the saddle horns.

"Burn everything and take scalps," Two Hawks said.

The old constable was sleeping in a chair outside the deputy sheriff's office when he caught a whiff of smoke and opened his eyes. He looked at the sky and saw black smoke billowing up to the clouds. He wasn't alone. Many people stopped on the streets to look to the sky as well.

For a few seconds, the old constable wondered what was burning, and then he jumped out of the chair and raced into the office. Deputy Sheriff Griffin was behind his desk.

"The mission is on fire," the old constable said.

Griffin ran out to the street and looked at the sky.

"My God," he said. By the time Griffin got twenty men together and they rode to the mission, an hour had passed. The church and hospital were still ablaze, but there was no chance of saving any of it.

The dead lay where they were killed. Some of the men were scalped.

"The stage is due at noon," Griffin said. "You men tidy up the dead. I have to catch the driver to send an emergency telegram to the army."

Nothing seemed real to Maria. With her hands tied to the saddle horn, she had no control of the horse, and it ran tethered to the horse in front of it. She knew Father Ramon was behind her, but she couldn't see him.

They rode for hours without stopping. The hot sun beat down on her face, and she had to close her eyes to avoid sun blindness. Her back started to ache from the constant pounding of being in the saddle, then her legs cramped. Still they rode without stopping. More backbreaking hours passed. Late in the afternoon, she passed out. When she awoke, it was dark and they rode by moonlight.

"Stop. Please stop," Maria cried.

Her plea fell on deaf ears, and they rode for many more hours.

She passed out again. When she woke up, it was dark and she was on the ground with her hands and legs tied. Her back ached and her legs were numb. Father Ramon was tied the same way. He appeared to be asleep or passed out.

Maria tried to speak, but her voice wouldn't come out. She looked at her captors, and in the moonlight she recognized Uday.

"Why?" she croaked.

Two Hawks brought her a canteen and he held it while she sipped water.

"We were kind to you. Why did you do this?" Maria said.

"Don't talk, and save your strength," Two Hawks said. "You're going to need it."

"Please give Father Ramon some water," Maria said.

"When he wakes up," Two Hawks said. "We ride before sunup. I advise you to get some sleep."

Exhausted, the solders fell asleep immediately upon getting into their bedrolls. Captain Roberts, Tom Horn, Jack, and Emmet stayed up on first watch. They sat near the campfire and spoke softly.

"We covered fifteen miles in both directions in that creek and found not a trace," Roberts said. "I don't see what good we're doing out here. I have my orders, but it's a waste of time if you ask me."

"Captain, this is their land," Emmet said. "They know it far better than we do."

"Captain, I'll go out at dawn and check to the south," Horn said. "Give me ten miles, and I'll be back before noon."

"Okay, Tom," Roberts said. "What do you say, Marshal?"

"Emmet's right. They know this land far better than we do," Jack said. "They could be camped a hundred yards from here and we'd never know it. Emmet and I will scout north ten miles, and maybe between the two of us we'll get some luck."

"Then you men grab some shut-eye," Roberts said. "I'll stand watch until midnight."

Maria opened her eyes when she heard Father Ramon sobbing in the dark. Still bound with rope at her wrists and ankles, she inched her way on the ground until she was close enough to the priest to whisper.

"Father Ramon, please be quiet," Maria whispered. "They will hear you."

"They killed everyone. They burned our church," Father Ramon sobbed.

"I know. Please be quiet," Maria whispered.

"Why?" Father Ramon said.

Two Hawks was suddenly standing over them.

"Keep that old man quiet," Two Hawks said.

"Why? Why would you kill and destroy a church?" Father Ramon said. "We've done nothing to harm you."

"So says you," Two Hawks said and kicked Father Ramon in the face. "Now shut up."

"Please don't," Maria said. "He is an old man."

"Keep him quiet," Two Hawks said. "Or I will cut off his tongue and silence him forever."

"This is the spot they entered the creek," Tom Horn said. "I'm heading northeast. I'll see you boys back at camp in a few hours."

"Take care, young Tom," Jack said.

Jack and Emmet crossed the shallow creek and turned southeast. They rode slowly, carefully searching for signs and tracks of horses.

"If we were two Apache riders out here on the plains, where would we go?" Jack asked.

"I would say that depends on the motivation," Emmet said. "That these two took to hiding their trail tells me they are headed somewhere they don't want known."

"We don't know their motivation," Jack said. "For all we know, it's two old Apaches covering their tracks because they don't want to get killed by the white man."

"That could be, but none of this gives us a clue where they've been and where they went," Emmet said.

"Split up," Jack said. "We'll cover more ground that way. I'll meet you back at the creek."

Emmet nodded, and they rode off in different directions.

At sunrise, Maria was back on the horse, and they rode at an even more brutal pace. After a few hours, her back felt broken, her shoulders ached, and her legs went numb. She had little strength left and passed out again in the saddle.

When she woke up, she was on the ground next to Father Ramon. Their legs were tied again at the ankles, but their wrists were free. Father Ramon had passed out, and the right side of his face was purple and swollen.

Two Hawks and his men were eating flatbread. He approached her with a piece of the bread and a canteen of water. "Eat," he said. "We have many hours left to travel."

"Father Ramon?" Maria said.

"Hey, wake up," Two Hawks said and nudged Father Ramon with his boot.

Father Ramon opened his eyes and looked up at Two Hawks.

"She wants you to eat and drink," Two Hawks said. "I'd listen to her. We have a long way to go."

Jack returned to the creek first, dismounted, and rolled a cigarette. Emmet showed up a few minutes later and dismounted next to Jack.

"I couldn't find so much as a blade of grass disturbed," Emmet said.

"Same here," Jack said. "I am of the same opinion as the captain, that we are wasting our time."

"Here comes Horn," Emmet said.

Tom Horn approached them from the north and dismounted when he arrived.

"I think we're chasing a damn ghost, if you ask me," Horn said.

"Let's get back to the captain," Emmet said.

They mounted up and rode back to camp in time for a hot lunch.

"My orders are to report to Fort Dodge in seven days," Roberts said. "I don't see why we can't patrol north into Kansas over the next seven days."

"Suits me," Jack said.

"Men, after morning chow, break camp," Roberts ordered.

After eating the bread and sipping water, Maria and Father Ramon were tied to the saddle again, and the backbreaking ride continued. They rode into the afternoon sun, and Maria passed out in the saddle. She awoke at dusk and was surprised to find that they had reached a higher elevation. After a while, they were in the mountains, but she had no idea where.

Guided only by moonlight, Two Hawks led them through a canyon pass and up the steep side of a mountain to flatter ground. In the distance, Maria saw the red dots of campfires. She wasn't sure if the red dots were real or she was seeing things from exhaustion and weakness.

As they rode closer, Maria realized the dots were indeed campfires. Several of them. Suddenly, she was in the center of an Indian campground. She was cut from the saddle and flung to the ground. The men shrieked at her. The women laughed. Two Hawks grabbed her by the hair and threw her into a dark tipi.

A few moments later, Father Ramon was thrown in beside her.

"Father, are you all right?" Maria whispered.

"I'm not seriously hurt," Father Ramon said.

The flap of the tipi opened and a woman holding a torch entered. There was a circle of stones in the center of the tipi filled with firewood. The woman set fire to the wood and left.

"What do they want with us, Father?" Maria asked.

"I don't know," Father Ramon said. "But they spared us for a reason."

Two women entered the tipi. One held wood bowls filled with hot stew. The other held a canteen of water. They set the bowls and canteen on the ground and left.

"They wouldn't feed us if they intended to kill us," Father Ramon said. "Better eat, child. We need to keep up our strength."

Outside the tipi, the men conversed loudly in their native language. Father Ramon understood a few words, but couldn't follow what was being said.

After they ate, Maria ripped off a piece of her shirt and washed the bruise on Father Ramon's face.

"I don't think it will get infected," she said.

Two Hawks suddenly entered the tipi and stood over them.

"If you try to escape, you will be caught and tortured horribly," he said. "You will be bound with wet ropes and left in the sun. You will die a very painful death."

"What do you want with us?" Father Ramon said.

"That is my business," Two Hawks said and left the tipi.

There were blankets on the ground. Maria and Father Ramon wrapped themselves up and quickly fell asleep from exhaustion.

CHAPTER NINETEEN

Captain Roberts inspected his men. They were worn out and filled with aches and pains from a month in the saddle, but ready and willing to give their all. "We will patrol north past the Arkansas River into the Oklahoma Panhandle and stop in Guymon to resupply, then head into Kansas and back to Fort Dodge. Scout Horn, lead the way."

Tom Horn led the patrol north. Roberts followed closely behind. Jack and Emmet followed the two columns of soldiers, figuring to take the railroad in Dodge City to Tulsa and switch trains to Forth Smith and home.

At sunrise, two warriors entered the tipi. One grabbed Father Ramon, the other grabbed Maria, and they dragged them outside.

A crowd of warriors and women were seated around several campfires. They were having breakfast.

Two Hawks approached them. "Sit with the women and eat," he said.

Maria and Father Ramon slowly approached the circle of women and sat with them. They were handed wood bowls of stewed vegetables and deer meat. The women stared at them as they used wood spoons to eat.

"Do any of you speak English or Spanish?" Father Ramon asked.

"We all speak English," a woman said. "And it would be

unwise to open your mouth again, except to put food into it."

As soon as breakfast was over, Two Hawks came to the circle of women. "Take the woman and the priest to the creek to wash," he said. "They smell like wet goats."

"Move your arm and fingers," Jefferson said.

Amy stretched her arm, moved it over her head, and made a fist with her fingers.

"Very good," Jefferson said. "Now I don't want you using that arm much for a few more weeks at least. I'm leaving you a sling to wear when the arm gets tired and starts to ache."

"Thank you, Doctor," Amy said. "For everything."

"My pleasure, Amy," Jefferson said. "By the way, where are Chao-xing and the girls?"

"In the barn, milking the cow," Amy said. "Here they are now."

Carrying a large milk bucket, Chao-xing led Mary Louise and Sarah to the porch.

"Hello, Doctor," Chao-xing said.

"You've been an excellent nurse, Chao-xing," Jefferson said. "Her arm will be as good as new in a few weeks."

"Will you stay for lunch, Doctor?" Chao-xing said.

"You wouldn't happen to have made those wonderful dumplings, have you?" Jefferson asked.

"Girls, go inside and set a plate for the doctor," Chao-xing said.

At noon, Roberts called for a thirty-minute rest. The men ate cold cans of beans with water. Tom Horn, always on alert, spotted the rider in the distance first.

"Captain, rider coming in the distance from the north," Horn said.

Roberts used his binoculars to zoom in on the rider.

"That's a cavalry rider," Roberts said. "And from the way he's riding, he has news."

Jack and Emmet watched as the rider grew closer.

"Man's in one hell of a hurry," Jack said.

Several minutes later, the winded rider arrived and dismounted beside Captain Roberts.

"The colonel asked me to find you, Captain," the rider said, gasping for breath. "He wants you and the others to return to the fort immediately."

"What's happened?" Roberts asked.

"Indian attack on the mission they were building west of Lubbock," the rider said.

"Yellow House Canyon?" Emmet asked.

"I don't know the name," the rider said. "All I know is it's near Lubbock."

"Was anybody killed?" Emmet said.

"Everybody," the rider said.

"Everybody?" Emmet said.

"Yes, sir, they found no one alive," the rider said.

Emmet turned and walked to his horse.

"You won't make it on that nag pinto," Jack said. "It's thirty miles or more south of here. You'll just wind up killing her and be stranded on the Llano."

"Don't try to stop me, Jack," Emmet said.

"I'm not trying to stop you," Jack said as he went to his horse. He took the reins and walked his horse to Emmet. "I have two extra boxes of bullets for the Winchester. You might want to take your ammunition for your Dragoon."

Emmet took the reins from Jack. "Thank you, brother," he said.

"I'll wire the judge from Dodge," Jack said. "Oh, if he pulls to the left just yank him straight again."

Emmet looked at Roberts. "Captain," he said and mounted

Jack's horse. Jack dug out a box of bullets for the Dragoon from the saddlebags on the pinto and tossed them to Emmet.

"Jack," Emmet said.

"Emmet," Jack said.

Jack watched Emmet ride south on his horse.

"Do you know the people at this mission?" Roberts asked Jack.

"We took five nuns there a while back," Jack said. "There's a woman there Emmet wants to marry."

"Good Lord," Roberts said.

Doli and five other women sat on rocks and watched as Maria removed her clothing and waded into the shallow creek. The water came up to her waist, and she had to dunk under to get wet.

Doli had a rifle and a Colt pistol in her belt. She looked at Father Ramon. "Now you, priest," she said.

"It wouldn't be proper," Father Ramon said.

"Nobody here is interested in what's between your legs, priest," Doli said. "Take a bath or I will shoot you in the knee."

To emphasize her point, Doli cocked the lever on the rifle.

Reluctantly, Father Ramon removed his clothing and waded into the water.

Doli spoke to one of the women in Apache. The woman opened the bag she was holding, and removed two bars of soap and tossed them into the creek.

"What is that saying white women tell their children?" Doli said. "Oh, yes, don't forget to wash behind your ears."

Maria scrubbed her body with the soap and washed her hair. When she came out of the creek, a woman handed her a cloth to dry herself, and another woman gave her a native-made dress and moccasins.

"Your clothes are too filthy to wear," Doli said. "We will burn them."

Maria quickly dressed, then turned around as Father Ramon emerged from the creek. A woman tossed him a cloth. After he dried off, another woman gave him a pair of native-made pants and a shirt and moccasins.

"There," Doli said. "All pretty now. Let's go."

Emmet understood Jack's need for such a powerful horse now. The massive animal rode mile after mile without tiring or even breaking a sweat. They raced across the open plains south. Emmet didn't stop until they reached the Canadian River.

He gave the horse a short rest, and it took advantage of the time to graze on the sweet grass growing along the banks.

Emmet sat beside Jack's horse and smoked his pipe. He didn't want to think about the loss of Maria and the others, so he concentrated on the logic of the situation. For Two Hawks to attack and kill the more than twenty men and women working at the mission meant he'd amassed a large following of skilled warriors. How many at this point was a guess, but one thing was clear: Emmet's prediction of war was imminent.

The only question was when, where, and against whom?

Maria crept into his thoughts and he pushed the thoughts away. He mounted the saddle. Jack's horse responded, and was easily up to the task of crossing the high waters of the Canadian River as if it were a shallow creek.

Riding south, Jack's massive horse ate up the land, mile after mile, until the sun was low and darkness set in around them. Thick clouds enveloped the rising moon, and Emmet was forced to stop and make camp for fear of riding off course.

He removed the saddle, then built a fire and filled the fry pan with beans and bacon. Jack's flask of bourbon was in a saddlebag, and he added an ounce to the pan for flavor.

Then he filled the feed bag with a pound of grain. While Jack's horse ate, he brushed him for thirty minutes. Once the horse was fed and brushed, Emmet fed himself. He ate without really tasting the food, then filled his pipe and smoked a bowl of tobacco.

Twice in his life, he felt love for a woman. He lost the first to childbirth complications. He couldn't lose the second at the hands of a renegade Comanche, but the likelihood was that he did.

No one was found alive.

That's what the rider had said.

Emmet suddenly realized he was crying.

"Oh, Jesus," he said aloud.

Two Hawks counted his warriors around the council fire. Not including the women, the tally was nearly eighty. Their numbers had grown, but the band wasn't large enough to constantly raid in the valleys and along the rivers.

"Our numbers have grown, but it is not enough," Two Hawks said. "We need more brothers to join us."

"It is just a few days' ride across the mountains to the reservation," Uday said. "We can find more brothers to join us there. Comanche, Sioux, and Apache warriors."

"Most of the men on the reservation have grown tired and weak," Two Hawks said. "They have lost the spirits of our ancestors and replaced them with the infections of the white man's greed for gold and whiskey. They can't be trusted."

"Two Hawks, may I speak?" a warrior asked.

Two Hawks nodded.

"I am Snow Owl of the Crow Nation. I and others have traveled far from the Black Hills to escape the reservations. I know of many other Crow warriors who would join our cause."

"How far?" Two Hawks said.

"Five days' ride to the northwest," Snow Owl said.

"Take several of our warriors and leave at sunup," Two Hawks said.

Snow Owl bowed his head to Two Hawks as a sign of respect.

Seated to Two Hawks's left, Little Buffalo said, "What of the reservation police captain?"

"I am giving that much thought and consideration," Two Hawks said.

"Of the woman and the priest?" Little Buffalo said.

"They are useful to us as captives," Two Hawks said. "The white army won't attack if they know we hold their own as captives. When they are no longer useful to us, we will sell them back to the whites for gold."

"Of what use is gold to us?" Uday said. "It is too soft to make weapons out of and too heavy to wear as armor."

"To us it is useless," Two Hawks said. "To the whites it means everything, the way the buffalo once did to us."

Two Hawks stood and entered the tipi where Father Ramon and Maria were held captive. A fire burned within the circle of stones. He sat before the fire and looked at them.

"Are you harmed?" Two Hawks asked.

"No," Father Ramon said.

Two Hawks looked at Maria.

"No," she said.

"May I ask Two Hawks what his plans for us are?" Father Ramon said.

"Can you chop wood?" Two Hawks asked.

"Yes, of course," Father Ramon said.

Two Hawks looked at Maria. "Can you cook and wash clothes?"

"I can," Maria said.

"Those are my plans for you," Two Hawks said.

He stood up. "For now," he said.

Jack sat against Emmet's saddle and lit a cigarette off a wood match. Captain Roberts, holding two cups of coffee, sat next to Jack and handed him a cup.

"Thank you, Captain," Jack said.

"Worried about your brother?" Roberts said.

"Yes, but not in the way you might think," Jack said.

"How so?"

"He's tougher than you might assume from his looks," Jack said. "He wouldn't have lasted as chief of reservation police as long as he has without being tough and smart. He has a law degree from a college in Boston, you know."

"Why in heaven's name isn't he practicing law somewhere?" Roberts asked.

"His wife died in childbirth," Jack said. "He has two daughters to raise, plus our mother. Judge Parker appointed him a position with the reservation, and he naturally progressed to chief. He met this Mexican woman at the mission. You might call it love at first sight. If she's dead, it will all but destroy him. You see, Captain, I ain't worried about Emmet the police chief, but I am worried about Emmet my kid brother."

"I see," Roberts said. "And what about you, Marshal? Have you a wife and family?"

"Not yet, but if a certain woman back in Fort Smith will have me, I aim to have both," Jack said.

"I'm sure it will all work out," Roberts said. "We best get some sleep. We'll leave right after breakfast."

Amy sat on the porch and watched the stars and the waxing moon. The sky had cleared, and thousands of stars were visible overhead. It was a cool night and she wore a shawl over her nightgown. Summer ended early in the mountains, and it wouldn't be long before the leaves turned color and fell from the trees.

The porch door opened and Chao-xing came out with two warm glasses of milk. She sat next to Amy and gave her one glass.

"Can't sleep?" Amy said.

"I heard you get up," Chao-xing said. "I figured we both could use a glass of warm milk."

Amy took a sip of milk. "I guess as women we are natural-born worriers," she said.

"You are worried about your sons?" Chao-xing said.

"Yes," Amy said. "They've been gone a long time now. The last time Emmet was away from home this long, he was at law school in Boston."

"They are both good men," Chao-xing said. "They will be watched after."

"Good, but different as two brothers could be," Amy said. "When Jack returns, you will have your hands full taming that one."

"I don't wish to tame him," Chao-xing said. "He has a strong, fine spirit in him."

"I agree, Jack is spirited, and a braver man I never did see, but don't you let him bully you," Amy said.

"He doesn't bully me," Chao-xing said. "In a lot of ways he is like a little boy."

Amy smiled. "In a lot of ways all men are like little boys," she said. "Come, let's get some sleep."

CHAPTER TWENTY

At dawn, Emmet ate some cornbread with sips of water. He saddled Jack's horse, mounted up, and rode south at a slow pace to allow the horse to warm up and work out the morning kinks. Once the horse was ready to run, Emmet let him go hard.

They raced south. The horse ate ground like no other horse Emmet had ever sat atop before. He understood Jack's desire to own such a horse. He ran for about an hour without breaking stride, the need for a rest, or even breathing hard.

Emmet caught a whiff of acrid smoke in the air about a mile from where the mission was located. He slowed the horse to a walk and smelled the air. It was thick with the harsh remnants of fire.

Emmet yanked hard on the reins. "Go," he said, and they raced the mile to the mission in minutes. A hundred feet from the mission, Emmet stopped the horse and dismounted.

Everything had been burned to the ground. Church, dining halls, hospital, all of it, burned to ashes. He checked the grounds for signs the dead had been buried and found none.

Emmet jumped back into the saddle and raced toward the settlement town of Lubbock. He covered the distance in a matter of ten minutes and rode along Main Street to the deputy sheriff's office. There he jumped down from the saddle.

The old constable was seated in a rocking chair on the sidewalk.

"I remember you," the old constable said.

"The dead from the mission, where are they buried?" Emmet asked.

"See the deputy inside," the old constable said.

Emmet entered the office. Deputy Sheriff Griffin sat behind his desk.

"The dead from the mission, where are they buried?" Emmet asked.

"Who are you?" Griffin asked.

"Emmet Youngblood, chief of reservation police from Fort Smith," Emmet said.

"The constable told me you and the marshal was here," Griffin said. "To answer your question, they are buried in our cemetery about a hundred yards north of town."

"Do you have the names of the dead?" Emmet asked.

Griffin pulled out a desk drawer and produced a ledger book. He opened it to a page and turned the book around on his desk.

Emmet scanned the list. "I don't see Maria Lopez or Father Ramon on the list," he said.

"They were not found at the mission," Griffin said. "We believe they were taken hostage."

"Hostage?" Emmet said. "What the hell for? Of what use does Two Hawks have for a hostage?"

"We don't know," Griffin said. "The army, the Texas Rangers, and every US marshal between Texas and Kansas are on alert."

Emmet sat in the chair opposite the desk.

"There is nothing you can do, Chief Youngblood," Griffin said.

"Maybe not, but I can sure as hell try," Emmet said.

He stood and walked out of the office. The old constable was still in the rocking chair.

"Did you see all the dead folks from the mission?" Emmet asked him.

"I did. It wasn't pretty. Some were scalped," the old constable said.

Emmet nodded, took the reins of Jack's horse, and walked him to the general store. He purchased forty pounds of fresh supplies and loaded them into the saddlebags. Before he mounted the saddle, Deputy Sheriff Griffin walked to him.

"What are you planning to do?" Griffin asked.

"Track them as best I can," Emmet said.

"They're gone nearly a week," Griffin said. "The first good rain will wash everything away."

Emmet mounted Jack's horse. "Let's hope it doesn't rain," he said.

Two Hawks, Little Buffalo, and Uday inspected the camp. Warriors made arrows, bows, and tomahawks. Two hunting parties left at sunrise to hunt fresh meat. Snow Owl and a party of five also left at sunrise to ride to the north for Snow Owl's people.

Two Hawks led Little Buffalo and Uday into the woods for privacy.

"I want the whites to hear our voice all the way to Washington," Two Hawks said as he stuffed his pipe with fresh tobacco.

"They do," Little Buffalo said. "They must be aware of our activity by now. They have the telegraph to send instant messages."

"That's not enough," Two Hawks said.

"Our raids will send a clear message to the Washington chiefs," Uday said.

"They don't care about our raids," Two Hawks said. "They care about their gold and their women and children. They will answer our raids with thousands of soldiers and the repeating Gatling guns."

"What do you want to do?" Little Buffalo asked. "We will follow you into death. Just tell us what you want us to do."

"Leave me for now so I may ask for guidance," Two Hawks said.

Little Buffalo and Uday left Two Hawks alone, and Two Hawks walked farther into the woods. He spotted a fallen tree and sat upon it to smoke his pipe and think.

Father Ramon chopped wood for many hours in the warm sun. His hands blistered and finally bled. His parched lips chapped. Several warriors with rifles guarded him, but it never occurred to Father Ramon to try to escape and leave Maria behind.

The two warriors spoke English. Around noon, one of them said, "That is enough. Carry the logs to camp."

Father Ramon loaded a large wheelbarrow made of wood, with a metal wheel, and pushed it back to the camp. He needed to make five trips to bring to camp all the wood he had chopped.

A log was placed in front of the tipi he shared with Maria and he sat on it. All about him the warriors went about their tasks without a glance his way. Doli approached him with a leather pouch over her shoulder.

"Show me your hands, priest," she said.

Father Ramon held up his hands.

Doli removed a glass jar of salve from the pouch and rubbed some on Father Ramon's blisters, then wrapped them in white cloth.

"You will live," Doli said. "Priest."

"Can I ask who you are?" Father Ramon said.

"I am Doli, the woman of Two Hawks," Doli said.

"May I ask Doli where the woman Maria is?" Father Ramon said.

"She is at the stream washing clothes," Doli said. "If you are hungry, there is food and water."

"Thank you," Father Ramon said.

"Don't thank me," Doli said. "If I had my way, I would castrate you and feed your parts to the dogs before I removed your scalp."

The women simply got naked and brought the dirty clothing into the stream with bars of soap. Maria did the same. The women spoke in their native languages as they scrubbed clothing. When the clothing was clean, it was hung on a rope stretched out between two poles to dry in the sun.

Dry clothes were folded into wicker baskets and set aside. When the sun was in the noon position, the women spread blankets beside the stream and opened pouches of food. Maria sat on the edge of a blanket and kept silent. None of the women bothered to put their clothing back on, and it didn't seem to bother them one bit. Maria was given two slices of flatbread and two sticks of jerked meat. She ate without speaking.

"You, what is your name?" a woman asked in English.

"Maria."

"You are Spanish?"

"Mexican, but I was born in Texas," Maria said.

"What does Two Hawks want with you?" the woman asked.

"I don't know," Maria said.

Another woman said something in her native language, and all the women giggled.

"She asked if Two Hawks has put his tomahawk inside you yet," the woman asked.

"His . . . oh . . . no, he has not come near me," Maria said.

"If he does, Doli will take a knife to your throat," the woman said.

"I do not think he wants that from me," Maria said.

"We shall see," the woman said.

★ ★ ★ ★ ★

Emmet studied the hills behind the burned-out mission. Even with all the horses that had disturbed the tracks, he had little trouble following the trail going back up the hills.

He walked Jack's horse up the hills and counted at least fourteen different sets of tracks going down and sixteen going up. They took Maria and Father Ramon hostage.

At the top of the hill, Emmet mounted the saddle and followed the tracks in an easterly direction. He rode for several hours until the afternoon sun was low in the sky. He stopped to eat a few biscuits with water and allow Jack's horse to graze a bit on grass.

After he ate, Emmet inspected the tracks carefully. Maria's horse was in tow, probably roped to another horse. He could tell from the tracks, which were close to the other horse and nearly parallel.

Maria's hands were probably tied to the saddle horn to prevent her from falling out of the saddle. The same for Father Ramon.

Why did Two Hawks spare them? Emmet was grateful to God that he did, but the question was puzzling, to be sure.

In the days before the treaties were signed, Maria would have made a fine slave and concubine for a tribe. An incident of that sort hadn't been reported in nearly two decades. And what of Father Ramon? What reason would Two Hawks have for taking a priest?

Emmet continued walking Jack's horse, following the tracks. Finally, he mounted the saddle and followed tracks until the sun was low in the sky.

Tom Horn rode into camp after scouting ahead for several hours. He dismounted beside Captain Roberts.

"Damnedest thing, Captain," Horn said. "I tracked a war

party of six for ten miles northeast of here."

"A war party? Tom, are you sure?" Roberts asked.

"I'm sure," Horn said. "One of them is carrying a feathered lance."

"That's a war party, all right," Jack said. "One warrior is elected war chief and carries a decorated lance to show his authority. That authority lasts as long as the war party is together."

"Tom, are we in a position to capture this war party and bring them with us to Fort Dodge for questioning?" Roberts asked.

"They're not exactly riding the best mounts," Horn said. "We should be able to outrun them on a straight field."

"I suggest not," Jack said. "A war party will most likely turn and fight, and we'd have to kill them all."

"I agree," Roberts said. "What do you advise, Marshal?"

"Good moon tonight," Jack said. "We can come upon them while they're asleep and take them all alive."

Roberts looked at Horn. "Can we get the jump on them?"

"Like the marshal said, good moon tonight," Horn said. "Even if they post a lookout, we can sneak up on them. Most likely they won't have no fire."

"Captain, have a few men ride over to that stream we passed a few miles back. Take a few pots and make mud," Jack said.

Emmet followed the tracks until dark. Where Two Hawks was going was a mystery. He could have taken a southern route from the mission and skirted around the hills and mountains, but he chose the more difficult route that would slow him down. Given he had two horses in tow, that didn't seem a wise move.

After building a fire and putting food on to cook, Emmet tended to Jack's horse. The horse had taken a liking to Emmet, and as he brushed him, the horse turned and nuzzled Emmet's hands.

Before he sat down to eat, Emmet filled the feed bag with about a pound of grain. "We're doing some riding tomorrow, so eat every bit," Emmet said.

After eating, Emmet extinguished the fire and got into his bedroll to ward off the chilly night air. He didn't bother to hobble Jack's horse. He was well trained and wouldn't wander more than twenty feet during the night to eat grass.

"So where are you going, Two Hawks?" Emmet said aloud before he closed his eyes.

"Cover every part of your body that might reflect moonlight," Jack said. "Face and hands. Captain, leave two men behind to tend the horses. And remove your boots. We'll go in barefoot. Handguns only. Young Tom, you lead the way."

Horn led the patrol northeast for a mile. The full moon illuminated the ground, and Horn had little trouble retracing his path to the war party. A hundred yards from where the six in the war party were sleeping, Horn gave the hand signal to stop.

"No lookout," Horn whispered softly.

"Probably didn't feel the need," Jack whispered. "Captain, have the men form a circle, and we'll walk in and surround them. Nobody shoot unless you have to."

Jack led the circle, and they silently closed in on the sleeping war party. Jack gave the hand signal to stop when the war party was surrounded.

"Young Tom, do the honors and wake them up," Jack whispered.

Horn cocked his revolver and fired a round into the dirt. The six warriors jumped awake. One of them reached for his lance, and Jack moved forward and smacked him across the face with his Colt revolver.

"Don't," Jack said. "Just don't."

★ ★ ★ ★ ★

Two Hawks entered his tipi and found Doli already under the blankets. A fire burned in the pit, and the interior of the tipi was warm. He removed all of his clothing and got under the blankets beside Doli.

Her eyes were closed but she was still awake. He reached for her breasts and she swatted his hand away.

"No," she said.

Two Hawks tried to kiss her on the neck and Doli moved and said, "No."

"What is wrong?" Two Hawks asked.

"Why do we need that Mexican woman?" Doli asked.

"She and the priest are prisoners," Two Hawks said.

"I know what they are," Doli said. "I asked why we need her."

"Take that tone with me, and I will remove your nose and put it in the stewpot," Two Hawks said.

"Do you want her for this?" Doli said and reached under the blanket, found Two Hawks's testicles, and took a firm hold.

"Watch what you have a hold of, woman," Two Hawks said.

Holding his testicles with her left hand, Doli squeezed forcefully, and Two Hawks winced in pain. She reached for the knife hidden beside her and placed it to Two Hawks's throat.

"Do you want her for this?" Doli demanded and yanked on his testicles again.

"No," Two Hawks said.

"Swear on the spirits of your ancestors," Doli said.

"I swear," Two Hawks said.

"Than what use is she?" Doli said.

"To us, none," Two Hawks said. "To the whites, they will pay in gold to get her back. The priest, too. They took what we value. I will do the same."

Doli stared at Two Hawks, then released his testicles, and

lowered the knife.

"Damn it, woman, you hurt me," Two Hawks said.

"Don't be a baby," Doli said. Very gently, she took hold of his testicles again. "Come and put this to good use."

Roberts had a supply of wrist shackles and leg irons, and his men shackled the six warriors together before a campfire.

Jack held the war lance and stood in front of the six warriors. "Who carries this lance?" he asked.

The six warriors kept their heads down and didn't respond.

"I'll ask again, who carries this lance?" Jack said.

The six warriors kept silent.

"Maybe they don't speak English, Marshal," Horn said.

"They speak English," Jack said. "Spanish and probably French, too. Reach into my saddlebags. I got a nice sharp pair of scissors in there. I'm going to give these boys a haircut."

"A haircut?" Horn said.

"And then I going to take my shaving razor and shave their heads bald," Jack said.

Roberts looked at Jack.

"Captain, have some of your men hold these boys down while I barber them up," Jack said.

Horn handed Jack the scissors. Jack pointed to the warrior who'd grabbed for the lance. "Start with him," Jack said.

Two soldiers seized the warrior, and Jack came up to him with the scissors. "You carry the lance, don't you?" Jack said. He took hold of the long black hair.

"Stop," the warrior said.

"See, Tom, the King's English," Jack said.

"What king?" Horn asked.

"Never mind. So, war chief, what's your name?" Jack asked.

"I am Snow Owl of the Crow Nation."

"Crow?" Jack said. "You're a mite far from home, aren't you?"

"There is no law that says a man can't travel upon the land he was born on if he travels in peace," Snow Owl said.

"That's true," Jack said. "Except that a man traveling in peace usually doesn't carry a war lance."

"I found it on the plains," Snow Owl said.

Jack ran his fingers along the feathers on the tip of the lance. "Is that why the pitch on these feathers is still wet?" he said.

Snow Owl looked at Jack.

"Ever hear of a war chief called Two Hawks?" Jack said.

Snow Owl turned his head and looked straight ahead.

"He's not going to tell us anything here," Roberts said. "We'll take them to Fort Dodge for questioning in the morning."

Jack looked at Snow Owl and then broke the lance in two by snapping it across his raised right leg.

CHAPTER TWENTY-ONE

Emmet opened his eyes to look down the barrel of a cocked revolver. The man holding it was filthy with yellow teeth, greasy hair, and a messy beard. His two companions were equally filthy, and they grinned rotten smiles at him.

"Sit up slow like," the man holding the revolver said.

Emmet slowly sat up.

"Get his gun," the man holding the revolver said.

One of the other two men removed Emmet's gun from the holster and stuck it in his pants.

"Now we been riding double on one horse for quite a spell, so we thank you kindly for the use of that fine big horse of yours," the man holding the revolver said.

He smacked Emmet across the face with the revolver, and he fell over onto his side. Blood streamed into his left eye from a cut on his forehead. He was dizzy, but not unconscious.

"Now put the saddle on that horse," the man with the revolver said.

Emmet stayed still and heard Jack's horse kick up a fuss at the intruders.

"Hold him still," the man with the revolver said.

Jack's horse reared up and kicked out with his front legs.

"He's a wildcat, this one," a man said.

Emmet felt his head clear a bit. He turned and saw Jack's horse kicking at the two men as they tried to put the saddle on him. Emmet reached for his knife and slowly drew the long blade. Jack's horse reared up and kicked the man holding the saddle in the head, cracking his skull in two. The man fell dead.

Emmet jumped up and shoved the knife into the back of the man holding the revolver. As the man slumped, Emmet grabbed the revolver from the man's hand, cocked it, and shot the third man in the chest.

Emmet pulled the knife from the man's back and rolled him over.

"All I wanted me was a horse," the man said.

"You picked the wrong horse," Emmet said.

A moment later the man closed his eyes.

Emmet sat down and dropped the revolver as his hands started to shake. Jack's horse walked to him and nuzzled Emmet's face. Emmet reached up and stroked the horse's neck.

"Should we waste time burying them or move on?" Emmet said aloud.

Jack's horse grabbed Emmet's shirt in his teeth and lifted him to his feet.

"You're right. We'll move on," Emmet said.

Two Hawks found a felled tree in the woods and sat upon it to smoke his pipe and think. He knew he would lose this war. The white army was too large and powerful to defeat.

But this war he declared wasn't about winning or losing.

It was about dying as a whole people.

As a small boy he used to see buffalo so vast in numbers, the herds blocked out the horizon. It once was that way for his people. It would never be the same again.

Two Hawks didn't want to die at so young an age, but he wasn't afraid to die either. All things that drew breath eventually died. Even the tallest, mightiest tree will succumb to death one day.

But if he must die as a young man, Two Hawks wanted his to

be a good death so that his spirit would join his ancestors.

Death as a free and whole man, as his ancestors once were.

There was a rustle of leaves behind him, and Little Buffalo appeared.

"Go back and tell everyone we will have a council fire shortly," Two Hawks said.

Maria looked out from the tipi and saw the men preparing wood for a large fire.

"Father Ramon, come look," she said.

He went to the opening and peered out. "They are getting ready for a council fire," Father Ramon said. "Odd. It isn't even noon. Two Hawks must have decided something important."

"About us?" Maria asked.

"I doubt he thinks of us at all," Father Ramon said.

Captain Roberts called for a thirty-minute rest.

"We should be in Fort Dodge by sundown," he said.

Jack opened a can of beans and ate them cold with a spoon, as did most of the men. "Captain, I'll be going with you to the fort if you don't mind," Jack said. "I'd like to find out more about old Snow Owl here before I leave for Fort Smith."

"I'm afraid most likely all that will happen is he and the others will be returned to the reservation," Roberts said.

Jack looked at Snow Owl. "They won't go, not this bunch," he said.

Snow Owl smiled at Jack.

"No, not this bunch," Jack said.

Two Hawks emerged from the woods and walked to his place at the council fire. Eighty warriors sat in a large circle around the fire. The women sat in a separate group behind the men.

Slowly, Two Hawks sat between Little Buffalo and Uday.

"Tomorrow morning at sunrise two raiding parties will leave camp," Two Hawks said. "I will lead one, and Uday will lead the other. Little Buffalo will be war chief until I return. Uday, pick your men and prepare provisions for at least a seven-day ride. Make sure each man has a dozen arrows and one rifle, plus a tomahawk. I will do the same. I will discuss the plan at the feast tonight."

Two Hawks stood and walked to the tipi where Maria and Father Ramon were kept prisoners and entered.

"Priest, go chop much wood for tonight's meal," Two Hawks said.

Father Ramon looked at Two Hawks.

"Go," Two Hawks said.

Father Ramon exited the tipi.

Two Hawks looked at Maria.

"And me?" Maria asked.

"Go help the women prepare the feast for tonight," Two Hawks said, then he turned and left the tipi.

Two Hawks walked across the compound to his tipi and entered. A moment later, Doli appeared behind him.

"You want that woman," Doli said in anger.

"And what if I do?" Two Hawks said.

Doli drew the knife from her belt and slashed out at Two Hawks. He grabbed her right wrist and bent it backward until the knife fell from Doli's grasp.

"I do not want her, but if I do, I will take her and you will do nothing about it," Two Hawks said.

Doli tried to bite Two Hawks. He laughed and bent her wrist and twisted her arm until she was kneeling on the blankets.

"Remove your clothes," Two Hawks said. "I desire you."

"I will if you release my arm," Doli said.

Two Hawks released Doli's wrist, and Doli punched him in

the testicles. Holding his crotch, Two Hawks slumped to his knees.

Doli picked up her knife, replaced it in her belt, stood, and said, "Touch her, and I will kill her."

"Then I will kill you," Two Hawks said.

"Kill me and you will never see your son growing inside my belly," Doli said and walked out of the tipi.

Two Hawks flopped onto his back and looked up at the point of the tipi.

"All women are crazy," he said aloud.

By midday, Emmet had tracked the horses to a stream that ran southeast from the Canadian River. He steered Jack's horse into the shallow water and tried to pick up the trail, but it was hopeless. The moving waters had removed all traces of tracks left behind.

He crossed to the other side of the stream and checked for tracks. There were none. He dismounted, deciding to make camp and eat a hot lunch. While beans and bacon cooked in a pan, Emmet removed all his clothes, took a bar of soap from the saddlebags, and waded into the stream. He scrubbed the cut on his forehead and washed his hair. When he emerged from the stream, lunch was ready, and he ate naked to allow his body to air-dry in the warm sun.

After he dressed, Emmet decided to ride along the stream for a while in hopes he would spot something. He crisscrossed from one embankment to the other and rode for miles without seeing so much as a disturbed blade of grass.

"They could be anywhere," Emmet said aloud. "They could have gone anywhere."

He rode for several more miles until the sun was low in the sky. He was about to leave the stream when the sun struck something in the shallow water and glinted at him.

"Hold up, boy," Emmet said.

He dismounted, stood in the foot-deep water, and reached for the shiny object. It was the chain and crucifix Maria had worn around her neck. It was broken at the hasp and had simply fallen into the stream.

Emmet pocketed the chain and then mounted Jack's horse.

"They had to come out somewhere," he said aloud.

He stayed in the creek. The thing about tracking on grass was that grass was very resilient. Hours after even a large herd trampled over it, the blades started to spring back. After a day or two of new growth, tracks all but disappeared.

As he rode, Emmet noticed dark clouds forming to the north. "Looks like we're going to be in for it," he said.

Emmet rode Jack's horse out of the creek on the south side and traveled southeast for a while as he looked for shelter. He rode several miles and spotted an abandoned Overland Stage Company way station building.

"Let's go, boy," Emmet said to Jack's horse, and they raced to the building.

The corral and barn were dilapidated, but the way station building seemed intact. The front door and windows were boarded shut, and it took a while for Emmet to pry off the boards. The interior had been stripped of furniture and beds. A Franklin stove against a wall was intact.

Emmet led Jack's horse into the building, dug out the small ax from the saddlebags, and went outside to chop wood. The fence posts were dry and easy to chop, and he brought in enough wood to last the night.

After making a fire in the woodstove, Emmet tended to Jack's horse. "That storm's going to hit soon, and I expect there will be thunder and lightning, so don't get skittish," Emmet said as he brushed the thick coat.

Dinner was coffee boiled on the woodstove and a can of beans with a piece of cornbread. The storm hit while Emmet was eating beans from the heated can using a spoon.

Outside the way station, lightning flashed, thunder boomed, and a hard rain fell. Emmet looked at Jack's horse. He was falling asleep standing in the corner.

"I have to admit, brother, you trained him well," Emmet said.

Maria and several other women spooned stewed meat into the wood bowls before each warrior around the council fire. Once every bowl was full, Maria returned to her tipi and the other women took their places with the men.

"Eat," Two Hawks said.

Nobody spoke until all bowls were empty. Then Two Hawks stuffed and lit his pipe. "I have given this situation much study," he said. "Thanks to Uday, we know Emmet Youngblood, chief of reservation police, has been tracking us. Where Emmet is, his brother is, and by now so is every marshal and soldier in the territory. We will meet this challenge, and we will prevail. Emmet lives in a cabin on the reservation with his mother and two young daughters. Uday will lead one raiding party to Emmet's cabin and return with his youngest daughter. No one is to be hurt if possible, but we must have the youngest daughter. Even if our location becomes known, the whites won't dare attack. I will lead the second raiding party. Just before the reservation land, the man from Washington who is called the Indian Affairs Agent lives in a cabin. I will bring him here, and he will make our voice known to the chiefs in Washington. We leave at sunrise. Little Buffalo is war chief in my absence."

"Colonel Flynn, this is Marshal Jack Youngblood," Roberts said.

"I understand you've been quite helpful to Captain Roberts," Flynn said.

"Have you news on the mission that was attacked?" Jack asked.

"It's grave, I'm afraid," Flynn said. "Eighteen dead, two taken hostage."

"Hostages? Who?" Jack asked.

"Father Ramon and a young Mexican woman," Flynn said. "I'm, sorry, but I don't have her name."

There was a knock on Flynn's office door. It opened, and his assistant stepped in. "The mess hall is open, Colonel. The cook is preparing a hot meal for the men who just returned."

"Captain, why don't you and the marshal grab a hot meal," Flynn said. "Then you can put him up at our guest quarters."

"Colonel, I'd like to be there when you question the prisoners," Jack said.

Flynn nodded. "All right, Marshal. I don't see why not."

"Thank you, Colonel," Jack said.

"I want to go with you in the morning," Doli said.

"That would not be wise," Two Hawks said.

"I can fight as well as any warrior," Doli said. "My bow is as true as any. My knife as sharp."

"And the baby in your belly won't appreciate it if you got hurt," Two Hawks said.

They were under the blankets in the tipi.

"The baby isn't yet the size of a pebble," Doli said. "I can ride and fight."

"Do not ask again," Two Hawks said. "I will be gone less than seven days. You will see to the women and prisoners while I am gone."

Doli sighed heavily.

"And if the Mexican woman is harmed while I am away, I will not be happy when I return," Two Hawks said.

★ ★ ★ ★ ★

The post cook prepared a steak for each man in Roberts's patrol. Each steak came with potatoes, carrots, and as much bread as each man wanted. Flynn had instructed him to allow two glasses of cold beer per man with the midnight supper.

"Best steak I've had in years," Jack said as he soaked up the last bit of gravy with a piece of bread.

"The hostages, the priest and the Mexican woman, is the woman the one Emmet went after?" Roberts asked.

"I believe so," Jack said.

"So by now he knows she survived and was taken captive."

"I expect so," Jack said. "I'm hoping he'll meet up with me in Dodge, but knowing my brother, he might try to track them."

"On his own?"

"Know what a fisher is, Captain?" Jack asked.

"Nasty little creatures," Roberts said.

"I saw one once, couldn't have weighed more than ten pounds take on a forty-pound porcupine," Jack said. "The fisher would run in and bite the porcupine on the face, and then run off. He'd run in, take a bite, and run out. This went on for half an hour or more, until the porcupine was so weak the fisher was able to kill it. Emmet's a lot like that little fisher, tenacious with no quit in him. If he starts to track them, he won't stop until something stops him."

"He's gone after the woman?" Roberts said.

"Bet on it," Jack said.

CHAPTER TWENTY-TWO

Snow Owl and the others were given a full breakfast in the post jail, and then Snow Owl was escorted to Colonel Flynn's office. Jack, Captain Roberts, and two armed guards were also in the room.

"You speak English?" Flynn said to Snow Owl.

"I speak English very well," Snow Owl said.

"So you'll understand what I am about to say?" Flynn said.

"I understand you perfectly," Snow Owl said.

"Good," Flynn said. "This inquest is to determine why you were so far away from your reservation and picked up in the vicinity of recent hostile raids conducted by Two Hawks and his followers."

"I am familiar with the white man's law of the reservations," Snow Owl said. "I am free to leave when I choose if I harm no one. I have harmed no one."

"You had a war lance in your possession," Flynn said. "If you meant no harm, why would you have such an item?"

"I told your captain I found it on the plains," Snow Owl said. "Perhaps your Two Hawks dropped it in his travels."

"Where were you going when you and your men were picked up?" Flynn asked.

"The reservation in Montana," Snow Owl said. "In the Bighorn Mountains."

"The Bighorns to where you were picked up in the Texas Panhandle is a far piece," Flynn said. "Wouldn't you say?"

"Indeed I would," Snow Owl said.

"What prompted you to take such a long ride?" Flynn asked.

"Restlessness," Snow Owl said.

"And why were you going back?"

"Restlessness."

Flynn sighed as he sat back in his chair. "I'll tell you what I think, Snow Owl," he said. "I think you went to join up with Two Hawks, and you were returning to get more recruits to join his cause."

"You are free to think what you want about anything you want," Snow Owl said. "Have I broken any of your laws?"

"Not that I can determine as yet," Flynn said.

"Yet I am your prisoner," Snow Owl said.

"Being held for questioning," Flynn said.

"And you have asked your questions," Snow Owl said. He looked at Jack. "The big man. If you left us alone, I have the feeling his questions would take a different form."

"I run this post," Flynn said. "Under the supervision of a dozen soldiers you will be taken by railroad back to the reservation in Montana. Captain Roberts will lead the contingency. The train leaves Dodge at noon. Guards, return Snow Owl to his cell to prepare for the trip."

Two Hawks mounted his horse and looked at Uday.

Uday nodded.

With the entire population watching, Two Hawks nodded to Uday, and both war parties rode out of camp and down the eastern side of the mountain.

Doli waited for them to be out of view before she sought out Maria. She found her carrying a basket of laundry with a dozen others to the stream.

Doli waited until the women had removed their clothing and waded into the water, and then she drew her knife and waded into the water behind Maria. Before Maria could react, Doli had the knife to Maria's throat.

"Do you see how quickly your life can end?" Doli said in English.

"I am not afraid of you," Maria said.

Doli lowered the knife and spun Maria around.

The two women stared at one another.

Doli placed the tip of the knife to Maria's left breast. "Perhaps I shall remove it and make a tobacco pouch for Two Hawks," Doli said.

"Why not take them both and make a pouch for yourself as well?" Maria said.

Doli flicked the knife, and a drop of blood appeared on Maria's left breast.

"When Two Hawks no longer has use for you, I will remove your skin and leave you to bake in the sun for the ants to feast upon," Doli said.

Maria turned and continued washing clothes.

Emmet stepped out of the way station and right into a large puddle of mud.

"Well, any hopes of picking up a trail are certainly gone now," he said aloud.

He went inside to walk Jack's horse out and then mounted the saddle. "We can make Dodge City in three days, meet up with Jack, and take the train to Forth Smith," he said.

Jack's horse whinnied.

"What? You want to run?" Emmet said.

With a tug of the reins, Jack's horse took off at a moderate speed. Emmet kept the slower pace for a few miles to allow Jack's horse to warm up his muscles and expand his lungs. Once the horse was thoroughly loosened up, Emmet tugged on the reins again and the horse responded by doubling his speed.

They rode for several hours before Emmet stopped to rest the horse for thirty minutes. They had been traveling north and slightly west. While Jack's horse ate grass, Emmet had a hard biscuit, a stick of jerky, and some water.

He was about to stuff his pipe when he noticed something in the distance. He pulled the binoculars from the saddlebags and zoomed in on a dozen Apache and Comanche riders traveling east.

Emmet put the binoculars away and grabbed Jack's horse by the neck. "Sorry, big fellow, but we're a bit exposed here on the plains," he said and bent the horse's neck toward the ground.

To Emmet's surprise, Jack's horse understood and immediately lay down on his side in the tall grass. Emmet placed his body over the horse's neck and rubbed him gently. "My brother trained you very well indeed," he said.

It took several minutes, but finally the riders rode past them less than a hundred feet away. "Steady, boy," Emmet whispered. He waited about five minutes and then stood up and gently rocked Jack's horse back to his feet.

"I guess Dodge City can wait awhile," Emmet said aloud. He stuffed his pipe and sat under a tree to smoke it. Jack's horse busied himself eating grass. "We'll give them an hour to put some distance between us," Emmet said.

Jack and Captain Roberts shared a table at the Long Branch Saloon in Dodge City. Each had a shot of bourbon whiskey. Jack rolled a cigarette and lit it with a wood match.

"What are your plans, Marshal?" Roberts asked.

"I'm tempted to go with you, Captain," Jack said. "But I think I'll stick around Dodge for a few days and see if Emmet shows up."

Roberts tossed back his shot and then extended his right hand to Jack. They shook, and Roberts stood up.

"Well, I have a train to catch," Roberts said.

"Good luck," Jack said.

"You, too."

Jack sat for a few minutes to finish his drink and cigarette, then left the Long Branch and walked several blocks to the telegraph office. The operator was at his desk.

"Marshal Youngblood, it's been a dog's age," the operator said. "I heard you rode in with the army and some captive Indians."

"They're on their way to Montana now," Jack said. "Is Marshal Adams in town?"

"Had to ride to Topeka. The sheriff's here though."

"I'll stop in and see him," Jack said. "First I need to send a telegram."

Emmet followed the tracks from a safe distance. The war party was about an hour in time and five miles in distance ahead of him. Jack's horse could have easily overtaken them, but outnumbered a dozen to one, that wouldn't be a wise decision.

He needed to find out where they were going, although he had no doubt they were riding to join up with Two Hawks.

Wherever Two Hawks was, there he would find Maria and Father Ramon. Emmet believed Two Hawks took them hostage for a reason, and that reason wasn't just to kill them. Two Hawks had a purpose and a plan for what he was doing. He wasn't wasting time or energy on things that didn't advance that plan.

Something caught his eyes about a thousand feet away. "Hold up, boy," he said and brought Jack's horse to a stop. He dug out the binoculars and zoomed in for a closer look.

It was a dead horse. Its rider was nowhere in sight.

Emmet replaced the binoculars and rode slowly to the dead horse, with his every nerve on the alert. He reached the horse. It had three arrows in his neck. He had broken his right front leg, probably from a hard fall.

The rider had removed his supplies from the horse and walked directly north toward the Arkansas River. The others rode on.

Emmet thought for a moment. What would Jack do in this situation? he asked himself.

"Oh, goddamn it," Emmet said and turned Jack's horse to follow the rider who'd set out on foot.

Emmet rode hard, following the tracks for several miles. Then he spotted a dot in the distance. He didn't need the binoculars to know the dot was the fallen rider. Emmet opened up Jack's horse to a full run, and the dot grew larger.

The gap closed quickly. When about a hundred feet separated Emmet from the Apache warrior, the warrior turned around. Emmet stopped Jack's horse, and the two men stared at each other.

The warrior was around thirty years old, a handsome specimen. He held a bow in his right hand and had an arrow pouch on his back. Emmet recognized the markings on his face as war paint.

Emmet drew his Colt Dragoon revolver.

"I can't let you live," Emmet said. "That war paint tells me you aren't traveling in peace. I can't risk you joining up with another war party that we'll only have to fight down the road."

The warrior stared at Emmet.

Emmet cocked the Dragoon.

The warrior closed his eyes and began to sing his death song.

Emmet lowered the Dragoon to his side for a few moments and listened to the war chant. The warrior dropped his bow to the ground, finished the chant, and stared at Emmet.

Emmet raised the Dragoon, aimed it at the warrior, and shot him in the chest.

"God forgive me," Emmet said.

Judge Parker stared from the window in his office while he waited for Witson and Reeves to arrive.

Reeves got there first.

"You sent for me, Judge?" Reeves asked upon entering the office.

"Have a cup of coffee, Bass," Parker said. "Witson should be here any minute. I don't want to explain this twice."

There was a ceramic pot of coffee and cups on the conference table. Reeves filled a cup and then took a seat. He rolled a cigarette and sipped from the cup. A few minutes later, Cal Witson arrived.

"Judge," Witson said.

Parker sighed. "Have a seat, Cal," he said.

Witson filled a cup with coffee and sat next to Reeves.

"Got a report from Youngblood," Parker said. "He and an army patrol based out of Dodge City picked up a war party on the plains. It's believed they were on their way to recruit more warriors for Two Hawks. The leader of the party is a warrior called Snow Owl. A Crow from the reservation in the Bighorns."

"Crow?" Witson said. "That's hell and gone from here."

"I'm afraid Two Hawks's influence is more widespread than we first believed," Parker said.

"What do you want us to do, Judge?" Reeves asked.

"Take a ride over and see Colonel Tate," Parker said. "Ask him if he would attend a meeting in my office. Stay the night. Tomorrow on your way back, stop by and pick up Henry Teasel at his home."

"Okay, Judge," Witson said. "When is Jack due back?"

"I'm afraid he and Emmet were separated on the trail," Parker said. "He's going to wait in Dodge for a few days to see if Emmet shows up."

"Okay," Reeves said. "We'll be back tomorrow, sometime late morning."

Emmet picked up the war party tracks and followed them until dark. They were at least four hours ahead of him, out of his range for seeing and smelling a fire. He made camp, built a fire, and put on a pan of beans with bacon and a pot of coffee. While the food cooked, he fed Jack's horse a pound of grain and brushed him thoroughly.

The flask in the saddlebags still had a few ounces of bourbon left in it, and Emmet added an ounce to his coffee. He smoked his pipe while he drank a cup and tried not to think about the Apache he killed earlier.

The warrior was willing to die freely for the cause he believed in. How many other people could say the same?

The willingness to die for a cause made for a frightening adversary.

Emmet decided to keep tracking the war party. If he could learn the location of Two Hawks, maybe more bloodshed could be prevented.

He stuffed his pipe and smoked, thinking about Maria and Father Ramon. Two Hawks's reason for capturing them had to be leverage. The attacks on the farms and mission were to get attention and amass a following. Two Hawks had proved himself to be more than just a warrior. He was a planner and leader, as well. Maria and Father Ramon were protection against attack. Two Hawks knew full well that he wouldn't be attacked so long as he held living hostages.

Emmet raised his cup. "Here's to you, Two Hawks," he said and took a sip.

Maria and several other women served the evening meal to the warriors as they sat around the campfire. When the large wood pot was empty, Maria returned to the cauldron to fill it. As she passed Doli, Doli stuck out her foot and tripped Maria.

Maria fell hard, and the wood pot splintered under her weight.

"What a clumsy bitch she is," Doli snickered.

Maria slowly stood up and looked at Doli, then walked to the pile of wood pots to grab another. As she walked past Doli, Doli shoved her from behind.

Maria spun around, swung the heavy wood pot, and hit Doli straight on the chin with it. Doli was unconscious before she hit the ground.

Maria looked around at the warriors and women who stared at her.

"What?" Maria said.

Chao-xing and Mary Louise were playing checkers at the kitchen table while Sarah watched.

Amy, no longer wearing the sling, entered the kitchen.

"Girls, bed," Amy said.

"We're almost done," Mary Louise said.

"You've played her every night for a month and have yet to win a game," Amy said. "We're going to town in the morning, and we need to leave by eight. Bed, and right now."

"We can leave the board as it is and finish the game tomorrow," Chao-xing said.

Sarah looked at Chao-xing. "Are you coming?"

"In a while," Chao-xing. "Your grandmother and I are going to have a cup of tea first."

Mary Louise took Sarah's hand. "I'll stay awake until you come to bed," she told Chao-xing.

"You'll do no such thing," Amy said. "March."

After Mary Louise and Sarah went to the bedroom, Chao-xing boiled water at the woodstove and prepared two cups of tea.

"It's a beautiful night. Let's sit outside," Amy said.

After the tea brewed, they went outside to the porch to drink it. The sky was bright and clear, and thousands of stars were visible.

"Fall is coming quickly," Amy said.

"They've been gone a long time," Chao-xing said. "Is this how you felt when your husband was away from home?"

"Always," Amy said.

"Perhaps they can do something else?" Chao-xing said. "They don't have to be lawmen."

"Emmet, I agree with you," Amy said. "He'll put his law degree to good use and soon. Jack is another matter. Some men are just born to be lawmen. My husband was like that, and so is Jack I'm afraid."

Chao-xing sipped tea. "Men can change," she said.

"If it came down to a choice, would you want Jack to choose a life that made him miserable?" Amy said. "Can you see him clerking in a store or hauling freight?"

"Jack clerking in a store?" Chao-xing smiled. "No."

"Wearing a white shirt and bowtie with an apron around his waist," Amy said. "Can you picture Jack in a getup like that?"

"A bowtie?" Chao-xing burst into laughter. "No, I cannot," she said.

"I'm afraid, dear, that if you truly want Jack, you'll have to take him as he is," Amy said.

Chao-xing nodded.

"But as he is, Jack is a pretty damn good man," Amy said. "Come on, let's go to bed. You don't want to keep the girls waiting."

Jack sat in a chair on the porch of the Hotel Dodge, drank coffee, and smoked a cigarette. He was debating with himself about what to do next: leave Dodge and try to pick up Emmet's trail, or take the noon train to Fort Smith?

He would hate to face the wrath of Amy if he came home without Emmet. On the other hand, he could spend weeks tracking Emmet only to find he'd gone home.

Then there was the matter of Chao-xing. If she had left Fort Smith and gone to San Francisco as she threatened, what would he do?

Jack searched his heart.

The answer was both complicated and simple.

He would turn in his badge, go to San Francisco, and find her.

Simple, in that traveling to San Francisco was a week on a train.

Complicated, in that San Francisco had a population of a quarter of a million, and thirty thousand of them were Chinese.

And if he did manage to somehow find her, would she even want him anymore?

The telegraph operator approached the hotel, climbed the steps to the porch, and handed Jack a slip of paper. "Finally got a reply," he said.

"Thanks," Jack said and took the paper.

The judge wrote two words.

Come Home.

CHAPTER TWENTY-THREE

Henry Teasel had been an Indian Affairs Agent for thirteen years. Five in Montana, three in Nebraska, and the past five years in Fort Smith. He was college educated, having earned a degree in economics from Yale. He put that degree to very good use.

As the Indian Affairs Agent and liaison to Washington, Teasel was responsible for every penny of funds directed to the reservation. From food, clothing, and medicine, to building supplies and education, not a nickel was funded without Teasel's approval and signature.

He took great pride in his job and cared deeply about those under his care on the reservation. So he thought nothing of it when, after breakfast, he kissed his wife and two daughters goodbye and headed off to town to mail his monthly report to Washington.

The buggy ride to town took no more than twenty minutes. It was a fine bright morning, crisp and warming up quickly. The dirt road to town wound through the hills, making for a pleasant trip.

Teasel's briefcase contained a dozen requisitions for various items. As Washington was always slow to respond, he needed to send the requests three months in advance.

These requests were for the coming winter months, when traveling was more difficult and . . .

As the buggy came out of a turn, Teasel suddenly found

himself face-to-face with Two Hawks and a dozen warriors.

Teasel and Two Hawks stared at each other.

"I know you, Two Hawks," Teasel said.

"I know you, too, Henry," Two Hawks said.

"You've been causing some trouble," Teasel said. "It's going to take some straightening out."

"I appreciate your concern," Two Hawks said. "Now if you will kindly get down from that buggy, we have a horse for you to ride."

"A horse?" Teasel said. "I'm afraid I'm not going anywhere with you."

"I'm afraid you have no choice," Two Hawks said.

Two Hawks held up his right hand, and a dozen arrows were suddenly aimed directly at Teasel.

Chao-xing and Mary Louise led the buggy from the barn to the front of the house.

"Go fetch your sister and grandmother," Chao-xing said.

Mary Louise ran to the house, up the stairs, and inside. A few moments later, Amy stepped out with Mary Louise and Sarah.

"Girls, don't forget . . ." Amy said just as something down the road caught her attention.

"Don't forget what, Grandmother?" Mary Louise asked.

"Girls," Amy said. "Get in the house."

"But, we're going to . . ." Mary Louse said.

"Inside right now," Amy said. "Chao-xing, get up here."

Chao-xing ran to the porch.

"Inside, quick," Amy said.

They went into the cabin, and Amy grabbed the wood plank and placed it over the slots to bolt the door.

"What is it, Grandmother?" Mary Louise asked.

"Go to your room and get under the bed right now," Amy

said. "Chao-xing, lock all the back windows and shutters."

"Come," Chao-xing said and took the girls to the bedroom.

"What's wrong?" Mary Louise said.

"Get under the bed and be very still and quiet," Chao-sing. "Don't make a sound or come out until we tell you to."

"My doll," Sarah said.

Chao-xing grabbed the Chinese doll off the bed and gave it to Sarah. "Now under the bed, both of you," Chao-zing said.

After the girls were under the bed, Chao-xing closed every window and shutter and locked them. When she returned to the living room, Amy was at a window, holding a Winchester rifle.

"Can you handle a Colt?" Amy said.

Chao-xing looked at the Colt revolver on the table and picked it up.

"Bring it and the box of bullets to the other window," Amy said.

Chao-xing took the Colt and box of bullets to the window and looked out. A dozen or more Indian warriors were standing beside the buggy where they had dismounted their horses.

"What do they want?" Chao-xing asked.

"See the one holding the feathered lance?" Amy asked.

"Yes."

"He's the boss, and what they want is us," Amy said.

"We haven't harmed them," Chao-xing said.

The Indian with the lance gave the signal and then dozen warriors moved toward the cabin.

Amy cocked the lever of the Winchester and shouted, "That's far enough."

The leader and the warriors stopped.

"What do you want?" Amy asked.

The leader removed an arrow from his pouch, aimed his bow, and fired an arrow into the door.

"That's what I thought," Amy said and fired the Winchester,

striking a warrior to the leader's left in the chest.

The leader grabbed his tomahawk and charged the house, along with his warriors.

Chao-xing fired the Colt. She struck a warrior, and he went down. She fired five more times and as she went to reload, an arrow flew through the window and struck her in the chest just above the left breast.

As she fell to the floor, a warrior came through the window.

Amy turned and shot him.

Another jumped through the window. Amy cocked the lever and pulled the trigger, but the Winchester was empty. The warrior came at Amy with his tomahawk raised and Chao-xing, having reloaded the Colt, shot him in the back.

A warrior came through Amy's window, grabbed Amy, and held a knife to her throat.

Chao-xing lowered the Colt and tossed it away.

The warrior turned Amy around and cracked her in the jaw with the flat side of his tomahawk. Then he removed the plank from the door, opened it, and the leader and the others walked in.

"Find the girl," the leader said.

The warriors spread out. A few minutes later, one of them returned with Sarah, kicking and screaming, in his arms.

Chao-xing crawled along the floor toward Sarah.

"Stop," Chao-xing yelled. "She's just a little girl."

The leader kicked Chao-xing in the face, knocking her unconscious.

Emmet followed the trail of the warriors for many hours and many miles. He realized the trail led into a pass through the Oklahoma side of the Ozarks. The pass twisted and turned and rose higher.

The trail took him through a small canyon and then to

another very narrow pass. The pass wound around the base of a mountain. Emmet followed the pass until it ended at a narrow V-notch between two mountains.

Emmet dismounted and studied the trail markings.

"They went up," he said aloud.

Jack settled Emmet's pinto into the boxcar on the train. He removed the saddle and gave the horse a few carrot sticks while he brushed him thoroughly.

"We'll be home in about ten hours or so," Jack said. "I wish I could say the same for your owner."

Emmet found a safe place to make camp, even though there were still hours of daylight left. He needed to scale the mountain, and that would take half a day. He didn't want to risk getting lost in the dark, especially with how cold the mountains got after dark.

He made a fire and cooked an early supper. He fed Jack's horse a pound of grain and if he was still hungry after that, there was plenty of grass for him to graze on.

After eating, Emmet smoked his pipe and watched the sky darken and the stars come out one-by-one.

If Two Hawks was in these mountains, so too was Maria.

"That's all you think about," Emmet said aloud.

"Mary Louise, quit your crying this instant," Amy said.

"They took Sarah," Mary Louise said.

"I know that," Amy said. "Right now Chao-xing has an arrow in her chest, and she'll die if we don't get it out. Get your play bucket and go outside and make mud."

"Mud?"

"Yes, and hurry."

Mary Louise went to her room for her bucket and then went outside.

Amy helped Chao-xing off the floor to the sofa. She was bleeding heavily from the arrow in her chest.

"They took her! They took Sarah," Chao-xing said. "Why?"

"We'll get her back," Amy said. "I have to get that arrow out before you bleed to death."

Amy went to a cabinet and returned with a bottle of whiskey. Then she fetched a clean linen tablecloth and cut it into strips with a kitchen knife.

Mary Louise returned with the bucket of mud.

"Set it down beside the sofa," Amy said.

Mary Louise put the bucket down.

"Chao-xing, this is going to hurt a great deal," Amy said.

Chao-xing nodded.

"Mary Louise, hold her hand."

Mary Louise took Chao-xing's right hand.

"Look away," Amy said.

Chao-xing turned her head. Amy took hold of the arrow. The entire arrowhead was embedded in Chao-xing's chest. Slowly, Amy pulled the arrow out. Chao-xing gritted her teeth in pain and started to cry as the arrow was pulled from her flesh. Then it was free, and Amy tossed it to the floor.

"That's the worst of it," Amy said. She opened the bottle of whiskey and poured some into the wound. Chao-xing winced again in pain.

Amy sighed, then said, "The hell with it," and took a drink of whiskey.

"Grandmother," Mary Louise said.

Amy grabbed a handful of the mud and poured whiskey onto it, and then stuck it against the wound. "Help me sit her up," Amy said to Mary Louise.

Chao-xing was close to unconscious, but they were able to sit her up. Amy tied clean linen around the mud to hold it in place. Then Amy lifted Chao-xing in her arms.

"Mary Louise, grab the Colt revolver and the box of bullets," Amy said, and she carried Chao-xing outside and placed her into the buggy.

Amy and Mary Louise sat on the sofa of Doctor Jefferson's home and waited. Amy sipped tea from a cup while Mary Louise held her Chinese doll.

"Why did they take Sarah?" Mary Louise asked.

"I don't know," Amy said.

"I wish Papa and Uncle Jack were here," Mary Louise said.

"So do I," Amy said.

Jefferson entered the living room. "I cleaned and stitched the wound," he said. "She's sleeping. I'm going to keep her here for a few days. Can you stay the night? I'm going to town in the morning to report this to Judge Parker."

"We can stay," Amy said.

"Will she be all right?" Mary Louise asked.

"Yes, child, she will be all right," Jefferson said. "Thanks to some quick thinking from your grandmother."

Jefferson sat in his favorite chair and sighed heavily. "I knew Two Hawks was a troubled man, but I never dreamed it would come to this," he said.

"What does he want?" Mary Louise asked.

"The plague of all mankind, honey," Jefferson said. "He wants war."

CHAPTER TWENTY-FOUR

Jack stepped off the platform leading Emmet's horse and immediately got the sense that something was terribly wrong. As he walked to the center of town, people stared at him. When he neared the courthouse and saw the sixty army horses in the courthouse corral and the soldiers at rest on the great lawn in front of the courthouse, he knew something awful had happened in his absence.

Jack mounted Emmet's horse and raced the last five hundred feet to the corral, dismounted, and tied him to a post. Then he rushed up the back steps of the courthouse to Judge Parker's office.

Emmet cut off a piece of Jack's saddle rope and made a sling for Jack's Winchester rifle, then slung it over his right shoulder. He took the canteen and binoculars and looked at Jack's horse.

"I expect you to be here when I get back," he said and started up the mountain.

Emmet estimated the climb to the top at around four thousand feet. If he could make one thousand feet per hour, he could reach the summit by noon.

In Judge Parker's office were Colonel Tate, Witson, Reeves, and Doctor Jefferson. Parker did all the talking.

When Parker was finished, Jack simply turned and walked to the door.

"Marshal Youngblood, where are you going?" Parker asked.

"To the doctor's house," Jack said.

"I best get back myself," Jefferson said.

"Marshal," Colonel Tate said. "I sent a patrol to your mother's house to remove the dead."

Jack nodded and walked out. He walked to Emmet's horse and said, "I need you to run ten hard miles without dropping dead on me," and mounted the saddle.

The last thousand feet were the toughest. The angle was sheerer and the terrain was burdened with loose rocks that skidded and fell underfoot. Emmet slipped a few times but was never in danger of falling. When he finally reached the summit and flat ground, he lay on his back for a few minutes to catch his wind.

Finally, Emmet sat up, took a few sips of water, then stood. The summit was reasonably flat and stretched out several hundred yards. He walked to the opposite edge of the summit and looked down at the valley between the mountains.

For a moment, Emmet was stunned and didn't believe his eyes. He used the binoculars to zoom in closer at the hundred or more tipis dotting the landscape.

Jack jumped from the saddle, ran up the porch steps to Jefferson's house, and burst through the front door.

Amy was seated on the sofa with her knitting yarn. She stood up and looked at Jack.

"Ma," Jack said.

"She's in the bedroom," Amy said.

Jack rushed past Amy and entered the bedroom. Mary Louise was seated in a chair beside the bed. Chao-xing, sitting up against a pillow, stared at Jack in disbelief.

"Uncle Jack," Mary Louise said.

"Hi, honey," Jack said.

Chao-xing looked at Mary Louise. "Could you ask your mother to put on some tea for your uncle?"

Mary Louise nodded and left the bedroom.

"Tea?" Jack said.

"You were gone so long," Chao-xing said and started to cry.

"I thought you went to San Francisco," Jack said.

Chao-xing held out her arms, Jack sat on the bed and she hugged him. "You're an idiot," she said. "And you need a bath."

Judge Parker and Colonel Tate were in Parker's office when a sergeant knocked on the door.

"Enter," Parker said.

The sergeant opened the door and stepped inside. "Excuse me, Colonel, Judge, but there's a man downstairs who claims to be the Indian Affairs Agent."

"What?" Parker said. "Did he give his name?"

"Henry Teasel, sir."

"For God's sake man, bring him in," Parker barked.

Jack sat on the sofa with Amy and did his best to get his very large finger through a very delicate tea cup. He looked at Amy in frustration and said, "Ma."

"Never mind the tea, Jack," Amy said. "Finish telling me about Emmet and this woman Maria."

Mary Louise entered the living room. "The bathtub is nearly full, Uncle Jack," she said.

"Thank you, honey," Jack said.

"Bring some tea to Chao-xing," Amy said.

"Yes, Grandmother," Mary Louise said.

After Mary Louise left the room, Amy said, "Go on, Jack."

"Like I said, we took these nuns to the mission on the Llano," Jack said. "It took us off the trail, but we couldn't leave them there with Two Hawks on the loose. We stayed overnight, and I never saw anything like it, Ma. I swear, it was a case of love at first sight with those two."

"Unlike you and Chao-xing, only your brother has the good sense to know it," Amy said.

"Ma, please," Jack said.

"In that bedroom is a woman who saved my life twice and nearly died protecting Sarah, and you've treated her rather shabbily, Jack," Amy said. "What do you plan to do about that?"

"Do you want to hear about Emmet or not?" Jack said.

"Go on," Amy said.

"After we left the mission and rode north, we met up with an army patrol out of Dodge," Jack said. "A messenger from the fort caught up with us with the news that Two Hawks and his followers attacked the mission and burned it down. Emmet took my horse and rode back to the mission. His pinto could never keep up with my horse, so I rode to Fort Dodge with the army."

"Were there . . . ?" Amy said.

"Survivors? I don't know," Jack said.

"Dear God," Amy said.

Jack stood up. "I'm going to see about that bath," he said.

"Don't forget to shave," Amy said. "And a little lilac water wouldn't hurt."

"After he took me hostage, we rode west for several hours," Teasel said. "Then we stopped, and he forced me to write out his terms on the back of the document I was going to mail to Washington."

"His terms?" Colonel Tate said.

"His words, Colonel." Teasel said.

"And exactly what are his terms?" Judge Parker asked.

Teasel opened his briefcase and withdrew a document. "These are his words exactly as he stated them."

"Yes, yes, get on with it," Parker said.

"Item one," Teasel said. "Two Hawks wants one hundred pounds in gold bars for each hostage he is holding. At . . ."

"Gold?" Parker said. "Since when does Two Hawks care about gold?"

"He said you would say that, Judge," Teasel said. "His answer to that is he doesn't, but he knows that we do."

"How many hostages does he have?" Tate asked.

"Three at this time," Teasel said. "A priest, a young Mexican woman, and the Youngblood girl."

"Three hundred pounds in gold? He's lost his mind," Parker said.

"What else?" Tate asked.

"He wants a new treaty."

"Now I know he's lost his mind," Parker said.

"What kind of treaty?" Tate asked.

"He wants Washington to acknowledge that every Native American tribe has the same rights as every white man," Teasel said. "That a tribe, if they feel so inclined, can leave a reservation and hunt and live on the land as the white man does without having to assimilate into the white man's ways."

"Washington will never agree to any of that," Parker said. "The government has a no-blackmail policy that it won't break for another government, much less the likes of Two Hawks."

"He said you'd say that," Teasel said. "He said to tell you that failure to comply would result in an all-out attack in the spirit of his ancestors in the war of fifty-eight."

"He'll attack Austin, Texas?" Parker said.

"No, Judge, Fort Smith," Teasel said.

"Good God, man, these are modern times," Parker said. "The country is growing, and he wants to relive the wars of his ancestors. He has to know Washington won't allow this to happen."

"Judge, I had the very distinct impression that Two Hawks

simply doesn't care what Washington thinks," Teasel said.

Emmet tightened the saddle around Jack's horse and then mounted.

"We have two hours of daylight left. Let's make the most of them," Emmet said.

With a flick of the reins, Jack's horse raced forward and kept a steady pace for the next two hours, covering a distance of fifteen miles. At dusk, Emmet made camp. He built a fire and put on a pan of beans with bacon and made a pot of coffee. While the food cooked, he fed Jack's horse grain and brushed his coat.

"You didn't even crack a sweat," Emmet said. "So tomorrow when I ask you to make it to Fort Smith in a single run, it shouldn't be much of a problem."

Jack gently lifted Chao-xing into Amy's buggy.

"Now don't go bouncing her around for a few days," Jefferson said. "Those stitches could pop open. If she needs it, give her the laudanum, but only if she needs it. Best get going before it gets dark. I'll be by tomorrow to check on her."

"Don't worry, Doc, I can find my way home blindfolded," Jack said. "Ma, follow me."

The ride to Amy's house took about an hour, because Amy drove the buggy very slowly so as not to cause any bumping to her passengers. The sky was dark, and the moon rose by the time Jack dismounted at the corral and Amy drove the buggy to the porch.

"Jack, Chao-xing's fallen asleep," Amy said. "Carry her into the house."

Amy went into the cabin first to light a few lanterns. Jack gently lifted Chao-xing and carried her into Emmet's bedroom.

Mary Louise pulled down the sheets, and Jack lowered Chao-xing into the bed.

"She's asleep," Jack said. "Let's leave her be to rest."

Amy was making a pot of coffee in the kitchen when Jack and Mary Louise joined her.

"Mary Louise, go wash and change your clothes," Amy said.

"Then can I sit with Chao-xing?" Mary Louise asked.

"Yes, but only if you don't disturb her."

"I won't."

Amy filled two cups with coffee, and she and Jack sat at the table.

"What does he want with Sarah?" Amy asked.

"As a hostage," Jack said. "He won't harm her, or he loses his leverage."

"His leverage against what?"

"Being attacked."

Amy nodded. "She's just a little girl, Jack. Emmet couldn't deal with losing her."

"He won't, Ma. I promise," Jack said.

Amy sipped some coffee. "Jack, in that bedroom is a really good woman," she said. "She deserves far better than you've shown her."

Jack sighed. "I know that," he said.

Mary Louise entered the kitchen.

"Chao-xing is awake," she said. "She wants to see you, Uncle Jack."

"I am to return to the spot where Two Hawks set me free in five days with the response from Washington," Teasel said.

"You know what the reply will be," Tate said.

"Yes, Colonel, I do," Teasel said.

"And when his demands aren't met?" Parker said.

"Two Hawks and all of his followers will ride into Fort Smith and attack with everything they have," Teasel said. "I can promise you, Judge, he will do it."

"He can't have amassed that large of a following willing to die," Parker said.

"Judge, a hundred Comanche, Apache, and Sioux warriors can destroy this town even if every last one of them is killed," Tate said. "At full strength, I have eighty men and four Gatling guns, and that won't be enough."

Parker looked at Tate.

"Colonel, I guess we have some emergency telegrams to send," Parker said.

Jack sat in the chair beside the bed and looked at Chao-xing.

"Since you are a clumsy oaf and afraid to speak your feelings, I will speak first," Chao xing said.

"I'm not . . . okay, go ahead," Jack said.

"I sold my shop for a good price," Chao-xing said. "I fully intended to move to San Francisco if, when you returned, you did not want me. Many things have happened while you were away. Your mother broke her arm, I was shot with an arrow during an Indian attack, and I've grown to love Amy and the girls. I'll make this simple for you, Jack. Do you want me or not?"

Jack stared at Chao-xing. The words he wanted to say, the words he'd thought about while on the trail seemed to get stuck in the back of his throat.

Chao-xing sighed.

"Let's try this," she said. "If you want me, nod. If you don't, shake your head."

CHAPTER TWENTY-FIVE

Emmet tightened the saddle on Jack's horse, then rubbed his massive neck and patted him gently.

"I've grown right fond of you, big fellow," Emmet said.

Jack's horse turned his neck and nuzzled Emmet.

Emmet mounted the saddle and yanked gently on the reins.

"Let's go to Fort Smith," Emmet said.

Jack slept in the chair beside the bed. When sunlight filtered in through the window, he woke up feeling stiff in the back and legs. Chao-xing was still asleep. He stood, stretched out his back, and followed the aroma of fresh coffee to the kitchen.

Amy was at the woodstove making breakfast. Mary Louise was setting the table.

"Morning, Ma, Mary Louise," Jack said.

"Is Chao-xing still asleep?" Mary Louise asked.

"Yes," Jack said. "I didn't want to wake her."

"Sit and have breakfast," Amy said. "There is a clean shirt and pants for you in my bedroom."

Jack took a seat, and Amy served him scrambled eggs, bacon, toast, and coffee.

Amy sat opposite him with a cup of coffee. "Mary Louise, go see to the cow," she said.

"Yes, Grandmother."

After Mary Louise left, Amy said, "You'll be going to town to see Judge Parker?"

"Soon as I eat and change," Jack said.

"Will you be back tonight?"

"I'll be back."

"And Emmet?"

"If he doesn't turn up in a day or two, I'll go look for him."

Jack finished eating and then went to Amy's bedroom. A clean shirt and pants lay on the bed. He had forgotten that he left a trunk of clothes a while back. He found the trunk in the closet and lifted the lid. All the shirts and pants were clean and pressed.

He changed and returned to the kitchen.

Amy and Mary Louise sat at the table.

Jack's holster was slung over the back of the chair. He reached for it and slowly placed the holster around his waist.

Amy watched as a transformation in Jack took place. As the holster went on, her son went from happy-go-lucky goof to grit-and-steel lawman. She could see the change in his eyes.

"I'll be back before dark," Jack said.

After Jack left, Chao-xing walked into the kitchen.

"What are you doing out of bed?" Amy asked.

Chao-xing smiled and took a chair.

"What are you grinning at?" Mary Louise asked.

"Your uncle nodded yes," Chao-xing said.

When Jack arrived at the courthouse, Reeves and Witson were standing on the front steps. Two dozen army tents were pitched on the grass in the park, and sixty soldiers milled about, mostly drinking coffee.

"Besides standing around with your thumb up your ass, what else are you boys doing?" Jack said.

"Waiting on the judge," Reeves said.

Jack rolled a cigarette and lit it with a wood match. "I see the army decided to move into the park," he said.

"That's right, you weren't here when Teasel showed up," Witson said.

"Teasel? Henry Teasel?" Jack said.

"I'm going to get a cup of that army coffee," Witson said. "Why don't you tell him about Teasel, Bass?"

"Get some coffee for us," Reeves said.

"I saw something this morning that reminded me very much of my husband," Amy said.

Amy and Chao-xing sat in chairs on the porch. The morning was unusually hot for the time of year. Each woman held a cup of tea.

"I watched my son strap on his holster this morning," Amy said. "It was as if a switch was thrown inside his head. The lovable dope who is Jack, my son, was suddenly replaced by the very dangerous lawman, Marshal John Youngblood. Do you understand?"

"Yes," Chao-xing said. "But allow me to ask you this. If you could go back, knowing how things would turn out, would you still marry your husband?"

"Yes, I would," Amy said. "Without hesitation."

When a deputy fetched Jack, Reeves, and Witson to Judge Parker's office, Henry Teasel and Colonel Tate were already present.

"We're waiting on a reply from Washington," Parker said.

"The President, the State Department, and Congress are never going to agree to those demands," Jack said. "We all know that. Why pretend we don't."

"I'm afraid I stand with the marshal on that opinion," Tate said.

"What are you saying, that we declare war upon Two Hawks and his followers?" Parker said.

"Judge," Jack said. "He's already declared war upon us. If four more days is all we have, I suggest we prepare for it, or he'll burn this town to the ground."

Parker looked at Teasel. "Henry?"

"I'm afraid I have to agree with that, Judge," Teasel said.

"Judge, you're a federal appointee," Tate said. "You can have the railroad shuttle every citizen in Fort Smith to Little Rock in a matter of two days. You can get authorization to have troops from every outpost two days' ride from here so that Two Hawks will be greeted with everything we have without harming civilians."

"And what of the hostages?" Parker asked. "Do we just let them die at the hands of Two Hawks?"

Neither Tate nor anyone else had a response to the judge's question.

"I suggest we wait to hear from Washington before we do anything else," Parker said.

When Two Hawks and his warriors rode into camp, Uday and the others were already there. They had the Youngblood girl captive in the tipi with the priest and the Mexican woman.

"Prepare a council fire," Two Hawks said. "We will council as soon as I see this little girl."

Sarah was sitting beside Maria in the tipi when Two Hawks entered. Immediately Sarah jumped into Maria's arms.

"Are you harmed?" Two Hawks asked Sarah.

She shook her head.

"Your father is Emmet Youngblood, chief of reservation police?" Two Hawks asked.

Sarah nodded.

"You won't be harmed," Two Hawks said and walked out.

Father Ramon stood up and looked at Sarah.

"You father is Emmet Youngblood?" he asked.

"Yes," Sarah said.

She turned into Maria and started to cry.

Maria and Father Ramon looked at each other.

"Small world," Father Ramon said.

Maria stroked Sarah's hair. "Indeed," Maria said.

Two Hawks sat before the blazing council fire and looked around the circle at his ever-growing number of warriors.

He held up his right hand to quiet the chatter. When all he could hear was the crackle of the fire, he said, "Every warrior here knows the white chiefs in Washington will never agree to our terms. We will make good our threat and attack Fort Smith on the day we promised. Some of us, if not most of us, will die on that day. It will be a good death, and we will join the spirits of our great ancestors at their council fire. Let us pray and contemplate our fate."

"Well, boys, I'm sick of sitting around," Jack said. "Let's find something better to do than turn our asses to stone."

Jack stood up from the courthouse steps just as a railroad courier came rushing to the courthouse. He held a leather briefcase under his arm and paused at the steps. "Special correspondence for Judge Parker," he said.

"We'll take it," Witson said.

"No, sir," the courier said. "I have to place it in the judge's hands."

"Well, go ahead then," Witson said.

After the courier entered the courthouse, Jack sat on the steps and rolled a cigarette. Five minutes later, the courier returned and said, "The judge said if his marshals are around, to tell them to report to his office."

★ ★ ★ ★ ★

Looking out of the flap of the tipi, Father Ramon said, "Their meeting has ended. What do you suppose it all means?"

Holding Sarah, Maria said, "I don't know, Father, but I have the feeling something is going to happen, and very soon."

"Why did they take me?" Sarah asked. "My sister and I were hiding under the bed, and they came in and took me."

Maria stroked Sarah's hair and said, "Do not worry. I have the feeling your father is on the way."

Judge Parker sat at the conference table and looked at Jack, Witson, Reeves, Colonel Tate, and Henry Teasel.

"I'm going to read this exactly as written," Parker said. "The United States Government does not and never will negotiate with terrorists, criminals, and those who seek to harm it and its citizens. Take all precautionary measures to protect Fort Smith. Colonel Tate is authorized to send for as many troops as he feels necessary from surrounding territorial forts to accomplish the task. A peaceful resolution is priority, but if bloodshed is unavoidable, the conflict is to be ended quickly and decisively. The hostages are a priority and must be rescued safely. A representative from Washington will arrive sometime tonight."

Parker lowered the document.

"Well, there you have it," he said.

"Judge, this is exactly what Two Hawks wants," Jack said. "A war that will end in a blaze of glory for him and his followers."

"I think we all understand that," Parker said. "What do you suggest as a peaceful resolution?"

"I don't think there is one at this point," Tate said. "I best send some telegrams for reinforcements."

There was a sudden commotion outside the window, and Jack stood and went to see what it was.

"Son of a bitch," Jack said.

"What is it, Marshal?" Parker asked.

"Emmet's come to town," Jack said.

"Before you see the judge, there is something you should know," Jack said on the steps of the courthouse. "Two Hawks has Sarah. He attacked the cabin a few days ago before . . ."

Emmet started to walk past Jack up the steps, and Jack stuck his arm out.

"There is a whole lot more to this story," Jack said.

"That is an understatement, brother," Emmet said.

"Let's go see the judge," Jack said.

"War was his plan from the moment his wife died," Emmet said. "I'm sure of that fact. He knows full well Washington won't give in to his demands. That's why he took hostages, including my daughter. If he says he will attack Fort Smith, you can believe him."

"Colonel Tate has wired every fort in the territory and bordering states within a train ride for reinforcements," Parker said. "The railroad has agreed to send as many trains as necessary to evacuate all women and children. Those men who want to stay and fight are welcome to do so, although I'd rather they left as well."

"Judge, I followed the trail of a band of warriors into the Ozarks on the Oklahoma side," Emmet said. "Through a pass that I doubt any white man even knows exists. I stood on a summit and looked down, and do you know what I saw? I saw more than a hundred tipis and enough warriors to level Fort Smith and kill everybody in it."

"While everybody was combing the territory, he was in our backyard the entire time," Tate said.

"How far a ride to this spot?" Jack asked.

"I made it in eight hours, but that was on your horse," Emmet said.

"Can you show us on a map?" Tate asked.

Tate spread out a large territorial map, and Emmet used a pencil to trace his route.

"Here is where I followed them into the mountains," Emmet said. "Through this notch and then on a pass to their camp."

Jack rolled a cigarette and lit it with a wood match. "When Two Hawks attacks, he won't bring the hostages," he said. "He'll leave them behind. He'll probably leave the women to guard them. We can send a rescue party in after he leaves camp to come here. Colonel, give me a squad of men and . . ."

"I'll do it," Emmet said.

"You?" Jack said.

"My daughter and my woman are in that camp, Jack," Emmet said. "I'll do it. "Besides, you'll be needed here more than me."

"All right, brother," Jack said.

"We all know what to do," Parker said. "But for now, Emmet, go see your mother and daughter."

Amy, Chao-xing, and Mary Louise were seated in chairs on the porch. It was late afternoon, and they were expecting to see Jack ride in on Emmet's pinto.

Mary Louise spotted the pinto first.

"It's Pa!" she said and raced down from the porch to greet him.

Amy and Chao-xing stood. Amy wiped a tear from her eye.

"We best see to supper," Amy said. "We'll have a pair of hungry men on our hands."

After supper, after the dishes and pans were washed and put away, Jack, Emmet, Amy, and Chao-xing sat on porch chairs under a blanket of a million stars.

"You be very careful, Emmet," Amy said. "We don't want you getting killed in the process of rescuing hostages."

"Emmet can take care of himself, Ma," Jack said. "And he'll have a squad of soldiers with him."

"And why aren't you going with him?" Amy asked.

"Ma, it was Jack's idea to send a squad," Emmet said. "He volunteered first, but I told him I would go. He'll be needed in town when Two Hawks comes."

"Attacks, is what you mean," Amy said.

"Ma," Jack said.

"I swear sometimes that if men didn't have violence in their lives, they'd have no life at all," Amy said.

"I wish there was another way to get Sarah back, Ma, but there isn't," Emmet said.

"Do you think I don't know that?" Amy said.

Emmet sighed. "I best tuck Mary Louise in and get some sleep. That ride today has worn me out."

"I'll go with you," Amy said. "There are a few changes in the sleeping arrangements around here since you left."

After Amy and Emmet went inside, Jack looked at Chao-xing. "What do you say we go swimming in the barn?" Jack said.

"No, Jack, no more 'swimming' until you make an honest woman of me," Chao-xing said. "Besides, you need to find a place to sleep."

"What? What do you . . . ?" Jack said.

"Chao-xing, are you coming to bed?" Mary Louise called from inside the cabin.

CHAPTER TWENTY-SIX

Jack sat atop his massive horse while Emmet reclaimed his pinto.

"We'll be staying at the hotel until this is over," Jack said. "But I expect you'll be all right out here until we get back."

"Don't worry, Ma," Emmet said. "I'll get Sarah back."

On the porch, Amy nodded. Chao-xing stood next to her with her arm around Mary Louise.

"Let's go, brother," Jack said.

As Jack and Emmet rode away, Chao-xing ran down from the porch and after Jack's horse.

"Jack, wait," Chao-xing shouted.

Jack turned his horse and rode back to Chao-xing.

"I will make you a good wife," Chao-xing said. "Will you make me a good husband?"

"You bet," Jack said.

"In order for you to make a good husband, you need to come back alive," Chao-xing said.

Jack grinned. "Don't worry, hon, I'm not so easy to kill," Jack said.

As they rode into Fort Smith, the railroad station was crowded with citizens evacuating town. Three hundred soldiers and a dozen Gatling guns occupied the park in front of the courthouse.

They dismounted at the courthouse and Jack said, "Isn't that Captain Roberts over there?"

Emmet looked into the park. "It is. Do you see Tom Horn anywhere?"

"I believe I do," Jack said.

"Let's get upstairs," Emmet said.

Colonel Tate and Judge Parker were at the conference table. A large map of Fort Smith was spread out, and Tate was marking places on the map in pencil.

"There are only so many ways into town," Tate said when Jack and Emmet joined them at the table. "A squad of men and a Gatling gun will protect every entrance into town. In addition, wagons will block every street, and they will have to jump over them to gain access."

"Judge, how many fire wagons do we have in town?" Emmet asked.

"Two, and that's good thinking, Emmet," Parker said. "I'll make sure they're full and at the ready."

"And a full bucket brigade," Emmet added.

"They'll be ready," Parker said.

"Colonel, with your permission, I'd like to request Scout Tom Horn accompany me on the rescue mission," Emmet said.

"I'm not familiar with the name, but permission granted," Tate said. "What about the other men?"

"Captain Roberts and his squad," Emmet said.

"He's a fine officer," Tate said. "I'll see to it."

"Thank you, Colonel," Emmet said.

"Judge, where are Witson and Reeves?" Jack said.

"At the railroad station helping with the evacuation."

"Mind if I join them?" Jack said.

"Go ahead," Parker said.

"If you don't mind, I'll go down and see Captain Roberts," Emmet said.

"By tomorrow night, there won't be a woman or child left in town," Witson said.

"How many men you figure will stay and fight?" Jack asked.

"The unmarried ones," Reeves said. "Maybe."

"The hotels will stay open for us and the officers to stay in until the day before," Witson said.

Jack rolled a cigarette and watched as people boarded trains.

"Boys, both of you are married men," Jack said. "How do your wives feel with you being away from home so much?"

"My wife can't wait to get me out from underfoot," Witson said. "But if I'm gone too long, she gets to fretting."

"So she doesn't like it much?" Jack said.

"I been married four times," Witson said. "So either they don't like what I do, or they don't like me. I'll let you figure it out."

"What about you, Bass?" Jack asked.

"I was born a slave, Jack," Reeves said. "So was my Nellie. We got us eight kids. Did you know that? I worked a farm before Judge Parker appointed me in seventy-five. I earn more in two months as a marshal than I did in a year behind a plow. I love my wife and she loves me, but damned if she ain't glad to see me go on the road."

"Why?" Jack asked.

"She don't want no more kids, Jack," Reeves said. "What do you think?"

Jack grinned as he struck a wood match and lit the cigarette.

"This line of conversation wouldn't have anything to do with a certain Asian beauty who ran the barbershop," Witson said.

"I was . . . just wondering . . . is all," Jack said.

Reeves grinned. "Wondering won't get you no kids, Jack," he said.

★ ★ ★ ★ ★

Emmet traced the path through the Ozarks on the map at Roberts's conference table. "Here is the way in," he said. "Through this notch and then this pass."

"I suggest a full squad of twenty men, Captain," Tate said.

Roberts nodded. "With myself, Emmet, and Tom here, it should be enough," he said.

"Don't sell the women short," Emmet said. "They can be as fierce as the men, and we might have to kill a few in the process."

"It has come to my attention that Two Hawks favors sunrise for his attacks," Tate said. "At least that's the information I have received."

"I believe that's true," Emmet said.

"So he would have to leave after dark in order to reach Fort Smith for sunrise," Roberts said. "If we waited until the women went to sleep, it would make for an easy surprise attack and rescue."

"I concur, Captain," Tate said.

"I suggest we leave first thing tomorrow morning," Emmet said.

"Good idea, Captain," Horn said.

"Colonel?" Roberts said.

"Make it so, Captain," Tate said.

After having supper at the hotel across the street from the courthouse, Jack and Emmet had a drink at the bar. Except for the bartender, they were the only two in the room.

"I suggest you take my horse if you want to make it in one day," Jack said.

"I was thinking that very thing," Emmet said.

"Here's how," Jack said and tossed back his shot of whiskey.

"Here's how," Emmet said and downed his.

Jack looked at the bartender. "Two more," he said.

The bartender refilled the glasses.

"Jack, on the odd chance that I don't . . ." Emmet said.

"Do you need to even ask, brother?" Jack said.

Emmet nodded.

"Here's how," Jack said and sipped his drink.

Emmet lifted his glass. "Here's how."

Jack watched Emmet mount his horse at the courthouse corral. He patted his horse's rump. "Take care of my beast, Emmet," he said.

"It's more the other way around, Jack," Emmet said.

Captain Roberts and Tom Horn took the point. Twenty soldiers in a column of two waited behind them.

"Young Tom Horn," Jack said.

"Marshal," Horn said.

Roberts gave the signal, and the squad rode out of the corral and down the street.

Jack turned and walked to the center of town. Most of the stores and shops were closed for business. The blacksmith was open, as was the large dry goods store. He entered the dry goods store.

"Marshal, what can I do for you?" Greenly asked.

"I need a box of ammunition for my Sharps rifle," Jack said. "Better make it two boxes."

Greenly turned around and removed one box of ammunition from the shelf. "I'll have to get the other box from the storeroom."

While Greenly went to the storeroom, Jack walked over to a locked case of women's jewelry. It was filled with necklaces, bracelets, rings, and pendants.

Greenly returned with the second box of ammunition and set it on the counter. "Two boxes Sharps ammunition. Anything else, Marshal?"

"I understand there is such a thing as an engagement ring," Jack said. "At least I read about it."

Greenly stared at Jack.

"Pick me out one," Jack said. "And a box of your best chocolate."

Greenly grinned.

"Keep grinning and when I walk out of here, your front teeth will be in my back pocket," Jack said.

"Step over here, Marshal," Greenly said.

Jack left the dry goods store with a ring box and a box of chocolates. Both were gift wrapped in fine gold paper and placed in a brown paper bag. He walked to the blacksmith's shop.

"Charlie, your boy around?" Jack asked.

Charlie, the longtime blacksmith in Fort Smith was pounding shoes and paused. "Out back. Why?"

"I need a favor. Call him out here," Jack said.

"Hey, son, come out here," Charlie called out.

A moment later, Charlie's sixteen-year-old son appeared.

"With your pa's permission, I'd like you to run an errand for me," Jack said. "I'll pay you ten dollars."

"Judge, Henry ain't paid to take this kind of risk," Jack said.

"I'm inclined to agree with the marshal, Henry," Parker said.

"As the Indian Affairs Agent it's my . . ." Teasel said.

"I have final sway over the reservation, Henry," Parker said. "It's for me to say who goes and who doesn't."

"But Two Hawks is expecting me to . . ." Teasel said.

"Two Hawks is expecting an answer, Henry, and he shall have one," Parker said. "Now leave me be with my marshal."

Teasel nodded and left Parker's office.

"Are you sure you want to do this, Marshal Youngblood?" Parker asked.

"Want and need are two different things, Judge," Jack said.

"And you said it yourself; I'm the best man you got."

Parker sighed heavily and nodded his head. "How is your mother, Jack?"

"Fine, Judge."

"I understand you have a woman now," Parker said.

"You might say that, Judge."

"Don't make her a widow before she's a wife," Parker said.

Mary Louise looked out the window and said, "Grandmother, there is a boy in the yard."

Amy went to the screen door and opened it. "Who are you?" she said.

"My name is Charles, ma'am. I'm the blacksmith's son."

"What are you doing out here?" Amy asked.

"The marshal asked me to deliver this bag to his lady friend, ma'am."

"Bring it up here," Amy said.

Charles dismounted and brought the bag to the porch. "I have to get back right away, ma'am," he said and returned to his horse.

As Charles rode away, Amy turned to Mary Louise. "Where is Chao-xing?"

"In the garden."

"Fetch her to the porch."

While Mary Louise went to the garden behind the house, Amy took a chair on the porch. A few moments later, Chao-xing and Mary Louise came to the porch.

"You best not be opening those stitches," Amy said.

"I'm fine," Chao-xing said.

Amy held out the bag.

"For me?" Chao-xing said.

"What is it?" Mary Louise asked.

"It's a bag of mind your own business," Amy said.

Chao-xing took the bag and sat next to Amy.

"It won't bite you," Amy said.

Chao-xing removed the ring box and chocolate box from the bag.

"It's gift wrapped," Mary Louise said.

Chao-xing stared at the ring box.

"It's not going to open itself," Amy said.

With shaking hands, Chao-xing removed the gift wrap and then slowly opened the ring box.

"It's empty," Chao-xing said.

Amy looked at the chocolate box. "My son is a mite warped in the head," she said.

Chao-xing removed the gift wrap from the box of chocolate and flipped off the lid. There were spaces for two dozen pieces of chocolate. One piece was missing and in the wrapper was the engagement ring.

Chao-xing picked up the ring and started to cry.

"There she goes being happy again," Mary Louise said and grabbed a piece of chocolate.

CHAPTER TWENTY-SEVEN

Riding a large army horse, Jack turned a corner in the road and stopped when, twenty feet ahead, he saw two mounted warriors.

They were fierce-looking man. Each wore war paint and carried a war lance. Rifles were tethered to their saddles, and they carried arrow pouches on their backs.

"I am United States Marshal John Russell Youngblood," Jack said. "Do you speak English?"

"We speak English very well," one of the men said.

"How are you called?" Jack asked.

"I am Uday. He is Little Buffalo."

"Mind if I ask you a question?" Jack said.

"Ask," Uday said.

"Why start a war you know you can't win?" Jack asked. "It just causes a lot of unnecessary bloodshed on both sides."

"We have already lost everything we once were," Uday said. "Our land, our heritage, our birthright. There is nothing left but to die as free and whole men."

Jack looked at them and then slowly nodded.

"I understand your outlook, but to be honest, dying ain't much of a future," he said.

"We have no future," Uday said. "Unless the chiefs in Washington agreed to our terms."

"I am sorry to say they have not," Jack said.

Little Buffalo's hand tightened around his lance, and his right arm moved a few inches.

259

"Don't," Jack said. "I will kill you both, and there is no honor in that. Your spirits will wander forever and will never have a seat at the council fire of your ancestors."

"You have the blood?" Uday said.

"My mother is part Sioux. My father was part Apache," Jack said.

"Two Hawks spoke of Emmet Youngblood, the chief of reservation police," Uday said.

"He's my brother," Jack said.

Uday nodded.

"We will deliver the answer to Two Hawks," Uday said.

"Ask him to reconsider," Jack said.

"What does that mean, recon . . . ?" Uday said.

"Change his mind."

"He won't."

"I reckon not," Jack said.

Uday nodded, and he and Little Buffalo turned their horses and rode away.

Jack watched them until they were out of sight, then turned the army horse around and rode back to Fort Smith.

"Must be a hundred and fifty tipis down there, Captain," Tom Horn said.

Roberts, Horn, and Emmet stood on the cliff overlooking Two Hawks's camp and watched through their binoculars.

"There must be two hundred or more warriors," Roberts said.

Emmet lowered his binoculars and looked at Roberts. "We need to find a place to camp for the night where we won't be spotted by any lookouts."

"I saw a place when I was scouting," Horn said.

"Take us there, Tom," Roberts said.

★ ★ ★ ★ ★

"Full war paint and war lances," Jack said. "I have no doubt that Two Hawks will attack at dawn the day after tomorrow."

Parker looked at Colonel Tate.

"Are we fully prepared and ready?" Parker asked.

"Judge, if we are attacked as we all believe we will be, my soldiers are prepared to kill every one of the attackers to protect and defend Fort Smith," Tate said.

Parker sighed heavily. "For the life of me, I can't understand why people are in such a hurry to die," he said.

"Heaven, Judge," Jack said.

"What?" Parker said.

"They want to go to heaven," Jack said. "They believe this is the only way."

"It can't be something that simple," Parker said.

"Judge, I'd feel a whole lot better if you took the train to Little Rock tomorrow," Tate said.

"The hell I will," Parker said. "My family left this morning, but I am staying right here."

"Judge, please be . . ." Tate said.

"Colonel, I've fired a rifle a time or two in my life," Parker said.

"At least can you fire that rifle from your office window?" Tate asked.

"My guess is they will leave at dawn and ride to within an hour from town and camp," Emmet said. "They will organize before sunrise and attack when the sun breaks."

"All we have to do is wait for dark, ride down, and attack," Horn said.

"After the warriors leave, can you scout the quickest, safest route into their camp?" Roberts said.

"No problem, Captain," Horn said.

"Captain, what do we do with the prisoners?" Emmet asked.

"Leave them," Roberts said. "What else can we do with them?"

"Nothing, I suppose," Emmet said. "The thing is, they will fight."

"And if they do, some of them will die," Roberts said. "It's their choice."

"Don't worry, Emmet. No harm will come to yours," Horn said. "I swear it."

"Thank you, Tom," Emmet said. "Captain, when Tom scouts a route down, I'd like to go with him."

"Granted," Roberts said. "Now let's get some food in us and catch some sleep."

"A deputy is posted at every street with the army," Jack said. "Every street into town is barricaded by wagons and bales of hay. One Gatling gun is assigned to every street corner into town. Some men, the young, unmarried men, have stayed to fight. All we can do now is wait for Two Hawks to attack."

Parker sat back in his chair and sighed. "How did it come to this?" he said.

Jack opened the liquor cabinet in the corner of the office and poured an ounce of bourbon into two glasses. He set one on the desk.

"Hate is a powerful fuel, Judge," Jack said. "It's said that faith can move mountains, but hate can destroy a country."

Parker took a sip of his drink. "I thought Emmet was the philosopher in the family," he said.

Jack took a chair, sipped his drink, and said, "For a long time I hated Emmet. I almost beat him to death because I blamed him for stealing the woman I wanted to marry. I probably would have, too, if Ma didn't stop me. The funny thing was, I didn't really love her and she knew it, and yet all I felt was hate toward the both of them."

"Do you mean Sarah?" Parker asked.

"She was a good woman and a good wife to Emmet, and I hated them both," Jack said. "It almost destroyed my family. That's the kind of hate Two Hawks carries around inside of him."

Parker sipped his drink. "How did Amy stop you?" he asked.

Jack grinned. "She hit me over the head with a bottle. I still carry a small lump."

"She's a tough woman, your mother," Parker said.

Jack tossed back the rest of his drink. "No shit," he said.

Maria, Sarah, and Father Ramon watched from inside their tipi as the warriors gathered around a great council fire.

"What are they doing?" Sarah asked.

"Praying, child," Father Ramon said.

"You mean to God?" Sarah asked.

"In a sense," Father Ramon said.

"Don't be afraid," Maria said.

"I'm not afraid," Sarah said. "I just wish my father was here."

Maria held Sarah's hand. "So do I," she said.

"They're singing," Sarah said.

"It's how they pray," Maria said.

"What do they want?" Sarah asked.

"Honor, child," Father Ramon said. "They want honor."

CHAPTER TWENTY-EIGHT

From a cliff a thousand yards away, Roberts, Horn, and Emmet watched as Two Hawks led his nation out of camp.

"There must be two hundred of them, Captain," Horn said.

"War paint and lances," Roberts said as he watched with his binoculars. "Not fifty rifles among them. How do they expect to defeat an army with bows and arrows and tomahawks?"

Emmet lowered his binoculars and looked at Roberts.

"They don't expect to win, Captain," Emmet said. "They expect to die."

Roberts sighed. "Tom, find us a way down," he said. "We'll go in after the women are asleep."

"Come on, Emmet, let's take us a walk," Horn said.

The bartender had left town earlier in the day, but the saloon was unlocked and open. Jack sat at a table with a mug of coffee and cleaned his Sharps rifle with a long-bore brush.

A dozen or so soldiers occupied tables, each with mugs of coffee as the colonel had ordered no liquor be served.

Reeves and Witson entered the saloon and went to the bar where a soldier was serving coffee. They took two mugs to Jack's table.

"How many times you clean that thing?" Witson said as he and Reeves took chairs.

"Twice," Jack said. "And I'll probably clean it once more."

"Will that improve your aim?" Witson asked.

"That reminds me of the time the master's son shot himself in the ass," Reeves said.

"Bass, how do you shoot yourself in the ass?" Witson said.

Grinning, Jack set the Sharps rifle on the table and started unloading his Colt.

"I was eighteen or nineteen at the time," Reeves said. "The master's son had a pair of 1851 Colt revolvers, the old cap-and-ball type. He took to twirling them out of habit, and one afternoon after too much whiskey, he was twirling them on the porch and one of them slipped out of his hand. The gun flew backwards over his head, hit the porch floor, the percussion cap ignited, and he shot himself in the left butt cheek."

"I don't believe that," Witson said. "Bass, did you make that up?"

"No, I didn't, but I did witness it, and I had to be the one to tell the master his son shot himself in the ass and was on his belly bleeding," Reeves said.

"And what did the master do?" Witson asked.

"He got so mad he took his own pistol and shot his son in the right cheek," Reeves said.

Jack and Witson stared at Reeves for a moment, and then they cracked up laughing.

"What?" Reeves said. "It be true."

Jack had stripped the Colt and was cleaning the barrel with a wire brush. "I got just one question," he said. "Who took the bullets out?"

A soldier on the street stepped into the saloon.

"The padre is holding a service on the courthouse lawn," he said.

"Come on, boys, we might as well get blessed before we get killed," Witson said.

★ ★ ★ ★ ★

Jack woke up and looked at his pocket watch. It was just after four in the morning. The jailhouse cot was hard and narrow, and his back was stiff when he stood up. The cell door was open. He walked out and down the narrow hallway lined with holding cells.

A prisoner stuck his arm out. "Hey, Marshal?" he said.

Jack paused. "What?"

"How 'bout you let me out so I can fight?" the prisoner said. "I fought in the war, you know. I'd rather die fighting Indians than having my neck stretched in Judge Parker's court."

"I'll mention it," Jack said.

He continued walking and entered the guard's office where a deputy was on duty.

"The coffee ain't good, but it's hot," the deputy said.

Jack lifted the pot off the woodstove and filled a tin cup. "Thanks."

"Marshal, do you really think we'll be attacked?" the deputy asked.

"He's killed thirty or so I know of," Jack said. "I believe Two Hawks will do as he says."

"I can fight, Marshal," the guard said.

"You'll have to defend the prisoners in case of the worst," Jack said.

"In case of the worst, I'll be in a cell with them," the guard said.

"Fire's out, and the camp is quiet," Horn said. "Moon is up and the sky is clear."

"How long will it take us to reach the camp on foot?" Roberts asked.

"About an hour."

"Hobble all horses," Roberts said. "Tom, Emmet, lead the

way."

Jack set the Sharps rifle against the wall of the courthouse roof and rolled a cigarette. Despite the large number of army troops in town, the streets below were eerily quiet. He struck a match and lit the cigarette.

Witson appeared on the roof with two mugs of coffee and gave one to Jack.

"Thanks," Jack said.

"Two hours to daylight," Witson said. "I guess we'll know then."

"Want to stay up here with me?" Jack asked.

"I'm no good for sniper work," Witson said. "I only have one good eye, unless you think I wear this patch 'cause it's fashionable in Paris. No, I'll stay below and do my work with a pistol."

"Bass?"

"He'll be front and center with the army boys."

Jack sipped his coffee. "Army coffee?"

"It's a mite better than the slop they have in the courthouse," Witson said.

"It is that."

"Well, I best find myself a front row seat to the party," Witson said.

Jack extended his right hand and they shook.

"Good luck," Jack said.

"You, too."

After Witson left, Jack watched the streets below and sipped his coffee. If it weren't for the fact that in a few hours they would be under a major attack, he would consider it a beautiful night.

Horn led the way into the quiet camp of tipis. Captain Roberts and Emmet followed, and the squad of twenty soldiers followed them. Each man had a Winchester rifle and a pistol.

Roberts held up his right hand, gestured to describe a large circle, and everybody spread out.

"Make some noise, Mr. Horn," Roberts whispered.

Horn aimed his Winchester at the ground and fired a shot. Surrounded by mountains, the noise was loud and echoed several times.

Emmet expected to see dozens of women rush from the tipis. As the last echo faded, the camp fell quiet again.

"There's nobody here," Roberts said.

"Sarah. Maria, where are you?" Emmet yelled.

His voice echoed and slowly faded. At the end of the camp, a flap on a tipi opened and Sarah emerged.

"Pa. It's Pa!" Sarah yelled and ran toward Emmet.

"Sarah," Emmet said and rushed to her.

Maria and Father Ramon emerged from the tipi. Maria looked at Emmet as he lifted Sarah in his arms, and she smiled.

Holding Sarah, Emmet walked to Maria.

"Somehow I knew you would find us," Maria said.

An hour before daybreak, Jack searched the dark outskirts of town. From the courthouse rooftop thirty feet above ground, he had the best vantage point in town. Past the streets, darkness hid everything. There could be a thousand warriors at the ready, and you wouldn't know it until the sun finally broke the night.

Jack turned when he heard a noise behind him. It was Judge Parker, and he was carrying a tray with two coffee mugs and some slices of cake on a plate.

"If you don't mind, Marshal, I'd like a bird's-eye view," Parker said.

"Can you keep your head down?" Jack said.

"I can keep all of me down," Parker said. "Have a piece of cake. Fresh made."

"Thanks," Jack said as he picked up a slice of white cake with a sweet frosting.

Parker set the tray on the edge of the wall and looked down. "People are going to die here today," he said.

"On both sides," Jack said.

Parker looked at the Sharps rifle. "Witson says you can hit a bird flying at a hundred yards with that thing," he said.

"As long as you plan on staying, maybe I can put you to work," Jack said. "The Sharps holds just one round at a time. You can save me seconds by handing me a round after each firing."

"I can do that," Parker said.

"The job comes with no pay." Jack grinned.

Roberts ordered a fire made and hot food cooked for Sarah, Maria, and Father Ramon before they tackled the climb to the horses.

"Did you know the women were going with them?" Roberts asked.

"Not until we saw them leave," Maria said.

"Did Two Hawks say anything to you?" Roberts asked.

Maria looked at Emmet. "He knew Sarah was Emmet's daughter," she said. "He knew you were tracking him. He also knew you wouldn't attack while he held her and us hostage."

Roberts looked at Emmet. "You ever hear of anything like this?"

"Comanche and Apache women can fight with the best of them," Emmet said. "If they're anything like my mother."

"Pa, I want to go home," Sarah said.

Emmet looked at Maria. "How about you? Do you want to go home?"

"Can she, Pa? She's really nice and she took care of me," Sarah said.

"How about it?" Emmet said to Maria.

"I would love to go home with you," Maria said.

"Captain, be light soon," Horn said. "We best move out."

Amy took a chair on the porch and sipped tea. A few moments later, also with a cup of tea, Chao-xing joined her.

"It will be sunrise soon," Chao-xing said.

"I lived through the Comanche Wars of thirty-six, the attack on Austin in fifty-eight, the Civil War, and the loss of my husband," Amy said.

Chao-xing took Amy's hand and squeezed it gently.

Amy smiled.

"Let's watch the dawn," she said.

Jack chambered a massive round into the Sharps rifle. In the distance, the first hint of light reached the clouds, which glowed light pink.

"Any minute now, Judge," Jack said. "I wouldn't be surprised to see Two Hawks and his warriors come riding down Main Street."

Parker looked at his pocket watch.

"I hate to admit it, Jack, but I'm scared right down to my boots," Parker said.

"You'll be fine, Judge," Jack said.

"How about you, Jack, do you ever get scared?"

"A United States marshal can't afford to get scared," Jack said.

"How do you not?"

"I don't think about it," Jack said.

"It's that simple?"

"I've been told by many that I'm a simple-minded man," Jack said with a grin.

The first hint of orange sun appeared on the horizon.

"Here we go," Jack said.

Two Hawks faced the horizon and watched the first glint of light break the darkness. He closed his eyes and tilted his head toward the sky. He prayed for strength and for strength for his warriors.

The task was nearly at hand.

Slowly, heat reached his face.

Two Hawks opened his eyes.

It was a glorious Comanche sunrise.

Slowly the sky lightened as the sun rose.

From the courthouse roof, Jack and Judge Parker looked at the streets below. There wasn't a warrior in sight. Not Two Hawks, Uday, or Little Buffalo. The soldiers, poised and ready for an attack, looked around in confusion.

"I don't understand," Parker said. "Was he bluffing?"

"A Comanche doesn't bluff," Jack said.

"Then where is he?" Parker asked.

Jack looked at the confused soldiers below. Then he turned and looked west.

"That fox," Jack said. "That son of a bitch fox."

"What? Who?" Parker asked.

Jack turned and rushed to the door and down the steps. He exited the courthouse and ran to Colonel Tate.

"Marshal, I don't understand . . ." Tate said.

"Colonel, Two Hawks said he would attack Fort Smith, and that's exactly what he did," Jack said.

Tate looked at Jack with confusion in his eyes, and then he slowly understood.

"My God," Tate said.

★ ★ ★ ★ ★

The Fort Smith army outpost was built on twelve acres of land and surrounded by a sixteen-foot-high wood fence. The corporal of the guard was on the catwalk just before dawn. Colonel Tate had left behind twenty soldiers to guard the fort while the rest went to protect the town.

It had been a long, uneventful night, and the corporal was looking forward to some hot chow and his bunk.

As the sun rose and the sky lightened, the corporal peered down into the shadows. At first he thought his tired eyes were playing tricks on him as he thought he saw something in the distance.

The corporal stared at the dimly lit horizon. As the sun rose and the ground brightened, he looked at fifty warriors on horseback. Each warrior held an arrow in his bow. Each warrior struck matches and ignited the whiskey-laced cloth wrapped around the arrow shaft just below the arrowhead.

The corporal looked to the west, south, and north, and fifty warriors with flaming arrows sat on each side.

"Indian attack!" he yelled.

A moment later, two hundred flaming arrows struck the fence and fire erupted.

A bugle sounded.

The warriors charged.

Two Hawks shook his war lance at the sky and emitted a loud, piercing war cry.

It only took minutes for the gates to burn enough for the warriors to charge through them into the fort and attack the helpless soldiers.

The soldiers, most in their underwear, put up a gallant fight, but they were overmatched and hopelessly outnumbered.

The slaughter was over in minutes. Every scalp was taken.

Two Hawks sat atop his horse and called his warriors around him.

"Ride to your homes and reservations with a full heart," Two Hawks said. "I am the one who will be hunted, but first they must find me. Uday, Little Buffalo, and Doli will ride with me to the Wyoming Bighorns and council with the great chief Geronimo. We will all meet again one day, I promise you, my brothers."

Two Hawks, Uday, and Little Buffalo rode from the still-burning fort to where Doli waited on a hillside.

She smiled at him as Two Hawks rode by, then she turned her horse and followed him.

Colonel Tate, Jack, and most of the soldiers arrived at Fort Smith while it was still smoldering.

The devastation was complete.

"I will hound him for as long as it takes, but I will find and capture that man," Tate vowed.

"Capture?" Jack said. "I wouldn't count on that, Colonel. But, good luck anyway."

Jack turned his horse and took a slow ride back to town.

Most of the soldiers were gone and the streets were deserted when he rode down Main Street. A train sat at the station preparing to leave for Little Rock. By tonight the saloons would be full and music would be heard from one end of town to the other.

But for now Jack was content to sit on the courthouse steps, smoke a cigarette, drink lousy coffee, and wait.

Until a weary-looking Tom Horn led Captain Roberts and his squad of soldiers into town.

Jack stood and smiled brightly as Emmet helped Sarah down from the saddle. Emmet dismounted and then helped Maria down from her tall army horse.

"Emmet," Jack said.

"Let's go home," Emmet said.

EPILOGUE

"More tea?" Chao-xing asked.

"Yes, please," Maria said.

Chao-xing filled Maria's cup and then sat next to Jack.

"That's a beautiful ring," Maria said.

"Thank you," Chao-xing said. "Jack picked it out."

Emmet looked across the porch at Jack.

Jack shrugged.

Amy came out from the cabin and took the last chair on the porch. "Honestly, those girls," she said. "Trying to put them to bed is like plowing a field full of rocks."

Sarah appeared at the screen door. "Maria, are you coming to bed?"

"Be right there," Maria said, then she stood and went into the cabin.

A moment later, Mary Louise opened the screen door. "Chao-xing?" Mary Louise said.

"Coming," Chao-xing said and went inside.

Jack and Emmet exchanged glances.

Amy sighed.

"We'll need a bigger house," she said.

ABOUT THE AUTHOR

Ethan J. Wolfe is the author of the popular western series, The Regulator. His other western novels include *The Last Ride, The Range War of '82, Silver Moon Rising* and *The Devil's Waltz*.

The employees of Five Star Publishing hope you have enjoyed this book.

Our Five Star novels explore little-known chapters from America's history, stories told from unique perspectives that will entertain a broad range of readers.

Other Five Star books are available at your local library, bookstore, all major book distributors, and directly from Five Star/Gale.

Connect with Five Star Publishing

Visit us on Facebook:
   https://www.facebook.com/FiveStarCengage

Email:
   FiveStar@cengage.com

For information about titles and placing orders:
   (800) 223-1244
   gale.orders@cengage.com

To share your comments, write to us:
   Five Star Publishing
   Attn: Publisher
   10 Water St., Suite 310
   Waterville, ME 04901